BOGFOKE

Michael Nicholas Richard

Cover art by Zach Giles.

I wish to offer grateful acknowledgment to Sherri Richard and Steve Jarman for their proofreading skills and enthusiasm.

Table of Contents

ONE:

The Dreams Of The City

Night came near again and Skag's eyes opened to the darkness of his barrow. He sighed and rolled onto his feet. He peered through the cracks in the barrow door. The world beyond the cemetery wall was bathed in the auburn glow of fading twilight, but beneath the twisted cedars, great oaks and spreading sycamores the shadows were dark. He put his shoulder to the rusted iron and shoved the door open. The night air was as moist as the arms of the earth.

Caw!

Skag's heart pounded against his ribs as he twisted and hurled himself away from the sound. Looking up he expected the red eyes and black wings of Father Daugth's crow. Instead, he saw Welken sitting atop the brick barrow and holding his sides as laughter trembled his body. His mimicry had been perfect and he was well pleased with the effect.

Skag cursed and flung a pine cone. Welken slipped easily down the curve of the barrow and the cone clattered against the gray coquina wall of the cemetery. Then the tangle-bearded face appeared again with a barely constrained smile. Welken held up an open palm of truce.

"I've no time for you, moss-brain," snapped Skag. He turned away and scampered over the nearby graves.

"Go ahead!" shouted Welken. "It will be of no use! Robbis has found something special for Mother Crabba."

Something special? What could that belly-creeper, Robbis, have found? Skag made his way into the growing dark shrouded around a lonely oak. Sitting with his back to the gray bark he looked past the coquina arch and the bars of the cast-iron gate. Sometimes he would sit here and watch the city dream.

The spirit of the city remembered everything, the red men wandering through the great forested lands to set the first dwellings between her two rivers. Then the white men who came with the rising sun at their backs, gliding over the water upon ships with sails billowing like great clouds. She had held them all, and she had changed them all.

Skag was sitting in wonder at the misted dreams when he saw a spider web strung between the fork of a small branch. A streetlamp sent a finger of light to dance upon the gossamer strands. Like a shadow, the spider continued working across the elusive, glittering spray of light.

Skag marveled at the fragile beauty. Carefully he reached with long, clever fingers to snap the branch a hand space beneath the fork. What could Robbis have found? Holding the branch gently Skag hurried along beneath the unchanging gaze of granite angels.

If Mother Crabba deemed his gift suitable, what tale would he have her raise? Ah, Cornbread Jack, the tale of the dark skinned man whose sweat had bound the pale gray stones of the cemetery wall to the master stonemason's pattern. Cornbread Jack, who knew of the city's dreams and who was one of the last of the few men to ever see Skag's kind. He had called them by the only name they knew for themselves, *bogfoke*.

The bogfoke had plagued the stone-worker. They had knocked over his work during the night and stolen his tools. Cornbread Jack had cursed them and the idle morass that was their existence. With the sweat of his effort he built the wall, and with knowledge beyond the ken of other men he had bound the bogfoke within so that they lived a furtive existence amidst the dilapidated and crumbling tombs and mausoleums they knew as their barrows.

Skag went to the gathering place, where men had raised a monument to the gray-cloaked warrior from one of their seemingly unending line of conflicts. The statue was

stern faced with rifle and bayonet poised defiantly. Huge
sweet-gum trees spread their broad leafed canopy above the
flagstones, with moss hanging from their branches like the
unpent hair of old women grieving.

Upon the granite dais of the gray-cloaked warrior sat
Father Daugth. His back was against the warrior's stone legs.
Upon the warrior's broad brimmed hat perched Father
Daugth's crow, with its red eyes glowing like hot coals. Father
Daugth held in his hand a stout length of sweet-gum that
ended in a cudgel-like knot. It was old and dry. The surface
was lined with cracks but it could still bring pain and the
memory of pain.

Father Daugth was a broad, gaunt figure, with limbs
seeming twisted by their own strength. His dark eyes glittered
from amidst the filthy white swirl of unkempt hair and beard.
His shroud-like rags were adorned with the skulls of rodents,
birds and even pieces of human bones scrounged from
neglected tombs.

At his feet, sitting directly on the flagstones, was
Mother Crabba.   She was so fat that her bloated flesh swelled
through the gaps in her rags. Her nut brown face was affixed
with a leering grin beneath a crooked nose. She was bald, but
draped Spanish moss over her scalp like a bedraggled wig.

The light of the rising moon filtered in lonely
patterns through the canopy of sweet-gum. A half dozen of
Skag's kith had gathered around the obese matriarch. No one
else had bothered to seek out a gift for Mother. They had all
heard of Robbis's find. Robbis was vain and lascivious, but he
had not the dark heart of his cousins, Slignan and Kribble.
Whatever tale he desired would be reluctantly accepted by the
others.

All faces turned toward the foolish Skag as he
brought forward his gift. He held the branch so that the
moonlight shimmered on the spider's web. Mother Crabba
reached with plump fingers to snatch it from his hand. She
held it against the moonlight with narrowing eyes. Then those
dirt encrusted fingers plucked the spider from the web and

dropped it into her wide mouth.

Snickering laughter burst from those gathered and the branch was tossed to the base of a tombstone. Skag faded back into the dark edge of the gathering as Robbis came swaggering up to Mother Crabba. Smiling broadly he held out a bottle of wine, three quarters empty. He had found the secreted stash of one of the grounds keepers. The smell of it was on him. It was easy enough to figure where at least some of it had disappeared.

Mother Crabba had been waiting. Word of his discovery had come to her and she accepted the gift with eager hands. She looked at Robbis accusingly as she swirled the liquid in its container. He mustn't be allowed to think he could deceive her. Then she turned the bottle up to greedy lips. With long, gurgling swallows she drained the last of the wine. Then she wiped her mouth on the back of her gnarled hand.

"What tale would you hear, Robbis?" asked Mother Crabba. Her voice was like the dry clatter of tree limbs in winter.

The chill of it caused Robbis to pause a long moment before he replied, "I would hear of the planter's widow."

In the dark beyond the gathering Skag pursed his lips in distaste. This was the tale of a rich man's widow who became a prostitute in the face of adversity. It was a tale more despairing and bitter than erotic, but Robbis would suck and scrape at the salacious tidbits as though they were sweetbread. Nearly all the bogfoke took delight in any tales of misfortune to befall the lives of men.

Excepting Skag. There was no entertainment in those tales for Skag. Such stories disturbed him, although he could not reach past the darkness that clouded his mind for a reason why. So he ambled away from the gathering back toward the lonely oak. As he moved among the monuments of death his feet sank into the soil of a fresh turned grave.

He stepped back, kicking dirt from between his crooked toes onto the squares of turf mounded in front of a tombstone. Leaning close he ran his fingers over the design engraved upon the granite monument. These were the words of men set for the life of the stone. He wondered what they might say.

"Jeremiah Simms. . . His courage has taken him from us -- "

The words were ended by the scramble of Skag's feet as he dove behind the tombstone. When at last he'd roused the nerve to peek around the granite slab he saw the faintest image of a man sitting casually atop the grave. Twice in one night Skag's heart had tried to pry its way past his throat. He calmed himself and stepped from behind the tombstone. He realized that he saw no living man. He cocked his head to one side and perched his hands upon his hips in uncertain defiance as he inspected the wraith before him.

This was not entirely unusual. Sometimes the city held them for a short time. There was no knowing why, unless it was to impress the memory of them upon her dreams. This had been a right tall fellow by the looks of him. He was all misty, making it impossible to tell what color had been his eyes, hair or skin. Skag could discern what he thought to be the features of a white man in the hazy image.

"You are a . . . bogfoke," observed the wraith with a distant voice.

Skag frowned. No dream of the city had ever spoken to him before. What was this? He edged back again as caution struggled with curiosity.

"Are you Jeremiah Simms?" he finally managed to ask, feeling ridiculous for speaking to the misted remnant.

The faint image of a head nodded, "Yes. Or at least I was. It is difficult to know that I might be now. This is not unpleasant, however, because the city dreams of the promise beyond."

Skag sat down. This was more interesting by far than any tale raised by Mother Crabba. She had extraordinary skill at raising images, but they were smaller and less real somehow for all their color and motion. Besides which, you were never sure if you were seeing images the Mother raised in your head or outside of it.

Skag scratched his stubbled beard as he observed this phantom. It seemed a little less interested in him. Its eyes appeared to be looking somewhere beyond this place.

"How came you to know what I am?" Skag demanded of the ghost.

That which had been Jeremiah Simms grinned and the eyes focused upon the bogfoke. "There is a little colored fellow who watches over the gate to this hallowed ground. Cornbread Jack he names himself. He tells of you when we enter. When we enter this place he tells us of you so that we mightn't be too fearful of where our souls are to pass eternity. It is his burden for the curse he wove. It is a thing for which he must atone."

"You talk like a black robe," snorted Skag, meaning the priests and ministers he'd heard from his barrow over the years. "You won't be here for eternity."

"So it is understood, but you are ugly creatures and mindful of unpleasant possibilities."

Skag frowned again. He looked at the cryptic symbols chiseled into the granite. "Why did your courage take you from them?"

The wraith looked up beyond the squat form of a young cedar, "I drowned. I was fishing down by the river. A boat floundered in the water. I heard the cries of despair. I heard children and the anguish of their parents. I dove into the river. . . foolish. They climbed onto the capsized boat. I drowned."

"You leaped into the river to save them?" said Skag, shaking his head. "That *was* foolish. So now you are dead. Would seem to me courage is a foolish thing."

"Perhaps. I was not a very good swimmer, so it took courage to go into the water. It does seem foolish, but I will not make light of one of mankind's great gifts -- misused as it might too often be," replied the ghost-man. "I am not one to wallow in the shortcomings of my kind. Someone once said to me that only man kills his own kind. What nonsense. Can you believe such a notion? Mankind has committed only one evil upon this earth not done by any other species. That one evil would be to ever commit evil knowing it is evil."

Skag shrugged. "I don't care. Why do you tell me this?"

The wraith paused, seeming diminished. "I don't know. I suppose I was talking to myself."

"I've seen tomcats kill and even eat kittens," mused Skag.

"My people have a purpose in this life," sighed Jeremiah Simms. "A gift. A gift of knowing. And, knowing, we are to build, to reach, to grow. We have risen from the sea and the soil and shall grasp for the stars! We reach too for things that cannot be measured or weighed."

"And rats kill each other," said Skag, nodding his head. "Why do you want the stars?"

"To grow, to build and to reach. To understand when a thing is not right, when it is out of proper order, and to correct it, to know when a thing is in proper order and appreciate it. A gift and a duty."

Skag arched his eyebrows. He'd seen stars on occasion. Usually the bogfoke didn't look up to the sky, unless it was to curse the light of the moon which might betray them to the eyes of men, or to be wary of Father Daugth's crow. He was going to ask Jeremiah Simms about this growing and correcting business, but there was a scurry of leaves behind him.

"Look at light-head Skag," smirked Kribble. His eyes glittered as black as his soul. "Talking to the ghost-man."

Skag hissed and tossed a handful of leaves in a gesture of disdain. Kribble chuckled and scratched at his rag covered belly, then leaned over and spat on the freshly re-laid sod.

"So much for you and yours, ghost-man!" he shouted. Then he jumped behind the tombstone, shoving his shoulder against it. The monument tipped forward and thudded atop the grave. Kribble was wracked with laughter at his own handiwork and pointed derisively at the solemn form of Jeremiah Simms.

Skag was enraged. He grabbed for Kribble, pounding with his fists. They rolled across the grass, wrestling, clutching and cursing. Finally Kribble managed to break free and ran off into the darkness. His curses drifted more slowly behind.

Panting and shaken, Skag turned back toward the new grave. He grabbed the tombstone and pulled. It was too heavy. He sat down for a moment, trying to think of a way he might right it. It was just too heavy.

"Do not mind that," whispered the wraith. "The grounds keepers will straighten it in the morning. It was a noble thing you did. An act of courage. You saw a wrong, and you sought to change it."

Skag scratched his stubbled chin. Was it? Yes, he supposed it was. From where had this come?

"It was borne on your anger," explained the ghost-man, who somehow knew Skag's thoughts. "But, it came from something deeper. I can go now, Skag. The city is done with me. Farewell, I have a journey to undertake."

The wraith of Jeremiah Simms faded like fog melting in the morning sunlight. Skag was sorry to see him go. He tried to move the stone again -- it was no use.

He rose to his feet and wandered between the long rows of graves. Why had the city shown him this? The city with all her dreams, each tumbling over the other. He sat against a cedar tree, bored but not wanting to go back to the gathering. He was tired of all this. Their lives were like a quagmire of darkness, despair and endless waiting.

Change it. The thought rolled over in Skag's mind -- *change it*. The world unfolded beyond that gray wall. He thought then of Father Daugth sitting like a pending nightmare upon the stone dais. It made his heart weaken, but his eyes still glittered.

Skag's hand grasped a fallen branch of cedar. It was

stout and of good length. He brought it under his nose, inhaling the clean, sharp-edged scent. He peeled away a strip of feathered bark from the red-veined wood. It was a strong wood, and he swung it through the air. The sound of its passing whooshed in the night -- Skag smiled.

From where he was sitting, Skag could see the stone arch above the cast-iron gate. The Weeping Arch it was called. The superstition of men was that anyone touched by those tears would next pass through that gate in a coffin. But the city dreamed of cleansing waters washing away the hold of the living upon the spirits of the dead.

The moist night air was condensing upon the gray blocks. A few drops had seeped through the porous stone and fallen to the ground below. Skag wondered about those tears. What could they cleanse besides the souls of men? He gripped tight the length of cedar and began walking back to the place of the gathering.

He found Mother Crabba gesturing with one hand, while the other held the empty wine bottle. The last words of the tale were woven by her slurred and rasping voice. The wine had diminished her hypnotic power. Father Daugth sat with his eyes half lidded. He might have been sleeping.

The other bogfoke were sitting around in varying degrees of interest. Robbis was crouched near Gristel, and the intrusive intent of his hands pestered at her. She absently knocked his hands away, or hissed disapprovingly. Her sister, Tegmina, sat nearby, tense and fearful of Robbis's lewd attention turning to her.

Welken and Weart seemed disinterested, gazing more into the space above Mother Crabba's head than at the matriarch's face. When Kribble saw Skag at the edge of the gathering he elbowed Slignan and they both chuckled as though sharing a joke.

Skag stepped onto the flagstones near Mother Crabba. The matriarch's narration faltered and all the other bogfoke stared at him. Except perhaps for Father Daugth -- Skag hadn't the courage to look.

"Sit down," ordered Mother Crabba, with her voice masking any surprise at his sudden intrusion.

"Shut up!" retorted Skag. Before the Mother could speak again he lashed out with the cedar stave, knocking the wine bottle from her hand. It skidded over the flagstones and shattered at the base of the dais.

Then came the steady tapping of Father Daugth's staff against the granite, like the footfall of doom. Skag was forced to look up. He hefted the cedar, seeking courage. The eyes that met his were black as the dark between the stars. As Father Daugth shifted to his feet the skulls adorning his rags clattered against one another.

"Go back to your barrow, Skag. The night is over for you," ordered the Father. His voice was a shadowed whisper, but the venom of it lingered after the words had faded.

Skag felt his heart go cold, and fear began to crack at the foundation of his courage. The utter dark refuge of his barrow called for him. Instead, he jumped to the dais. He could hear the drawn breaths of the others, but in his mind he heard again the words, *change it.*

Father Daugth made to strike, but Skag was faster. The cedar crashed upon the sweet-gum. The gray shaft was torn from Father Daugth's hands and clattered on the granite. This stunned the patriarch and upset his balance so that he toppled onto his side.

Then came the sound of wings stroking the night air. Skag glanced up to see the crow wheeling high into the canopy of branches. Then he felt Father Daugth's hand wrenching at his ankle. He struck down at the hoary fist. Father Daugth's scream of pain entwined with that of the crow's anger.

Skag flailed the cedar stave wildly above his head. The crow curved away, but the talons scraped the back of the bogfoke's hand. The bird disappeared into the dark above the gathering place. Skag's gaze darted over the tangle of branches in desperate search. Then the sound of those black wings came from behind him.

Skag swung the stave at the red-eyed shadow. It brushed the bird, and he caught sight of the creature rising sharply. He crouched in defense, but the night was filled with a sudden shriek.

His eyes found the crow. The momentum of its flight had impaled the wretched creature upon the gray-cloaked warrior's bayonet. Drops of blood dripped down onto the flagstones, like crimson tears. The dark form was still, dead beyond all doubt. Those unnatural eyes were forever dimmed.

Skag turned to his kith and kin. Gasping for air, he was unable to speak and could only stare at their uncertain faces. Kribble moved a little forward, but was halted by the flex of Skag's hand upon the cedar. Nearby a low moan issued from Daugth.

"Try something, Kribble," Skag finally managed to snarl. "I'll pound your black soul from out of you."

All was quiet, except another low moan from Father Daugth, and the occasional splatter of the crow's blood. Skag leaned forward to gaze into each and every face. "We are changing all of this."

His stave waved out as if to encompass them all. Their eyes were blank, but his were firm. "We can leave this place, tonight. We can cross the river and go into the Great Wood."

"How, with the wall of Cornbread Jack binding us?" asked Welken.

"Through the Weeping Arch," replied Skag, and he nodded at their amazement. "We will go down into the storm drain and follow the water down to the river. The city has dreamed often of the way."

Even Kribble showed a spark of curiosity in his dark eyes and ventured to speak, "Why?"

"To grow, to build and to reach," sighed Skag, knowing that only a morsel of understanding could pass to them. He barely understood himself, but he would move them with the force of his will. "To the arch, if you would be free."

They started moving, but Mother Crabba hesitated. "If we are touched by the sweat of Cornbread Jack, then surely we will die."

Skag shook his head. "The tears of the arch. The sweat of Cornbread Jack. We will only be cleansed of the darkness and strengthened to our purpose. That is the dream of the city."

Again they started toward the gate. Skag turned to the prostrate form of Father Daugth. He picked up the gray staff and broke it in two. The elder bogfoke was weak and uncertain. It seemed to Skag that some power had gone out of the Father when his ghastly familiar had been destroyed. He took Father Daugth's arm and helped the old bogfoke to his feet. "Come along, Father Daugth. Even for you there lies a path out of this place."

Daugth wavered, unsteady on his feet. Skag motioned with one hand to encompass the cemetery around them. "Would you stay here alone? In this place of men?"

With a death rattle sigh, Daugth let himself be led to the Weeping Arch. The others were waiting for them at the cast-iron gate. They were frightened, as though perched near the edge of an abyss. Using the stave, Skag pushed open the gate. The hinges were shrill upon being disturbed, but beyond lay the city streets.

Skag stepped over the threshold. The tears fell from above, wetting his face. On the other side he paused. He wondered what would happen. It was only water, and he felt no touch of doom He felt the birth of possibilities.

He looked around, realizing what he had done. He was outside. He was free of the ancient binding. Then he felt something—it welled through him and found its way to his lips. Skag smiled, nearly he laughed, and the other bogfoke followed as that smile lured them past the Weeping Arch. Though he lingered to the last, even Father Daugth finally made his uncertain way onto the street.

Then, with every face streaked by the tears from the coquina blocks they followed Skag toward the storm drain as the city folded the memory of them into the tumble of her dreams.

***

Skag shepherded the other bogfoke down into the culvert. There was enough room for a man to walk hunched over and the bogfoke could easily enough make it standing. They followed the stream of water. The darkness of this place served to comfort and calm them. Their kind possessed an innate skill in the dark. They could see with very little light, and they could sense by sound after all the long years of night.

The water began to deepen and soon they found themselves sloshing ankle deep. The brick lined sewer terminated in a sudden descent into a large concrete pipe. They squeezed through this and continued on along a more ancient section of sewer for nearly three miles. Here they came upon a pool of black water.

Skag moved forward and stared into the water. He could see faint gray light glowing under the dark water. He turned back toward the others, nodding. "Just as the city dreamed. The light comes from the creek into which this pipe empties. The sun has risen outside and the light shines through the water. We will wait until twilight before we venture beyond this pool."

"How?" grumbled Slignan. The light from the pool was glowing in his eyes, revealing the doubt.

"We will go down into the water," replied Skag, with his fist tightening upon the stave. "If we can see the light, then we cannot be too far from the surface."

There was a rustle from amongst the other bogfoke, drawing together the thin strands of their courage. They looked at one another seeking a voice. Finally Slignan leaned forward, looking dubiously at the pool and then back to Skag.

"Why is it that you do this? Why do you let the city lead us away?"

"I have told you," replied Skag. "In time the understanding of my words will come to you in full. But you may return if you wish, to the binding and the despair. I will continue on. I will go into the Great Wood, where there are places upon which have fallen no eyes of men."

"There are darker tales of the Great Wood," hissed Mother Crabba.

"There seem to be tales of light and dark told of every place in this world," shrugged Skag. "I will risk facing the dark for the sake of the light. I will risk the uncertainty to never again face the certainty of the place we have left."

The faint grumbling from behind urged Slignan on. The black-hearted bogfoke scratched his crooked nose, wondering what to do. The hold of Skag's will was slipping. Then Gristel moved away from the cluster to stand nearer to Skag.

She looked down at the water's surface before turning to face the others. "Which of us has not dreamed of leaving the cemetery? Who has not dreamed of passing beyond the binding of Cornbread Jack? I do not understand all the words of Skag, but I remember those dreams whenever he speaks. I will go into the water. I will follow Skag."

The tenuous strands of courage unraveled and Slignan felt suddenly alone, squirming beneath the gaze of Skag. He edged closer to the others. Skag gestured with the stave back along the tunnel.

"Let us go back a ways," he told them. "Out of the water. After a time we will send someone to watch for the fading light."

They followed him with relief up the incline of the tunnel. They came back to a place where the pipe had long ago cracked wide and the storm waters had eroded a small cave in the clay earth. There was space enough to accommodate them all and they settled down for the passing of the day. Skag positioned himself at the mouth of this womb in the earth so that the others would be dissuaded from any thoughts of fleeing back to the cemetery.

He was resigned to a sleepless day. He looked at his fellow bogfoke. He had suspected that Gristel might be the first to side with him. Many times before he had seen the glint of resentment and pride in her eyes whenever she felt put upon by one of the others. Her sister, Tegmina, shared a dreamy nature, but was far too timid to help or hinder.

Welken and Weart, the womb brothers, would follow the strongest wind. They were the youngest of the bogfoke in temperament, although only Mother Crabba and Father Daugth might know how many years had passed since their coming into the world. The lives of the bogfoke stretched further than their memories.

Robbis? He was certainly the most difficult to figure. He was restless and mischievous. Sometimes he was a petty and bawdy creature, but without truly dark intent.

Kribble and Slignan, there was the dark intent. They were shadows of Father Daugth, greedy for power and desiring the subservience of others. Kribble was perhaps the less cruel but more clever of the two.

What of Father Daugth and Mother Crabba? The Father hadn't a word to say since the confrontation at the dais. Skag was not ready to trust that the old one's spirit was broken. The darkness shrouding that ancient soul was too impenetrable for Skag to be certain of anything.

He was not sure why he had urged the patriarch to come. The loss of his familiar had weakened Daugth, but Skag sensed that this was not permanent. He would need to be vigilant.

Mother Crabba would be trouble. Without the threat of Father Daugth to give her words weight she would turn to spiteful cunning. As trivial as her mischief might seem, it must be watched. She had dark insight into the workings of the world and the bogfoke mind.

There was no way to mark time in the darkness of the tunnel. The time dragged by for the sleepless Skag, with the rumbling snores and occasional coughs of his sleeping kith disturbing the quiet. Finally he nudged Slignan with the cedar stave.

"Wake up, black-heart," he hissed. Slignan stirred and

his eyes opened both blurred and angry.

"What is it?"

Skag pointed with the stave along the descending slope of the tunnel. "Go to the pool and watch. When the water darkens come back and tell me."

"By myself?"

"Yes, faint-heart, by yourself," snapped Skag. "Do you think I'd let you take one of the others so you could devise some dim-witted scheme?"

Slignan kept his grumbling well under breath and trudged down the tunnel slope. Skag sat back against the curve of the tunnel. He saw Father Daugth stir. Those dark eyes opened and peered at him a moment. Then the Father settled with a clatter of skulls and slipped back into sleep.

The time passed in another long stretch. Gristel and Welken both woke. Neither spoke, but only sat watching the tunnel for Slignan's return. Skag idly watched bits of leaves and other debris passing on the thin stream of water flowing by. The flow of water seemed to be increasing and he wondered if that was a cause for concern. Then there came the echo of footfall sloshing back along the incline.

"It is darkening," reported Slignan. "It was strange. I looked away, and when I looked back, the water was like charcoal."

"More likely you fell asleep," muttered Skag as he nudged the others awake with his stave. They staggered to their feet and followed Skag as he started down the tunnel. Slignan was right. The water was nearly as dark as a starless night.

"You go first, Kribble. Then Robbis. Then Gristel and Tegmina," directed Skag, sending them in an order he felt to be manageable. "Welken will follow with Mother Crabba. Then Slignan, followed by Weart, Father Daugth and myself."

Kribble waded tentatively into the black pool. He glanced back at Skag and then dove beneath the water. Robbis shrugged and followed. They all went, until Skag saw

Father Daugth's dark form merge with that of the pool. Holding tight the cedar stave with one hand he slipped into the cool water.

Kicking his legs, Skag used his free hand as a guide along the pipe. He was blinded by the black water for a moment, but then spied the vaguest gray. His hand found a hold upon a muddy tangle of roots and he pulled himself from the water.

It was raining. The others had clustered around the stump of a half sunken willow. Huge, black storm clouds filled the sky and lightning flicked above the marsh surrounding them. Skag moved to join the cluster as he surveyed the scene around them.

Tegmina had begun to weep and Gristel draped a comforting arm around her shoulder. The others sat silent and glum. Skag looked back at the pool of water. Not two-hundred yards away was a steep embankment sweeping up to a roadway of men. This mounding of earth had severed the pool of water from the small creek that ran into the river. Skag gestured for them to follow him.

He forged an unsteady path through the clumps of marsh grass. The other bogfoke followed him, tugged along by the seeming strength of his courage in the face of the storm. But even in *his* heart was a longing for the comforting darkness of his barrow. Somehow, in the rain and the lightning, the words of Jeremiah Simms and the dreams of the city were diminished. Skag clung to their fading power as he forced himself to plod forward.

The mud sucked at their feet and the long grasses snagged at their arms and legs. They struggled to the edge of the river. Skag began to use this as a guide, following the gray waters upstream. As the storm began to roll away he espied a spur of forest jutting into the marsh. He turned their course for this stand of pines.

The rain had slackened and the lightning began to fade. The bogfoke fell exhausted onto the needle carpeted ground. The trees provided modest shelter from the rainfall.

Skag stood up and looked out over the tawny marsh grass to the river and beyond. On the horizon he could see the dark edge of the Great Wood and a sense of purpose returned to him. He looked over to Slignan.

"It was only late afternoon, you moss-brain," he scolded. "The thunderstorm blocked out the light and darkened the water."

"How was I to know? We couldn't hear anything in the sewer," protested Slignan. You told me to report when the water had darkened, and I did."

Skag pursed his lips, and then reluctantly nodded as he realized Slignan was right. Still, he would have liked to rap the black-heart upside his head, but that was what Father Daugth would have done. Instead, Skag just nodded again and turned away.

They would have to pass the remainder of the afternoon in this spur of forest. At least it was removed from the dwellings of men. In the meantime they could look for something that might help them cross the river.

"Come with me, Kribble."

Kribble rolled his eyes but rose to follow Skag deeper into the wood. Water fell in large drops from the tips of pine needles and the wind came sluggishly from the river. Mushrooms were abundant in the swampy copse. The two bogfoke pulled the mushrooms from the moist earth, stuffing them into their ragged shirts.

Finally they came across a log lying a quarter way buried in the sod. It was the remnant of a cypress that had been struck by lightning and tumbled by a past storm. Skag poked it with his stave, nodding his head all the while. "This will do. It has dried out so that it will not be too heavy for us to move, but not so dry that it will waterlog as we cross the river. When the darkness comes we will drag it to the creek and then float out across the river."

"We can't all get on that log," observed Kribble.

Skag shrugged. "Some of us will take turns swimming alongside. Now, let's take these mushrooms back to the others."

Kribble crinkled his nose at the thought of swimming across the river. Splashing about in the fish pond back at the cemetery was one thing, but a river?

When they returned to the wood they offered the mushrooms for Mother Crabba's approval. She poked them, sniffed at them, and turned them over in her palm before acknowledging each one fit to eat.

Skag munched his slowly. He figured it could be no more than three hours to true dark. There would be a three-quarters moon, but the overcast should keep the night black. He ate the last of his mushroom and wished he had a fat goldfish from out of the cemetery pond.

When the gloaming had reached out over the marsh, Skag led the other bogfoke back to the fallen log. It was hard work, pulling, prying and pushing to loose the log from the sod. Once it was free they slid it with relative ease over the leaf strewn earth. The bogfoke puffed, cursed and pulled until their makeshift boat splashed into the dark water of a wide ditch that fed into the creek. A weak cheer went up from the younger bogfoke, but Mother Crabba and Father Daugth looked skeptically at the bobbing form.

"All right," sighed Skag, musing over the bogfoke gathered around. "Father Daugth, Mother Crabba, Gristel, Tegmina, Weart, Kribble -- you shall sit atop the log. Slignan, Robbis and Welken will swim alongside with me. We will switch when we grow tired."

"There might be snakes in the water," protested Slignan.

"Let us hope they will have more sense than to poison themselves on your black blood," snorted Skag as he gestured for everyone to take their places.

The water was warmer than they had suspected. Skag held onto the log with the fingers of the same hand that grasped the cedar stave. Those sitting atop the log stroked with their hands and feet. Slowly they began moving along the ditch and into the creek. The sluggish current of the creek helped them move more easily toward the river.

"When we get to the river the current will be against us," warned Gristel.

Skag nodded grimly and managed to reply between strokes, "We will follow upstream along the river bank. Then we will cross. . . We can drift down a bit. . . There is a creek on the other side. . . We will paddle into its mouth. We can follow it well into the Great Wood."

A muskrat popped out of the water ahead of them. The beady eyes looked with disbelief upon the jumble of bogfoke coming toward it, and then the rodent dove back into the water and out of sight.

"Cowardly bones," grumbled Weart. "That would have made a decent meal."

Gristel had been correct. When they came out of the creek into the river the current came slow but steady against them. Those who had been swimming changed places with those on the log, excepting Mother Crabba and Father Daugth. Skag used his cedar stave like a pole on the shallow side near the riverbank.

They struggled for more than a mile upriver. Those in the water kept glancing at Skag for some sign of relief. At last he gestured for them to guide the log against the riverbank. The bogfoke in the water threw themselves in exhaustion onto the marsh grasses.

"We will rest for a bit," Skag informed them. "It is possible that we four could run into trouble as we cross the river, if it is more difficult than I'm guessing. In that event we will need some of you to help us."

"But we just swam for over a mile," complained Kribble.

"You will help us or we drift down into the city. What would the sons of Cornbread Jack do with such a black-hearted bogfoke as you, Kribble?"

"It just doesn't seem fair," sighed Weart.

"Crossing the river will be the most difficult part,"

said Gristel. "We will all do what we must."

"These two haven't done a thing so far," replied Kribble, gesturing at Mother Crabba and Father Daugth.

Skag said with a smile, "Let us be gentle with them, black-heart Kribble. They are as old as they are mean. Besides, haven't they lost enough of their pride?"

There was no reply. Sympathy was an emotion unfamiliar to the bogfoke. It came only in subtle and creeping ways, as if their better nature must sneak upon them. At Skag's words a sullen quiet settled on the group as they waited.

After a few minutes Skag gestured for everyone to again take their places and the log was guided into the river. The way was not as difficult as they feared. The wind had picked up and was blowing them toward the opposite bank, and forcing the tidal waters further upstream than was usual. The moon shone faint behind the overcast like a lidded eye. Far downriver there glowed the lights of the city, reflecting on the greater river into which this lesser flow emptied.

They paddled the log into the mouth of the creek. The tidal flow was pushing them at a brisk pace. The banks were steep and wooded. Skag didn't like the look of them. Lights from the windows of a great plantation house confirmed his suspicion. He whispered to the others, "Gently now. The houses of men are built upon either shore of this creek. The water goes on as far as I can see."

Gristel sat erect, peering into the dark. Then she nodded. "There is a bridge ahead. How far do you suppose we will need to go?"

Skag pulled himself a little onto the log for a better vantage. "It is difficult to be sure. The Great Wood is perhaps three miles from the river, but I don't think the houses of men extend that entire distance."

Many of the houses alongside the creek were abandoned, having been left vacant since the great war had swept through this area. Many were little more than rotted shanties. When the bogfoke had glided beneath the arches of the bridge Skag called for a change of places. He clambered onto the foremost portion of the log just ahead of Mother Crabba. The old matriarch was grumbling and holding tight to her wig. Father Daugth sat like a shadow behind her, silent and still.

They had gone nearly another mile when the last houses of men were left behind. Willows and cypress crowded along the low lying shore of the Great Wood. The canopy of leaves and the ribbon of water beneath were equally black. The pale gray moss hanging from the tree limbs was lifted by the wind and floated wraithlike against the dark.

After a half dozen miles the creek began to widen and the force of tide had finally failed them. Marsh grasses sprouted between the clustered trees. Across the broadening stretch of water rose the mighty trunks of the forest proper. The northern edge of the woodland drained into this marsh and the resultant dark-water pool. From there the creek fed into the river.

"Hallo, what's this?" chuckled Weart as he stood up chest deep in the water. "Look, cattails—everywhere. This whole pool is shallow."

The other bogfoke excepting Mother Crabba and Father Daugth slid off the log. Slimy mud squelched between their toes. Skag gestured toward the Great Wood, "We will let the Father and Mother ride on the log. This water is becoming too shallow to support any more weight than that."

It was difficult going. Their feet were snagged by roots or slipped on the muddy bottom. The dark water pool stretched a half mile between them and the banks of the Great Wood. With grumbling, cursing and an occasional plunge into an unexpected hole they struggled toward the tall pines.

Several hundred feet from the edge of those pines the log began to scrape on the bottom of the pool. Mother Crabba and Father Daugth were compelled to relinquish their perches and the log was abandoned. Weart and Welken helped the Father along. Gristel and Robbis aided the Mother.

The last short distance was a tortuous tangle of innumerable roots, but at last they came sloshing from the black water and threw themselves wearily onto the ground under the towering pines. The dark was intense beneath the wood. They all gazed anxiously along the ragged forest aisles.

"So, this is the Great Wood," mused Weart, smoothing his sparse beard nervously as he spoke. "It seems much like the wood we left on the other side of the river, only taller."

Skag shook his head. "No, this is many times larger than the city itself. It spreads for miles and miles uninterrupted by the axs of men. We cannot rest just yet, however."

He led them eastward under the tall trees. The land began to rise and the pines gave way some of their domain to hardwoods. The bogfoke had been adept at moving silently through the cemetery but were now tired and in unfamiliar surroundings. The noise of their passing made Skag grimace.

They found themselves floundering through an intense tangle of briars, vines and thorn bushes. At times they were forced to squirm along on their bellies for short distances. The density of this stinging undergrowth was such that they had not even the room to rest.

At one time Skag chanced to pass the skeletal remains of some poor buck that had wandered into the briars many years ago. It had probably thrashed about in panic, trying to free itself of this nightmarish tangle until, finally exhausted, it had simply fallen and died. The bogfoke were luckier. After a hundred more yards of agony the prickly jumble began to diminish.

Skag urged on the other bogfoke, but when their stumbling made any progress a farce he reluctantly allowed a brief pause. They sat sprawled, with heads bowed; weary beyond any fear of the eyes of men. Skag scratched his bearded chin. They had struggled nearly six miles into the wood, and with any luck they could make another or maybe two before the light of day was strong upon the earth. That would put them far enough from the edge of the forest and the lives of men as was possible for now.

When the slightest movement began among his kith, and a few had begun to gaze about, Skag exhorted them to their feet. They began their straggling journey once again. A small herd of deer was startled some distance ahead and darted away.

Skag gestured with his stave. "That is a good sign. Bogfoke should be able to get along easily enough wherever a deer can go."

Driven by Skag's relentless determination the bogfoke increased their pace. They had in their natures a capacity for traveling that sons of Cornbread Jack could not have managed. They crossed a small creek by way of a tree that had fallen across the water. The land was descending again and an occasional cypress or willow indicated that a larger body of water was near.

The wood gave way suddenly to an expanse of black, starless sky. Just barely could they see the equally dark water spreading before them. Skag moved to the edge of the water and his keen eyes appraised the situation.

"A lake, I suspect, far too broad for a creek or a river. Well, this is it then. We can go no further this night. We will rest here and look at things fresh by the light of a new day," he decided aloud, turning to look upon the others. "The light of day, imagine that. We are free of the cemetery and the day shall be as much ours as is the night."

With languid movements the bogfoke began to make themselves as comfortable as possible. Skag settled between the knees of an ancient cypress. With his back to the trunk he watched over the others as they arranged themselves for sleep. A chill crept along his spine when he became aware of Father Daugth looking at him. Those dark eyes were unreadable, but the hint of a smile shown through the thick, white beard.

"You have freed them of the cemetery, Skag," whispered the Father with his first words since the struggle beneath the gray-cloaked warrior. The poison had not perished from his voice. "Do you not think they should be pleased?"

With the ever present clatter of his adornments the Father rolled onto his side so that his face was turned away. The final movements of the other bogfoke gradually stilled. In the lonely dark Skag stared at the overcast sky. He sighed as he realized that it had all actually just begun.

TWO

In The Great Wood

The lake was deep and broad, reflecting the blue sky above. Scattered along its edge stretched tawny marsh and small black water creeks. Skag nodded, for this seemed a good place. The other bogfoke, save the ever grumbling Mother Crabba and the silent Father Daugth, crowded behind him. The reflection of light off the lake shone in their wide brown eyes. This sunlit world was a wonder to them all, something they had only glimpsed from the cracks of their barrows and crypts. This forest was overwhelming with new sights, sounds and smells.

"We will need shelter," he mused aloud. "Something not easily found by the eyes of men."

"I doubt if any men could come past that tangle of briars we crept through," said Gristel. "If the ground here wasn't so low we could dig a barrow."

Skag nodded again, thinking of the rolling gullies and low ridges of the forest. "Perhaps we *can* build a barrow..."

He turned back toward the high southern bank of the lake. The other bogfoke dutifully followed. They clambered back along the incline until they stood at the edge of a particularly steep ravine. Skag gestured into it with his stave, "We can set logs across this and cover them with turf and pine straw."

"When it rains the bottom will flood," observed Gristel.

Skag scratched his stubbled chin. She had a point.

"We could lay logs about waist high above the gully floor and then more logs as a roof above those," suggested Robbis. "We can square out the sides of the ravine and use the dirt fill beneath our floor."

"A barrow," replied Gristel as the concept of the sandwiched design formed in her mind.

"Sounds like a lot of work," grumbled Slignan. An agreement of complaints echoed his feeling, so he continued. "Also, how safe is it here? What of the houses of men?"

Skag nodded. "That is a concern. Why don't you and Robbis scout further along the lake in one direction. Welken and Weart can do so in the other. Turn back when the sun is near to noon. Just look for any signs of men.

"The rest of us will scout back and along the edges of that nightmare tangle of briars and brambles."

It was nearing late afternoon when they all gathered again. No sign of men had been found and so it was decided to rest through the night and begin the work on the barrow at dawn. Skag insisted that they make the day as much their own as had been the night in the cemetery.

He slept deep into the predawn hours. It had been his only true sleep in several days. When the sun shone through the boughs of the trees on the eastern shore of the lake, Skag's hunger finally stirred him from slumber.

He rubbed his eyes, staring up into the green canopy swaying high above him. His gaze lowered and he saw Gristel sitting nearby. Tegmina was still asleep, with one hand holding to the sleeve of Gristel's torn shirt. Slignan was awake, staring glumly at the lightening water of the lake. All the others were still asleep.

Skag began nudging them awake with his cedar stave. The whole group stirred, stretching, yawning and scratching.

Mother Crabba sat up, and with one hand holding steady her moss wig she glared at Skag.

"We must eat," she half whispered in her dry voice.

Skag nodded. "Even so, Gristel, Welken and Slignan will go foraging. The rest of us will start on the barrow."

Gristel motioned for the other two to follow, and they headed off toward the lake. Skag turned his attention to the remaining bogfoke. "Kribble and Weart, I want you to track back to where we came out of those briars and brambles. There was a deer skeleton."

"I remember it," interrupted Weart.

"The antlers, bones and hooves might be useful for digging out the walls and cutting the trees," explained Skag. "While you are off the rest of us will dig as best we can with our hands and any fallen branches we can find."

"There are probably clam shells somewhere along the shore of the lake," suggested Mother Crabba as she listened to their conversation. "They will help you dig. Otters leave them in small middens. You may even find some live clams. They are very tasty."

"That will be easier than digging with our hands," replied Skag.

As Kribble and Weart left, the remaining bogfoke scavenged along the lake shore and found a midden with plentiful clam shells. They returned then to slide along the ravine to the places Skag had indicated. Tegmina had to help Father Daugth along, but he began to dig like all the others. First the pine straw had to be raked away, and the bogfoke scraped at the loam with the shells and worried out troublesome roots with the branches they had found on the forest floor.

There was a surprise find in the midst of this effort -- grubs and earthworms. One and all the bogfoke stopped working and began picking the squirming creatures from the soil. After the unfortunates were washed in a puddle of water a modest feast ensued. Buoyed by the meal the bogfoke returned more energetically to their work.

Kribble and Weart returned in mid-afternoon, weary and battered but with their arms full. They deposited the remains of the fallen buck in a clatter as Kribble told Skag, "We brought everything we could gather and carry."

"Well done," replied Skag. "You two come along with me and well get started on getting logs for the bottom of the barrow."

Skag led them several hundred yards through the wood, near to the lake. He led them into the midst of a stand of cypress. He gestured toward the a sapling smaller in girth than a bogfoke's leg. "This wood is water-tough and rot-stubborn. We will build the barrow with it."

"How do you know such a thing?" asked Kribble.

"Because I spend many days with my ear near the door of my barrow," answered Skag. "I learned many things listening to the ground keepers."

Kribble and Weart joined him in chipping at the base of a slender trunk with the edges of the clam shells. It was very slow going. They finally settled in with two of them working while the third rested for a bit or returned to the midden for more shells, since they tended to break with some frequency.

Sweating, cursing and wondering if this was futile, the shadows had grown long before the sapling fell. They still faced the task of stripping the branches and cutting the thing to manageable length.

"Let's go back to the ravine and see if Gristel and the others have found anything to eat," sighed Skag. "I doubt this tree will escape while we are gone."

"Would that it could," Weart chuckled. "Then we could force it, instead, to follow us."

When the tree-chippers trudged into the ravine they found the other bogfoke eating. A wealth of acorns and wild berries were heaped in their midst. Skag ventured a look to inspect the digging. It had gone well enough, much better than he would have expected in his absence. He settled between Gristel and Mother Crabba and picked up one of the acorns, eying it skeptically.

"They can be eaten," said Gristel. "I used to nibble on them back in the cemetery. One of Mother Crabba's tale mentions them being roasted. Evidently they were sometimes eaten that way by the kith of Cornbread Jack."

Skag wondered what other tales known to Mother Crabba might contain tidbits of useful wisdom. Certainly it must be with an alert ear that he listened to her words from now on.

"We saw hunters," Slignan reported, leaning close. Skag arched his eyebrows and Slignan nodded. "I don't think they'll come this way. It was several miles from here and beyond that tangle of briars. I was following a low rabbit trail, hoping to get us some meat. There's no way the men could have come through the bramble."

"Which appears to go on and on," interrupted Gristel. "I shouldn't be surprised if it reaches to the other side of the lake."

"Anyway," inserted Slignan impatiently. "These hunters, they have a hatchet"

"A hatchet?"

Slignan smiled at the interest in Skag's voice. Then he pursed his lips as if thinking. "What if we steal the thing? Imagine how much easier and quicker it would be to build the barrow if we had a hatchet."

Skag nodded slowly. "Yes, but to steal in the light of day?"

Now Slignan's smile spread to its greatest width beneath his crooked nose. "It is nearly twilight. They cannot clear the wood by dark. I saw no camping equipment, so they must have a cabin or lodge nearby. See, I too listen to the tales of Mother Crabba."

Skag pondered the idea. He hadn't realized how much responsibility he had bargained for, and it weighed heavily upon him. Now hunters, so close, with only the briars to ward them.

"Men," snickered Slignan. "Men couldn't spot a bogfoke in the shadows at their feet, never mind the dark of night. Clouds are building, so it will be a very dark night."

After a thoughtful moment Skag replied, "Well then, black-heart. I hope your feet are as stealthy as your head is sly."

***

Through the last gray reach of day, Slignan and Skag tracked the hunters. They fought their way past the tangle of briars and thorny vines that curved around the lake-wood. The going was difficult enough for the bogfoke that it gave them a sense of security against the risk of being discovered.

Once they came to the spot Slignan had first spied the party the signs became easy to read. It was a narrow track by the standards of the kith of Cornbread Jack and the bumbling men left much evidence of their passing. The bogfoke, however, found it to be uncomfortably wide.

They moved in the deeper shadows alongside the path, tense and alert. Once, the flap of wings caused them to cringe. Memories of the red-eyed crow stung them with fear, but it was only a small owl. Skag and Slignan shared a chuckle before setting off along the trail again.

A yellow light began to dart in and out of their vision depending on the twist of the path. They edged around a wide bend and spotted the hunting lodge ahead. It was little more than a clapboard shanty. A kerosene lamp shone on the porch and the windows glowed with faint light from within. The two bogfoke curled around the place so that the wind was in their faces. A long row of kennels housed a dozen hounds and the bogfoke neither feared nor respected anything so much as a dog.

"Where do you suppose they'd keep the hatchet?" whispered Skag.

Slignan gestured toward a chest sitting on the porch. "Could be in there, or nearby. I see some other gear laid around it. That belt is where the hunter I saw hung the hatchet."

The belt was draped over the chest. An unlit lantern sat nearby, along with a small-game pouch. Skag surveyed the unkempt grounds around the shanty. The sound of sudden and loud laughter caused both bogfoke to melt into the dark wood. A plan formed in his mind.

All bogfoke were quick, and had an instinct for blending themselves into the shadows. All were adept mimics with the ability to throw their voices. It had often been useful in the cemetery. The sound of a startled cat scrambling into the brush could distract a human who was passing too near a hidden bogfoke. The rustle of rats might deter an inquisitive eye or probing hand from exploring a bogfoke's barrow. All could be useful in this endeavor.

"Drunk, I'd expect. That could work to our advantage," mused Skag. "What we need is for their attention to be taken away from the porch. It is too risky to go into that light, but I can go around the back and make some noise. When you hear me, then you run up to the porch and try to find a hatchet."

"Let's hope they don't let loose the dogs," whispered Slignan, swallowing anxiously.

All Skag could do was shrug. He suspected they wouldn't loose the dogs in the dark of night, but who could be certain what drunken men might do? He began edging around to the back of the shanty. Twice the raucous laughter pressed him close to the loamy earth. The back of the place had a small, stoop-like porch. Several washbasins and a half dozen mason jars were stacked in one corner. Skag's bogfoke heart was elated at the possible mischief.

It was a stomach wrenching dash to the edge of the stoop. He scrambled under the floor and fought to calm himself. The weakness wouldn't leave his knees, and his stomach refused to un-knot. He finally managed to reach up and jerk the largest washbasin from off the porch. There followed a shattering of glass as the jars were knocked over, then the clatter of the fallen basin, and finally the bellowing from kennel of the startled hounds. Skag bolted from under the stoop, running hard for the wood.

From behind him came an eruption of surprise and anger. He heard the slap of the screen door and the thump of feet on the stoop. He heard Slignan mimicking the sound of some animal seeming to retreat into the forest in the opposite direction the bogfoke were going. There was confused shouting, and even some amusement. Speculation was bantered about, and annoyed curses punctuated the turmoil.

The sounds were lost as Skag slid through the underbrush. Thorns snagged at his ragged trousers, but he continued to hurtle through toward the rabbit path. His heart was cold with dread anticipation of the baying hounds being loosed in pursuit, but in the end there was only the sound of his own frantic retreat.

He burst through a tangle of wax myrtle and felt something crash into his side. Knocked to the ground, he rolled through the underbrush and was quickly to his feet again. He found himself staring into the bent-nose face of Slignan.

Surprised melted on both faces. They grinned sheepishly at one another, and then Slignan thrust forth his hands. He was holding the belt, with the hatchet dangling from it. Skag took the wooden handle and slid the tool from its case. Even in the dark he could see the glint to that keen edge.

Skag looked up from the wedge of steel and into Slignan's proud eyes. They had done it. Skag's finger brushed along the metal surface, but he jerked it away. Iron always unsettled him. He held the tool at arm's length, examining it, just an ordinary hatchet. He handed it back to Slignan.

"It is yours," he told the other bogfoke. Slignan's eyebrows arched in surprise, but Skag nodded. "It was your idea. You were the one to fetch it from the porch. You are the keeper of the hatchet."

Slignan smiled grateful and proud. He quickly sheathed the tool when large drops of rain began to sporadically fall. Skag motioned for him to follow. "Come along, sly-heart. I don't think they are going to release the dogs at night, in the rain, against an unknown quarry. Let's get back to the barrow. The rain will erase our scent in any event. Tomorrow you'll have plenty of work for your blade."

Together they made their way back to the barrow as the rain began to fall harder. Slignan's eyes were bright in the dark, and his smile was untainted.

***

The nights following the rain became chilled and the bogfoke worked with misted breath. The frosted pine straw crackled beneath their feet and the bite of the hatchet echoed among the autumnal hardwoods. At night they huddled around a fire that they were forced to keep short lived. Mother Crabba wove her tales, but only those chosen by Skag. His intent was not to tyrannize the others, but he did not want dark and despairing images to worry at their sense of purpose.

The barrow now gave them modest protection from the cold rains of autumn. Slignan wielded his hatchet with zealous energy, disregarding the envy of his comrades. They watched him work, sometimes desirous of his position and sometimes with wonder at the glittering dance of steel upon wood.

The Great Wood offered to the bogfoke a bounty that demanded only their cleverness and toil before earning its revelation. They were bogfoke still, with delighted squabbles and pine cones flung in half-hearted confrontations. Skag smiled often through his weariness as he watched them working.

Yet, there came times when the bustle was overwhelming to him. He tried always to work longer and harder than any of the others. In his exhaustion he grew tense at the silent, steady stares of Father Daugth and the endless grumbling of the Mother. On occasion he would wander into the deep wood, letting the solitude soothe him as he wrapped his mind around the purpose that had brought them to this place. Like a tired farmer shifting his grip upon the plow, he always found a reserve of energy.

After a particularly contentious morning he straggled along the lake shore, poking absently at the ground with his cedar stave. His way wove through a maze of cypress knees until he came to the huge stump of a once mighty tree that had cast its roots far afield. Certainly it had been as tremendous in girth as any tree he had ever seen. Testing its condition, he rapped at the trunk with his stave.

"Stop it!" came a shout that pierced the thud of cedar upon half rotten cypress.

Skag whirled around with the stave held defensively. It had been no bogfoke's voice he had heard, but also not that of a man. Only the slight shadows of mid-afternoon crouching beneath the forest were revealed to him. The thought of swift retreat filled his head, but from what? Which direction? Then there came from behind him a rustle like dried leaves.

"Back here, wood-knocker," sighed the same deep voice.

To Skag's amazement a great mound of fallen moss began to rise from the base of the cypress trunk. Not moss -- a tangle of hair draped atop a gnarled face. Skag stepped back with his stave poised defensively, but his bogfoke curiosity kept him from flight. Whatever this thing was, it towered man high.

The wide eyes were of washed out brown, and the hair grew along the shoulders and halfway down the back as well as swirling around a grinning face. The skin was gray-brown. It was naked and sexless so far as Skag could determine.

"A troll," it cackled in answer to the question unasked. It leaned forward to stare into Skag's face. "Least wise, that is what the witch called me. Hmm, I've seen the like of you afore, wood-knocker. Long ago, like peeking into someone else's dream."

"I didn't know that the stump was your home,"

apologized Skag, with his hands still firm in warning upon the cedar stave.

"My home?" mused the troll as it turned to look back at the cypress stump. The smile became tinted with sadness. "That, stump-thumper, is me. Or least ways it once was, in a manner of speaking."

Skag was confused, but willing to believe these words -- knowing nothing of trolls. The creature nodded its head in affirmation of some inner thought.

"I was that tree," it explained to Skag. "Or that tree was the home of my spirit. Depends on how you look at such things. Now *you*, or a man, or the witch, you are more completely both material creatures and spirit. Me? Well, I'm less creature than that. Or, I was. But, I dwelt in that tree as you seem to that body, but I was not limited to it.

"Well, in any event, the witch came. She sang to me and she seemed a pleasant thing. And I began to yearn for the freedom of men. I desired to stride with substance. To stride across the face of this world with nary a binding root. I, lord of the lake-wood, charged with the guiding dominion of water and forest. Lord of the lake-wood, so that nothing moved in this woodland without some inkling of it coming to me. She seduced me from the deep soil."

The thing that called itself a troll rose a little more erect and spread its twisted arms. A crooked smile snaked across the face. "You cannot say that she lied. I can move as freely as any man and swifter than most. But the cost. The shame. My dominion was broken. The strength of my spirit diminished to little more than these bones and this flesh."

The troll was shaking its head ruefully by the ending of the words, but then a cloud of suspicion settled on the troll's brow. "Are you one of her creatures?"

Skag shook his head. "I've seen no witch. I am a bogfoke."

The troll shrugged his hairy, leaf-tangled shoulders. "Never heard of such a thing. Still, you are remindful of something…"

"Is the witch still around?"

The troll arched its eyebrows to emphasize the confirmation before saying, "Certainly. And this is *her* wood now. Are all bogfoke as small as you?"

Skag shrugged to indicate give or take a bit here and there. The troll shrugged back to indicate that was what it had expected as it spoke again, "Well, two of you might could take a man in a fight. A small man, though. Very small. Though, I don't know about one of the witch's men. You look lean and tough enough to have some fight in you."

The bogfoke relaxd his grip on the stave and sat back on a clump of dried marsh grass as he replied, "I am named Skag. I have led my kith from the city that we might grow, build and reach."

"The city, with all her dreams," the troll sighed, and then nodded at Skag's wonder. "Yes, even the dreams of the city came to me --- in time. The city and I were kindred spirits. Guides and tenders we were. Well, I must tell you, Skag, that this wood isn't much of a place for growing and such with the witch around."

"Do you have a name?" asked the bogfoke.

"Ah, I have many. One I will not utter aloud. That one was given to me before even the beginning of this wood. That one not even the witch could seduce from me," replied the troll. He turned to look wistfully at the rotting cypress trunk. "You may call me Stump. It is short, and rings nicely to my ear. Like Skag."

The bogfoke looked past the troll, absently surveying mallards that floated across the blue-gray water of the lake. A witch, he thought, what misfortune. A few of the ducks began to ascend from the water, rested now and eager to be on their way again. Skag watched them trade the blue of the lake for the azure sky. He turned back to the troll who called himself Stump.

"I would assume this witch is human?"

The troll nodded grimly. Skag pursed his lips at the distasteful problem. "How many humans come around here?"

Stump's laughter was dry and crackling as he replied, "Very few, stump-thumper. I am not completely without power. And the witch, she don't like meddlers. Did you not come through that tangle of thorn, bramble and briar? It is called the ward of Yolande, for it is of her making.

"I'll tell you, by the deepest soil, it is near impossible for a man to pass that nasty stretch 'less she wills it."

"It wasn't so easy for a bogfoke, either."

"Well, perchance she mightn't bother you and yours, wood-knocker," offered Stump. "Could be she'll consider you little more than clever animals, like beavers or raccoons."

"Let us hope," the bogfoke sighed. "I must be getting back. We are building a barrow."

"I hear the bite of an ax," replied Stump, with more than a little distaste. "Mostly young cypress by the sound of it."

Skag squirmed uncomfortably, "I'm sorry about that."

The troll chuckled morbidly. "No need to apologize. It will let some of the other trees gain some breathing room. But leave be this bit of wood around us here. These are the off spring of the tree that was me."

The shaggy creature turned then and began wedging itself back into the shallow burrow beneath the cypress stump. Skag shook his head in wonder. Then he turned to maneuver his way through the knobby cypress knees and back to the barrow.

***

With the passing of each day the forest had drawn upon itself a little more of winter's gray gown. The nights were becoming bitter cold, with stars adamant against the utter black between. When the winds came rolling from the northwest the great trees would moan and creak in the grasp of the frigid air. Then one day this early winter seemed to vanish.

Skag woke in the gray predawn. The bogfoke were

not as susceptible to the cold as were the kith of Cornbread
Jack, but he was immediately aware of how warm the early
morning air had become. He crawled past the snoring forms
of his comrades and eased his way through the barrow door.

What had been a hard frost the night before was now
dew was dripping from the green points of pine needles. A
winter black bird fluttered to a nearby branch and cocked its
head to look at Skag. It seemed as confused by this weather as
was the bogfoke. The velvety touch of spring should have
been months away.

Skag sat with his back to the barrow listening to the
forest. No wind stirred and a solemn quiet had descended. It
reminded him of the cemetery, with the gray hardwoods
standing like tombstones amidst the pines. The winter-cold
lake had misted over and tendrils of fog eased along the
forest aisles.

Gradually the other bogfoke awoke. They looked in
suspicious wonder at a forest world held in the arms of
gentle warmth. The lethargy of the wood crept into their very
bones, as if any effort would be wasted. Slignan sat fingering
the handle of his hatchet with lips pursed in thought. He
finally went with Welken to scavenge for wood.

Father Daugth moved like a shadow beneath the gray
branches of a nearby oak. He settled against the rough bark
and his dark eyes roamed the surface of the misted lake as
though searching for the wraith of a lost memory. Mother
Crabba stood between the Father and Skag, studying the
scudding clouds high above. She leaned for a moment toward
the elder bogfoke, as though pulled by the magnetism of
habit, but then she shuffled over to sit by Skag.

She arranged her moss-wig and turned her brown
eyes to study the younger bogfoke. The crooked smile was
gone from her lips and the nut brown face was tense. Skag
arched his eyebrows in question.

"We are old, the Father and I," she whispered. As
Skag nodded, her brittle voice continued, "We have seen this
before. It is one of the great storms that come up from the

sea."

A chill ran along Skag's spine, but he managed a look of incredulity. "The sky is clear, and the season of great storms has passed, Mother. I can sense a movement of air but surely it is just the passing of one season into the next. These temporary reversals are not unusual."

A sigh bubbled from Crabba's bloated chest, "For the moment there are only those few low clouds moving overhead, while all seems still below, but the storm is coming. The forest waits. We have all seen these storms before. It is not unheard of that they should come even in the early winter. We can hope that it only brushes us, rather than descend with full fury."

Skag was trying to dredge forth some argument. He had as great a feel for the weather as any bogfoke, excepting perhaps the Mother. He had memories of the great storms, but never one so far into the winter. He was about to question her on this when the sounds of urgent shouting erupted from near the lake.

Skag leapt to his feet and, with the other bogfoke following, hastened toward the uproar. The first thing he saw was Stump. The troll's already ugly face was contorted with revulsion and he was standing knee deep in the lake. Skag then saw Slignan near the edge of the water brandishing his hatchet in a threatening manner. Welken was standing nearby holding a twisted branch as though it were a stave.

"Skag!" shouted the troll. "I am most happy to see you, stump-thumper."

Slignan cut his eyes to ascertain for himself that Skag was drawing near. He then stepped back away from the water's edge. Skag came to a gasping halt beside the hatchet-bearer.

"What is all this?" he asked.

Slignan gestured with his hatchet toward the troll. "We were walking along when all of a sudden this…thing…comes leaping out of the forest and grabs poor Welken by the shoulders. All the while it's shouting your name."

Stump shrugged, "You look alike to me, Skag. Truth is, I can't tell you much apart 'less I see you all together. I thought he was you."

Skag frowned, "Why did you want to grab *me*?"

The troll spread his arms like an oak reaching above the forest as he spoke, "I remembered where I'd seen the like of you afore."

Skag motioned for Slignan to put away his hatchet and then gestured for Stump to come ashore. The troll sloshed from the cold water, staring harshly at Slignan. He sat down upon the twisted roots of a cedar.

The other bogfoke drew up in a curious crescent behind Skag. Gristel was frowning and comforting her ever timid sister. Slignan kept one hand upon the handle of his hatchet while Welken still grasped his silly branch.

"What is this thing?" asked Gristel.

"A troll, more or less," replied Skag, who then turned his attention to Stump. "What did you remember?"

The troll scratched one of his shaggy shoulders nervously as he began, "I remember where I've seen your like. There used to be a whole jumble of your kind down by the big marsh. The red men, they called you cornbears, or marshbears. You used to steal their corn. Your folk said no one could own a growing thing."

"We've never lived in the marsh," snorted Kribble with indignant decision.

Stump paid him only little heed and continued, "Not *you*, but your *like*. The witch didn't appreciate you none. That's why I came to tell you what I remembered. It won't be safe for you around here."

Skag stood still for a long moment as he considered these words. "What happened to the cornbears?"

"They stayed mostly in their marshlands, especially after the coming of the white folk. But then there came the witch. They resisted her. I heard tell that she bound them all up in a big hill. I heard also that they went into the hill so as she couldn't get to them. When I was a tree I could hear their voices through the soil. You must remember that I couldn't actually see them the way I see you. I could only sense them. That is why it was difficult for me to remember where I'd run into your kind before. And this form fogs my mind."

"He was a tree?" blurted Welken.

Skag waved off the distraction. He kept his eyes riveted on the troll. "Why did the witch not like the cornbears?"

Stump rolled his pale brown eyes as he replied, "How should I know? It's not like I'm going to be sittin' around on her porch in the evening going on about things like the weather and why she hates cornbears. Most probably they resisted her will. That's usually enough."

"Well, thank you for the warning, my friend," sighed Skag. "I will have to think about this for a time."

Stump shrugged. "You'll not be having all the time in the world, but then, you can't leave just now. There's a storm coming in off the great-water."

Skag was about to point out, as he had to the Mother, that the sky was clear, but it was then that his gaze was snagged on the southeastern rim of the world. Like a great gray wall the clouds were piling high upon the horizon. He saw Mother Crabba nodding on the periphery of his vision. The troll glanced at Slignan and then back to Skag.

"May I go back to my stump now?"

"Certainly," smiled Skag. "I thank you, and my kith shall not harm you now that they know you for a friend."

"Unless you come jumping out of the woods and shaking us like old rags," added Welken, ruefully massaging his own shoulders.

Stump looked at them for a moment before shaking his huge, shaggy head. "I'm sorry...but by the deep soil, it is difficult to sort you lot out."

With a final chuckle the troll turned and stomped off

through the wood. The bogfoke clustered tighter around Skag. They wondered at all of this. Skag had told them nothing of witches, not to mention a troll that had once been a tree.

"Why have you hidden this from us?"

The Father's whisper lingered virulently, but Skag could see the question reflecting less harshly in the eyes of all the others. He nodded slowly, as when drawing to a much pondered conclusion.

"We have things to discuss," he admitted. Then he turned to look back at the eastern sky. "Yet, we also have to prepare for the great-storm."

In a straggling line the worried bogfoke followed him back to the barrow.

***

They worked intensely through the remainder of the day. The dirt filling beneath the barrow was shored up with lengths of sapling poles. They divided their food supply and buried each portion in a different place. They drove sapling stakes further along the gully in the hope of diverting and slowing any water running toward the lake from higher ground.

By the time of the gloaming the overcast had grown thick and the boughs were swayed by strengthening winds. The moisture could be smelled upon the air. Seagulls flew overhead, squawking as they fled inland.

The winds began to issue in strong gusts as premature dark settled on the premature gloaming. Now even the great trees were bending to the will of the storm. A fine rain began to fall, driven with stinging ferocity. The bogfoke sat around their fire as the wind and rain sang outside the barrow.

Skag saw all the faces with each featured etched sharp by the flickering red glow. Every eye was curious, save the glinting dark gaze of Daugth, which was as unreadable as ever. So Skag told them how he had met the troll. He told them also of the witch.

"Why did you not tell us before?" asked Gristel. She was disappointed that he had not trusted them.

Skag weighed the moment. He suspected it would take all his will to hold their loyalty. He poked the fire with his stave, brightening the flame and reminding them of the cedar's presence -- reminding them also of his victory over Father Daugth.

"I did not think the witch a danger to us," he explained firmly. "Stump didn't think so at first. If I had told you, would you have had the courage and determination to finish the barrow?"

No words were returned. They sat watching the fire as it danced just beyond the tip of the cedar, or the swirling smoke as it drifted into the rafters of the barrow. Long, pressing gusts of wind had begun to dominate outside. In the distance a rumble of thunder sounded and echoed in the dark.

"Without the barrow we would not have shelter from this storm," Skag reminded them.

"Without this barrow we would have been back in the cemetery," replied Father Daugth. The chill and darkness intensified his words. "We were safe in the cemetery. We had been safe for years beyond the counting. Safe from a time before there ever *was* a cemetery."

Skag tensed his hands upon the stave even as he fought his anger. He turned his head to look at the Father. Those dark eyes were ready to swallow all of Skag's courage, but he forced himself to dive into their depths without hesitation.

"We were dead in the cemetery," he said with the grim firmness of his voice challenging the elder bogfoke. "We were as dead as any corpse of man laid beneath the soil."

A bolt of lightning shone brilliant through the gaps in the barrow walls. The thunder that followed had rumbled away before the Father spoke again. "What gave you the right to judge such a thing?"

The calculating elder was turning Skag's own morality and convictions back upon him, but it struck Skag that this was a tactic he too could employ. He smiled, determined to reply calmly while echoing Father Daugth's dark arrogance. "What right had I? What right had any of us when you sat upon that dais in judgment? What right? By your standards, I had the right by way of this cedar, the blood of a demon crow, and a broken cudgel of sweet gum. Do you challenge that?"

Father Daugth said nothing. The tension between them suffocated all words. Outside the storm was descending, causing them to feel as if they were in a cocoon of simmering, strained silence. For the moment the iron will of Skag had held them, but the threat was not ended.

He shifted his gaze from Daugth back to the others. "I would not be as this one was in the days of our binding. I forced not one of you to follow me here. When the storm has passed you may go where you will, or we will decide together what to do."

As the bogfoke nodded grimly, sudden gusts of wind began to fiercely pound at the forest. The barrow was rattled by the force of them, creaking under the strain. Skag gestured for the fire to be put out so that it would not be spread by this angry wind. The darkness was nearly complete, almost blinding even the bogfoke.

Lightning flashed, lingering for a moment and then fading. The thunder rolled until it was lost in the sound of the wind tossing rain in drumming sheets against the barrow. Skag grimaced as he felt the water spraying across his face. The wind was driving the rain through any and every crack in the barrow roof or walls. They need not have put out the fire.

He crept near the door to the barrow and ventured a look through the gap in the logs. The night was like shadow upon shadow. The wind was assaulting the trees and ripping limbs from the forest canopy. The noise of this destruction was lost in the growing uproar of the storm.

A loud crack drew his attention and he saw a tall pine

fall prey to the slashing wind. It was snapped in two and crashed to the ground, quivering for a long moment. The wind worried at the fallen tree like a dog at a bone. Another burst of wind-tossed rain drove Skag from his peep hole. He returned to the center of the barrow.

He had barely settled back amongst the others when a great roar caused them all to cover their ears. There was a blur of splintering wood and a huge shudder tossed the bogfoke about. A squat cedar tree had been ripped from its perch along the rim of the ravine and hurled against the barrow. The branches of the uprooted tree had crumpled the outer wall.

"Slignan, bring your blade," shouted Skag as he rushed to the ruined wall. He pointed at the intruding branches. "Cut those away or they'll pry the wall completely apart. The rest of you, help me shore up these logs. Bring rope!"

The bogfoke rushed to do his bidding. Except Father Daugth, who stood with eyes seeming to glow in the night. Mother Crabba edged away from his grim presence. Despite the uproar around and within the barrow, Skag heard the Father's hoarse whisper, "The cedar is fallen."

Kribble thrust the coil of rope into Skag's hand. It wasn't very strong rope, made of twisted vines, but it would have to suffice to lash the logs together and bind this breach in their shelter. Slignan chopped frantically at the intruding limbs and roots. They knew this would likely cause the main trunk to lean more solidly upon the barrow, but the cedar was being thrashed around so much by the wind that the intruding branches were like pry bars in the wall.

While Slignan worked, the others lifted and shoved the displaced logs back into place. They also tried to use the chopped off branches to push the cedar trunk away from the barrow wall, but those branches were not stout enough. The damaged wall moaned as the trunk pressed more firmly upon it.

The wind driven rain soaked the bogfoke's ragged

clothing and matted their hair against their skulls. The logs were slick and difficult to maneuver, and with some of the logs missing there would be large gaps in what remained of the wall. Slignan's hatchet danced fierce in the flashes of lightning as he worked on the remaining intrusive branches.

Suddenly the fallen tree shifted when only a few branches remained. Almost the wind pushed it away and to one side of the barrow wall, but a slight lull caused it to settle hard. Several of the unlashed logs popped out of place, sending the bogfoke diving for safety. Slignan twisted away from the falling cedar and the hatchet was flung from his hand and skidded across the barrow floor.

It lay there a long moment. It was the hand of Father Daugth that finally grasped it. The other bogfoke climbed cautiously back to their feet. They stood uncertain between Skag and the Father. The dark glitter in Father Daugth's eyes pressed them to the edges of the barrow, and he moved slowly toward Skag. The sound of skulls clattered ominously even in the din of the storm. Skag did not back away, but held tight to his cedar stave.

"I know your sort, Skag," hissed Father Daugth. He lifted the hatchet. The blade was pale in the dark. "The touch of cold iron is your bane. The Mother could have told you. There have been others like you. Even during my youth there was one, dreams of the city, the pattern of the stars, a face upon the moon, endless ponderings. I dealt with that nonsense."

Skag frowned, not understanding what the Father was saying, but he saw the Mother sobbing into her hands as she huddled against the far wall.

"My own sister," the Father smirked, and he hefted the hatchet as though enjoying the feel of its weight in his hand. "The cold iron pounded the life out of her. It is the one tale I would not let the Mother weave, the death of Sloe. They called her Sloe of the golden voice, but I silenced her, and all memory of her."

Daugth pulled himself to his greatest height, half a

head taller than Skag. Taller than any bogfoke Skag had ever known, and the dark bulk of him became as one with the night within the barrow. Each of the adorning skulls looked as if to leer and laugh at the younger bogfoke. Father Daugth's own dark laughter pierced the storm.

"But the death of Skag shall be told, ever and again," spat the Father. He rushed with hatchet descending as he screamed, "Come to your death, sister's son!"

THREE

Remus Wolfe

Skag hurled himself from the path of the charge, but felt the stinging bite of the hatchet graze his right shoulder. Blood spread warm across his upper arm. He swung out with the stave, but the Father had already retreated. Those black eyes glared at him as the lips twisted into a sneer.

Skag circled carefully around the hulking form. He made a feint, but Daugth ignored it. All those times Skag had caught the elder bogfoke watching him, now Skag knew. The Father had been studying him, watching how he used the stave. So now Skag faced an old but crafty warrior. An opponent to who pain meant little.

I am faster, thought Skag. He moved in, attempting to drive the butt of the stave into the Father's stomach. The hatchet came down upon the cedar with a shallow bite. Father Daugth had anticipated the move, seeming to know even before Skag how the younger bogfoke would react to every situation.

Skag tried to use the stave to wrench the hatchet from the huge fist, but Daugth managed to pull it free. Skag retreated, haunted by the gloating, confident smile upon Father Daugth's face. His courage was wilting and he looked past the dark form of the Father. He looked toward the storm tossed forest beyond the barrow door. He could flee.

To grow, to build and to reach. The words sprang into Skag's head in that moment where he was suspended between flight or continuing the struggle. To grow and to build you must learn. It shone like a light in his mind.

Skag shifted his grasp on the cedar stave so that he led with his left rather than his right. He charged toward the Father, moving *toward* the hatchet rather than trying to avoid it. As he did so he struck out at the arm with which Father Daugth held the wedged weapon. Father Daugth's eyes were wide with confusion as the blow glanced off his forearm.

Skag whirled and struck again, but this time lower so that he struck the Father's thigh. The change in Skag's grip had altered the pattern and posture of his attack He was less adept than before, but the Father was less able to predict his actions, and still hadn't the speed to match Skag. The cedar blurred between them, crashing upon the dark one's shoulder.

Father Daugth roared his frustration and lashed out with the hatchet. Skag poked forward with the stave, catching the elder bogfoke in the stomach. Unbalanced, the Father tumbled through the barrow door and slid along the muddy sides of the ravine.

Swept away by his anger, Skag leapt after his adversary. The rain stung his eyes, filling his mouth and nose. Just barely he could see the Father ahead of him, struggling in retreat along the ravine. The younger bogfoke sloshed through the ankle deep water in pursuit.

Stumbling around the bend in the ravine he was surprised by the Father's ambush from above. The elder bogfoke came sliding down the embankment with the hatchet slicing within inches of Skag's head. The cedar stave licked out, knocking the weapon from the Father's hand. Then both bogfoke went crashing to the muddy earth under the force of the collision.

They scrambled to regain their feet, each desperate to reach the hatchet before the other. But Slignan had followed them and had jealously plucked the weapon from where it had fallen. Skag was turning back to the Father when there erupted a long rumbling roar, and then came a wall of water surging along the ravine.

In a flash of lightning Skag saw the nightmare turmoil of rushing water and the bitter face of Father Daugth as the water swept him into its embrace. Skag tried to crawl up the embankment, but his feet slipped uselessly in the mud. Then all was black and a hundred currents plucked at him and bashed him with their fury. He fought to hold his breath but had it knocked from him when the water slammed him against some unseen obstruction.

For a moment he felt his head rise above the roiling water and he gasped for air. The current pulled him back down but was less angry. He realized that he had never let go the cedar stave and began stabbing it at the sides of the ravine, attempting to break the hold of the churning water.

At last he had purchase enough to drag himself from the chaotic flood. He struggled up the side of the gully and dropped onto the soggy pine straw as rain pelted his back. What of the others? What of Father Daugth? What of the barrow?

Darkness was crowding his mind and he couldn't sort the tangle of his thoughts. Then he felt hands upon his shoulder and looked up to see Gristel leaning over him. Mother Crabba, Tegmina and Weart stood nearby, but no sign of the others.

"Let us help you up," said Gristel as Weart took hold of Skag's other arm. He got weakly to his feet but had to lean against Weart to walk.

"The barrow is gone, washed away," sighed Gristel. "The others are trying to find what supplies they can salvage. We have not seen Father Daugth. He was swept away by the water."

They made their way to the scant shelter of a fallen log. After a while Robbis, Welken and Kribble came straggling in with a few pouches of food. Slignan came along only a short time later. He looked toward Mother Crabba and then shook his head, "No sign of the Father."

Sitting in the rain and lightning, Skag drifted in and out of consciousness. Words rolled in his head, confused memories and insistent whispers. One thing came over and again, the hoarse voice of Father Daugth shouting in disdain, *sister's son.*

A great crash of thunder shook Skag from the shadows of half sleep and he looked to the form of Mother Crabba. She was staring into the dark of the storm with her rain drenched wig sitting crookedly atop her head as she rocked upon her heels. The sound of Skag's stirring caught her attention and she turned toward the younger bogfoke.

Memories once buried had risen in Skag's uneasy sleep and he looked with resignation upon Mother Crabba and said, "You must tell us the tale of Sloe."

"The golden voice," sighed Mother Crabba as she returned her gaze back into the storm. The hold of Father Daugth was shattered and she slowly, sadly nodded her head.

***

Delirium and fever, dreams were shallow things only teasing him with their memories. He remembered the tale of Sloe as woven by the Mother, a tale of sorrow and a crime of bitter jealousy. The story was like a dandelion puff, with its beauty scattered by the wind until he was left without the substance.

Vaguely he remembered the insistent voices of his kith calling for tales that danced upon the edge of their memories. Tales of bogfoke half remembered in dreams suffocated by fear of Father Daugth. The penitent Mother Crabba strove to bring into the light the memories long suppressed.

In the smoldering delusion of his fever-wracked brain, Skag thought they were building a barrow in which to bury him. He saw the skeletal frame rise above him. Then would come the face of Gristel or Mother Crabba and for a while the burning sickness would ease.

He had known all his life the hypnotic strength of the Mother's words, but never had he known the healing power of her hands. So much wisdom bound by a wretched existence in the thrall of Father Daugth. From her tales came knowledge of herbs, and chanted songs to ease the turmoil in his body and mind. With each day she drove a little more strength into him, washing away the frightful curses Daugth had unleashed in the battle of the storm. After many weeks he was finally able to rise and inspect the barrow they were building.

Gristel had designated the place, a shallow depression of some thirty feet in diameter. They had dug it deeper and used the excavated soil as an embankment along the rim of the place. No more ravines for them. No more rushing waters sweeping away their work.

Cypress logs had been raised in three concentric circles. One large log had been hoisted erect in the middle. To these had been lashed and notched a web-like grid of cypress rafters. Every day during his illness Skag had witnessed the weaving of saplings into this grid. Now it hid the sky from his eyes.

"We are weaving it as tightly as we can," explained Gristel. "Then we are going to cover it with sod and plant grasses and vine upon it and around it. By late spring it will be difficult to find. A hunter might walk right over it none the wiser, thinking it just a low swelling of the earth."

"I hope it is never put to that test," offered the Mother.

Skag was huddled close to the small fire, nodding. It had been hard, cold work for the other bogfoke, but the endeavor glittered as a fine light in their eyes. Their barrow could offer them little shelter at this time against the breath of winter, but it warmed them with promise.

They learned much, gleaning nuggets of wisdom from Mother's tales. Kribble had fashioned, after a great many failures, an oven of clay. He baked cakes from acorn flower, and roasted nuts. Mother Crabba had burned mullein on the fire so that it loosened the grip of congestion from Skag's lungs. Weart had devised a wine of blackberries. Gristel and Tegmina had sewn wine-skins from scavenged deer hides. Welken, not to be outdone, had left a skin exposed to the coldest night. From the half frozen wine he had poured a fiery brandy that defied the chill of winter.

One day when winter's hold was less severe, Skag found a place in the sunshine and sat with his back against a bare oak. Mother Crabba took a moment to examine his shoulder, clucking at her appraisal. "Finally it has knit complete. It should not have been such a stubborn thing, little more than a graze. The curses of Daugth slowed the healing, of course, but it is also told of those to whom the steel of men is like a poison. So it must be with you, Skag. Take heart! It is also said that such like are known to be gifted."

Skag managed a smile. "I do not feel gifted."

Mother Crabba turned a moment to survey the barrow and bustle around them. Her eyebrows arched and she winked before walking away. Skag considered the accomplishments their endeavors had brought. He felt a twinge of pride upon realizing what his courage beneath the gray-cloaked warrior's monument had begun. If that was his gift, then he was glad of it.

Nearby, Weart and Welken were arguing over the best method for catching crayfish. Kribble was painstakingly boiling acorns, in preparation for roasting, in a cast iron pot Robbis had found near the hunting lodge. Mother Crabba had gone to help Tegmina boil muskrat pelts with oak bark. The pelts were then stretched across frames of willow. They were using yet another scavenged item, an enameled basin Robbis had found on the shore of the lake.

The tanning was taking place downwind, but an occasional whiff would cause Skag's nose to wrinkle. The others were so busy they did not complain of the stench. In fact, they complained very little. It seemed down right un-bogfokish to Skag.

In the middle of his musings Skag realized that the dance of Slignan's hatchet had stopped. He looked up to the roof of the barrow where Slignan was fitting lengths of saplings into the grid. The hatchet wielder was gazing off toward the lake. He turned to Skag, gesturing as he spoke, "Here comes that troll thing again. It came to see you while you were sick."

Skag nodded at the barest memory of such a visit. The shaggy head and shoulders of Stump became visible along the forest path. The troll was ambling along with a crooked smile, and his pale brown eyes glanced warily at Slignan's hatchet—a sentiment Skag could understand. Then the once-tree saw Skag sitting in the sunshine and his smile reached around to each ear.

"Wood-knocker! It is good to see you up and about. They mayn't have told you, but I will. It seemed to us that death had two arms around you."

"That I knew well enough," replied Skag as he motioned for the troll to join him in the sunlight. "They have, however, told me that you came around to visit when I was ill. Thank you."

Stump folded himself to the ground, saying with breath misted by winter cold, "Did they tell you also that I found Father Daugth's robe. All covered with skulls and such, it was. All torn and bloody, it was."

Skag shook his head. Stump nodded and pointed toward the lake. "A big piece of it washed up on the shore. A grim thing. He were a grim fellow, eh?"

Skag closed his eyes and nodded slightly. The troll sensed that nothing more of such matters should be brought up. He looked around at the busy bogfoke, and the dark, mound-like roof of the barrow. "Your folk are working like beavers. A good sign. Though I hope they are nearly done with cutting and such. Ah, I was remembering something. Across the lake there used to be a farm. Ain't nobody lived there in many a year. Not since well before it was caught behind the warding of the witch. There was a sizable orchard. Apple trees, pecans, walnuts, pears and cherries they grew. The people are long gone, of course, and the house tumbled, but I would suspect the trees and their offspring are still fruitful. Not much left this late in the season, except maybe the nuts."

Skag frowned despite the temptation. "I can't remember the kith of Cornbread Jack ever giving up something they've taken."

"Unless they've just forgotten it," replied Stump. "This place hasn't been lived in for years. It was abandoned sometime after the yellow fever took so many of the human kind from this world. And how could they find it again behind that warding of thorn and briar?"

"How far across the lake?" asked Skag.

The troll shrugged, having no solid concept of measured distance a bogfoke would understand. "Across the lake, then twice as far from the shore as is this barrow. It were well beyond my roots, but not beyond my domain."

A little less than a half mile from the far shore, Skag figured. It was tempting. His own idleness was pricking his guilt. He turned so he could watch the blue waters of the lake. "Perhaps I can look into this. But, it is a good stretch to march around this lake."

Stump shook his head. "Just use a log and float to the other side. That was how you crossed the great river's sister, was it not?"

Skag chuckled, "It can wait until tomorrow?"

The troll shifted and scratched at the tangle of hair on his shoulders, "I didn't mean to be so insistent, stump-thumper, but I was thinking of going with you. If I'm to be rootless I may as well see what might be across the lake."

"But you told me what was there."

"Only what I sensed as a tree," explained Stump. "Not what I've ever seen with these eyes."

"Sounds dangerous to me," called Slignan from atop the barrow.

Skag gestured with his cedar stave toward the hatchet hanging from Slignan's belt. "Fetching that was dangerous, but well worth the risk as it turned out."

"We could leave tonight," Stump suggested. "It'll be safer crossing the lake in the dark. Won't be no gators about, with the water so cold."

"I can take some of the larger saplings and lash them together as a raft," offered Slignan. "Otherwise, that water is going to be cold enough to numb your feet."

Skag shook his head in bemused resignation at how these adventures evolved. Slignan came down from the barrow and began working on the raft. At least this latest creation would be useful regardless. Stump ambled off; promising to return after nightfall and Skag was left to sit alone in the sunlight with his thoughts.

***

The raft was more than a yard wide and six feet long. Slignan proudly pointed out the four stout pieces of sapling used as cross members upon which the others were lashed. This design raised the floating raft several inches above the surface of the water even with Skag and Stump aboard.

They sat nervously at first, but Slignan had done his job well. Gristel handed them a deer hide sack and a reed basket. As Skag grinned foolishly and waved, Stump took up a long sapling and began to push the raft away from the shore. The remaining bogfoke watched them for a moment, and then began to wander back toward the barrow.

The moon had set early and the two travelers glided over the surface of the lake beneath the faint light of the stars. Their progress was slow after the water became too deep for poling and Stump used a crude oar to move the raft. The winter night was quiet, without crickets, frogs or night birds.

"I used to enjoy the winter," Stump mused, with his voice low in deference to the solitude. "It is a dreaming time for trees. You're all done for the time being with reaching further and further into the sky. You are through for the season with driving your roots deeper and deeper into the soil. It is like a long sleep, with a slow parade of dreams."

"Isn't it odd?" asked Skag. "To ride a raft of wood?

Isn't it as if I were riding a group of bogfoke bodies lashed together?"

"What?" replied Stump, thinking about it. "I suppose in a manner of speaking. But trees and the spirits that might be in them are not the same as your sort and their spirits. It's just a way of expressing such things. As I have said, I wasn't actually a tree, just a spirit bonded to a tree for the taking care of things.

"Besides, it wouldn't be all that different from you carrying a deer hide bag, or drinking from a deer-hide wine skin."

"Ah, I suppose not in some way or the other," nodded Skag, returning to Stump's original musings. "Winter was a hard time in the cemetery, too cold for bugs, frogs or fish. The ducks abandoned the pond, which could sometimes freeze over. Always a hungry time for us. The rats would disappear. The ground would get hard as a rock and we couldn't go grubbing. Wasn't no use to hide food in the summer to hold us over. The grounds keepers would find it and throw it out, 'cepting what little we kept in our barrows. I don't miss it all in the least."

"Truth is," Stump chuckled, "I don't think your kith miss it either."

"Not most of the time," replied Skag as he stretched back on the raft and stared into the spray of stars across the sky. He delighted in the sky, the stars, and the moon. He delighted even in the sun now that he was free of the cemetery. Stump shook his head and continued paddling. Slowly one dark shore receded while another drew near.

Nearly two hours passed before the raft bumped against the knees of a cypress. Skag helped the troll guide the raft toward a narrow, sandy beach. They sloshed ankle deep through the cold water, dragging their raft onto the sand.

Skag hefted the reed basket and his cedar stave with one arm, while slinging the hide sack over his shoulder. His eyesight was a little better in the dark than was Stump's, so he led them in the direction suggested by the troll.

The underbrush was winter sparse and huge trees stretched above young pines and wax myrtle. Stump gestured toward the bare limbs rising against the star filled sky. "Those are pecans. Beyond them a bit are some walnut. The apple and pear trees would be to our right, near the old farm house."

"Wouldn't be any fruit left this late into winter," replied Skag. "Let's try our luck with the nuts. After that, we can look around the old house. We might find something useful. I might even find some apple and pear seeds to plant near the barrow."

The frosted ground crackled beneath their feet and the slightest wind caused the tree limbs to creak. Skag set the basket on the ground. Taking the sack he began to brush the earth with his free hand. After a short while he had picked a half dozen good pecans from the fallen leaves. Stump fared better with the walnuts, gathering several dozen.

"The heavy husk protects them," suggested Stump as he turned one between his fingers.

"Still, not much here," said Skag. "Too far into the winter, I suppose, but look at these trees, next year we can gather a bounty."

As they moved in the direction of the farm house the tall trees were left behind. They came across a wide stretch of dried underbrush. Stump kicked at a clump of brown vegetation. "Look here, this is corn that's seeded wild. Likely there's other crops done the same."

He quickly gathered several dried, smallish ears of corn for Skag's seed store. The bogfoke received them gratefully, but seemed bothered. "It has been many years since this place was occupied? Just seems to me all of this should be overgrown more than it is. It is also a long time for cultivated plants to survive after having gone wild."

Stump shrugged as he said, "Funny things can happen. Might be the deer keep down the underbrush. They'd be attracted by the fruit and wild corn. They have a liking for young saplings, though there are few deer within the ward.

"Ah, look over there, that tumble of vines. That's where the farmhouse should be. Is that overgrown enough for you?"

The tangle of vines rose in a ten foot high mound. Only the ivy was still green, but the chaos of dormant runners hinted at what a mass of green this must be in the spring and summer. As Skag and the troll proceeded cautiously lest they stumble upon an old well or cistern, they could see the rusted remains of the farmhouse's metal roof and a broken chimney.

"Seems to me this is the kind of place snakes might like," noted Skag as he let the sack drop to the ground.

"Too cold for snakes, wood-knocker. I reckon you could step square on one without getting bitten," replied Stump as he forced his way through the vines. The troll dropped to his knees and wriggled beneath the collapsed porch roof. Skag followed as the troll crawled through the gaping hole that had once been a window.

They emerged in a room of half-rotten clapboard walls and a ceiling with many slatted boards missing. A few stars could be seen through the vines cascading over the vacant windows. There was nothing in the room save debris that had drifted or been carried in by animals.

"Once a fine old place," offered Skag. "Glass in at least some of the windows. Clapboard and a goodly bit of milled timber."

"Ivy, jasmine, creeper, honey suckle, wild rose and such," added Stump as he cast his gaze at the intrusive vines.

The troll turned his attention back to the dark interior, standing uncertain in the dark. Skag had more familiarity with the dwellings of men thanks to the Mother's tales and the dreams of the city. He motioned for the troll to follow. They walked into a hallway, with another room facing them, and another to their left.

"These over here would have been for sleeping," explained Skag. He turned right and walked cautiously over the rotting floor. "The kitchen would be back here, see? That is the backdoor. The room that way would have been what they called the parlor."

A cursory glance found the parlor to be as deserted as the bedrooms. They turned toward the kitchen, squeezing through a collapsed portion of a breezeway that had later been enclosed and connected to the main house. Skag knew the kitchen and its pantries were most likely to hold whatever might be useful to the bogfoke.

They found that the kitchen had suffered least from the ravages of time and an intrusive forest. Skag's heart leapt with joy at the sight of canning jars lining the doorless cupboards. Two enameled washbasins hung above another that was sunk into the counter. A half-dozen baskets were hung from the sagging ceiling. There had to be two dozen earthenware jugs and jars on the counters. What a find this was—then the realization sprang upon him, forcing a low hiss from between his teeth.

"Stump, this place isn't deserted. There isn't any debris on the floor. There is food still in some of those canning jars."

The troll's bushy brow knotted in worry and he replied, "Over yonder, bedding and a cot."

Skag nodded. "A kerosene lantern. Oh no, this place is not--"

Suddenly Stump's wrinkled hand clamped over the bogfoke's mouth. Skag watched as the troll's widened eyes tracked something beyond the leaning walls of the house. Then he heard it as well, the sounds of frost crackling beneath footsteps, and then the rustle of vines being brushed aside near the kitchen door. The troll half dragged the bogfoke back toward the main house.

"Out, quickly" Stump breathed into his ear, all the while shoving him toward the window they had originally entered. Skag scampered across the decayed porch and squirmed past the collapsed roof. He snatched his hide sack and dashed for the shelter of a juniper stand.

Through the spray of leaves he turned to see Stump's head emerge from the vines. Even as the troll struggled free and began shambling across the open space, Skag saw a shadowed form come dashing from around the corner of the house, the form of a man. Stump saw it also and whirled to face it.

It was not a large man, but fairly tall. Stump could rise no taller than nose high to the oncoming form. Skag saw a pale face, with thin beard and bushy eyebrows. The man seemed taken aback by having stumbled upon this troll. A look of surprise gave way to anger. A nasty snarl twisted beneath the beard. Skag blinked hard, because it seemed as if the hair and beard had grown suddenly thick and coarse, and the teeth seemed long, white and fierce.

The man moved in a blur, nearly as quick as a bogfoke and swifter by far than any man Skag had ever seen. The initial rush knocked Stump from his feet. Skag heard the troll's gasp mix with the rolling snarl from the man. Stump shoved suddenly, tossing the man to the ground, but the troll was hardly onto his own feet before the man charged again. It was apparent that Stump was the stronger of the two, but he was also much less agile.

"There will be none of *her* creatures prowling here!" screamed the man as he pounded with his fists upon the troll's gray face. Stump's knees buckled beneath the ferocious assault, but his long arms wrapped around the man, pulling him also to the ground.

For a moment they struggled on the frosted earth. The man squirmed and snarled like a rabid beast, scratching at Stump with hands transformed by anger into something claw-like. Once again the troll hurled the man away and managed to stand. This time the fellow rolled back onto his own feet and his hand went to the pocket of his trousers. Skag saw it gleam in the weak starlight, a knife.

The man moved toward the troll with more caution this time, and his knife danced in advance. Stump backed away, eyes widening at the sight of the keen edge. Skag had seen that expression before, when the troll had faced Slignan's hatchet.

"Afraid of good steel?" the man sneered. He jabbed at the troll. Stump tried to move away, but was too slow and the blade grazed his arm. A pitiful shriek was torn from the troll as he stumbled and struggled to flee.

The man laughed and raised his blade for another strike. The knife flashed in the dark but never reached the troll's flesh. There was the sound of the cedar stave whooshing through the cold air and the crack of wood upon the man's arm. The bearded mouth was wrenched into a scream of agony and anger. The knife clattered against the hard earth.

Skag wasted no time in pressing his attack, swinging hard at the man's legs. Again the shriek of pain as the cedar connected. Skag could not even stand level with his opponent's chest, but the force of his blow upended the son of Cornbread Jack and sent him sprawling. The air burst in a huff from the man as he hit the soil. Skag slid in front of Stump, holding the stave defensively while trying to recover from his exertion.

The man lay still for a moment, gasping for air. Then he slowly managed to rise into a sitting position. He was gazing wide eyed at Skag and his narrow features were a mask of surprise.

"Cornbear," he managed between gasps. "But, cornbears are not her creatures. She hates them."

"Ain't neither of us her creature, you hollow-head son of a broken people," hissed Stump as he tossed a nearly frozen clump of dirt at the man.

"Then what *are* you?"

"I'm a troll, or so she said, used to be a tree and a tender of Creation until Yolande lured me from the deep soil."

The man's face shifted into a more gentle expression, an expression of sorrow. He nodded softly. "Then you would be the lord of the lake-wood. It was the sort of thing to be expected from her. I'm sorry. It's just that you're right ugly. The kind of creature she'd send snooping around here. My name is Remus Wolfe, and please don't laugh, I have reason enough to curse it."

"What would be funny about it?" asked Skag, lowering his stave a little. The savageness had dropped from the man as he sat on the cold ground with his breath misting and his eyes weary. It was strange. He seemed so different, so human. The hands were small and pale, not at all the claw-like things Skag had imagined. The beard was thinner than he'd first thought, and the lean features were rather pleasant.

"I guess a cornbear wouldn't' have heard of Romulus and Remus," chuckled the man. "Would that Yolande had not."

"What have you to do with the witch?" asked Skag nervously.

"It is a long story, master Cornbear," Remus Wolfe replied with a sighed. "But, you have nothing to fear from me. I am perhaps more her enemy than your own folk."

"He's not a cornbear. He is a bogfoke," explained the troll. "I am Stump. This is Skag. The bogfoke have come from across the river—"

The words were cut off by a warning nudge from Skag's stave. Remus Wolfe was studying the cedar-bearer. His brows were drawn together as some thought rolled across his mind. "He looks like a cornbear. I've seen them, the cornbears. Not many white men ever have. Yolande won't like it. She hated the poor creatures."

"Why?" asked Skag, as his heart sank.

Remus Wolfe sat still for a moment, with eyebrows arched at the question. Finally he could only shrug. "Who could know? Something about them just didn't set well with her. But, I'll tell you one thing, I'd never seen her hate anything that much without at least a seed of fear being buried somewhere within it all."

"What could the witch fear from us?" blurted Skag.

"I don't know," replied Remus Wolfe. "Are they all as adept with sticks as you?"

He laughed at his own quip, then leaned to pick up his knife from the frost-whitened earth, and got stiffly to his feet. "This troll that was a tree can tell you, though, that things are not always what they first seem. Maybe that includes bogfoke. In any event, it mayn't be cold for bogfoke or trolls that were once trees, but I'm near to freezing. Let's go into the house."

As he turned toward the vine shrouded building, Skag and Stump hesitated. Remus Wolfe turned back to them, gesturing as he smiled. "Well, come on. I can fix up something warm to eat and drink. You do eat and drink?"

The reluctant guests nodded to him, and glanced at one another. Then each with a shrug followed the man toward the back of the house. Remus Wolfe pushed aside a spray of vines and pulled open a side door into the kitchen. Man, troll and bogfoke stamped into the room. The door closing behind them kept out only a little of the cold. Remus Wolfe also pulled shut the door that opened to the breezeway and lit a kerosene lantern. He then began to feed short lengths of wood into the cook stove near the wall."

"This is not much, but the best I have to offer," he told his guests as he opened a bag of ground corn. He scooped it into a pan before adding a little water. "We'll have some grits. Warm, if not particularly tasty without butter."

"Why are you and the witch rooting on unsettled ground?" asked Stump, as he and Skag seated themselves on the floor.

"What? Oh, I see what you're asking," replied Remus Wolfe as he struggled to dip a bit of cold honey from an earthenware bowl. "Where she lives used to be known as Stone's Creek. Folk used to take their boats down the creek and into the big river, and even into the sound. Yolande began to tell everyone that she could see to it that they filled their nets every day, and that she could make it so they got top dollar for their catch. They knew that she had

enchantments and such, and it's hard to ignore words like that
when you're hungry and your children are hungry. Times were
lean. So her offer was tempting. Of course, she had a price."

The wood was beginning to burn steadily, so Remus
adjusted the flue and closed the front plate. He placed a lump
of honey into the gruel and placed the pot atop the stove.
"What she did, in return for something more than just a few
coins, was to place a charm on the fishermen's nets. Seems
harmless enough, but she also placed a curse on boats from
other towns. Our boats would return everyday with fish
stuffed into every nook. The boats of other folk would come
back mostly empty. If they caught anything at all they had to
venture out onto the ocean."

He sat on the edge of his cot, looking grim in his
thoughts as he shelled a handful of pecans. "It's sad, but I
believe the folk of Stone's Creek could've lived with that. We
had one church. A traveling preacher used it every other
Sunday. He began preaching against this fish enchantment.
He knew there was something dark at work.

"I thought maybe folk would listen. But instead they
decided the church was too expensive to keep up. They
closed it and started riding to the city for services.

Remus Wolfe shook his head, rising to stir the grits
and crumble in the pecans. Brushing his hands clean he sat
back upon the cot. "They made the ride, at first. Then, a few
at the time, they just started staying home. I guess the Bible
said the same thing in the city as it did at Stone's Creek. A few
families had enough of the wickedness and moved away. The
others were just too greedy. Eventually a few of the boats
from other towns had more than a little bad luck. There was a
schooner that went down in a freakish storm. Nine men
drowned, four of them hardly more than boys."

He stopped for a moment, seeming unsure if his two
guests could have any sympathy for the lives of men. He
pursed his lips and bowed his head so that he was looking at
the floor, "I thought maybe that would get through to
Yolande. It only made things worse. I suppose she refused to

look at the results of her deeds. She was denying to herself how wrong it all was.

"Other folk weren't blind. They saw our boats coming in with full holds. Talk spread. Folk around the area knew of Yolande. One night in town, old Nick Donner and his boys were beaten by an angry group of fisherman from another town. Nick died and that was the beginning of the end of it. You should've seen us. We marched down to the docks and set our boats on fire. Our own boats, we sent them to the bottom of the creek and Yolande's charms with them.

"After that most everyone packed up their belongings and left Stone's Creek. There was something dark come on that place. Maybe a half dozen men and their families stayed behind. I suppose their greed kept them with her. Some of them are with her still, but all it has gotten them is a prison of thorns. Ain't been anyone left Stone's Creek or the wood within Yolande's ward in five years, I'd reckon."

The grits had begun to make puffing sounds as the heat bubbled to the surface. Remus rose and stirred it for a while longer while they all waited in silence. Finally he spooned the contents into three bowls, handing a portion each to Stump and Skag. He then poured a clear liquid from a canning jar into three cups and passed two of them to his guests. "This'll warm you up. Moonshine, it will take the bite out of winter."

He smiled and took a long swallow. Skag took a cautious sip, having tangled with this concoction of men before, when the bogfoke had stolen the hidden cache of one grounds keeper or another. Stump drank his in a single gulp, unperturbed by the fiery spirit. Remus Wolfe smiled in admiration and took a mouthful of grits.

"Why are you still here?" asked Skag.

"Yolande made it impossible for me to leave," he sighed, seeming to lose his appetite as he stirred his spoon through the thin, gruel-like grits. "She put a curse upon me, the man-wolf. Now, it ain't what you might think based upon the old legends, 'bout the full moon and such. But, surely you noticed something odd when we first had our set-to out there?"

Skag frowned. "Well, I thought so, but it was dark and I was plenty frightened."

Remus shook his head. "I don't turn into a wolf. But something wolf like comes upon me. I can't control the anger, and I seem possessed of some fierce strength and speed. I think most of the rest is illusion, but it adds to the effect.

"Yolande used to tease me about my name. This curse is just an extra twist. Of course, I can't just go walking into the city with such a bewitchment hanging on me."

Skag took a longer swallow of his liquor, while wondering what kind of witch they were sharing this wood with. As he sat on the floor, the chill in his heart could not be eased by the heat emanating from the cook stove. Even the fiery chase of the moonshine only made him feel all the colder in comparison.

"What a glum face, wood-knocker," said Stump. He jostled the bogfoke with an elbow, grinning broadly.

Skag shrugged. "We have worked hard to build ourselves a purpose. The barrow, and a life that hints of something more than just survival. Now I see this witch threatening it all. I greatly fear that we shall have to abandon the barrow. From what Remus Wolfe has said, she is not likely to overlook us."

Remus shook his head and the long features were troubled. "I wish I could offer you some encouragement."

"What about the fear you spoke of?" asked the troll. "The fear that you suspect is the seed of her anger and hatred?"

Remus Wolfe looked hard at Skag. It was easy to see that he couldn't fathom what kind of fear the witch might find in such a bedraggled and sparse creature. He rubbed his bearded chin, but finally shook his head without replying.

"But it is there," insisted Stump. "Let us not forget

that she did not kill the cornbears. Neither did she kill me."

"You were the lord of the lake-wood," explained Remus. "How could she kill you? She lured you from the soil, from the forest. She bound you in a lesser form. I suspect that she sought to only sever you from the soil. What would have happened if she had attacked the tree? The spirit would have been unbound and a bitter enemy for her."

The wolf-man shook his head again and sighed. "No, she needed you bound in a more limited form so that you would not rival her power. Surely she made it seem a grand thing. There's a deceptively beautiful lie behind every evil, I think."

"Then, mightn't the cornbears have rivaled her in some way?" suggested the troll. "That might be why she entrapped them in the Weeping Hill."

Remus arched his bushy eyebrows at the possibility. "If this is so, then there was more to them than meets the eye. Is there more to you than meets the eye, my friend Skag?"

The bogfoke shook his head. "Less, I would suspect. We are quick, skilled at hiding. We are excellent mimics and can throw our voices so that it seems the sound is coming from where we are not. But, that's about it."

"Wait, wait, wait," interrupted Stump, sweeping a long gray arm so that his hair waved like Spanish moss in the wind. "What about that Father Daugth? Now he might be a dark-hearted wretch, but he certainly carried within him something more than meets the eye. Mother Crabba? Her ability to conjure tales seems not of this world. Maybe the cornbears had such like in their midst."

Skag shrugged. "Whatever may have been, I must discuss all this with the others."

"Be wary in any dealings with Yolande," cautioned Remus. He reached over to take their bowls and cups. As the man placed the utensils in the sunken washbasin the first hint of gray peeped through a gap in the vines draping over the window.

"We must be on our way before full light," the bogfoke reminded Stump. The troll nodded and rose stiffly to his feet. They were reluctant to leave the relative warmth of Remus Wolfe's abode, but finally stepped out into the chilled air of the fading night. Skag shivered, it was as cold outside as a rich man's funeral.

"We came to scavenge," Stump chuckled toward the wolf-man. "The bogfoke are woefully short of provisions, all the more so because of the storm. I fear we must return mostly empty handed."

"I have some things I can spare," offered Remus Wolfe. He disappeared for a few moments back into the house before returning with small sacks of nuts, dried fruit and a larger sack of cornmeal. "You may certainly return. This old place still offers a bounty when free of winter.

"There are a half dozen abandoned homesteads within the ward of Yolande. I'll keep my eyes open and gather up tools, implements and such as I can find. Wouldn't do for you bogfoke to go prowling too close to the village."

They all circled around the house so Skag could retrieve his deer hide sack from the juniper stand. He stuffed it with the gifts of Remus Wolfe. Then they walked together toward the lake shore, silent and lost in lonely thought. For Skag the knowledge of this witch and her power was another weight upon his shoulders.

The hint of dawn was a gray dream on the horizon when they came to the water's edge. Stump and Skag were preparing to shove the raft into the lake when the bogfoke suddenly stood erect, "I forgot the reed basket. Gristel will use my hide for the next sack if I leave it. I set it near the pecan trees."

"I'll help you look for it," offered Remus as he followed the bogfoke through the winter orchard.

"Hurry," grumbled Stump. "To be out on the lake in full light ain't something we want."

Skag and Remus searched the entire orchard but could not find the basket. Finally, Remus suggested they give up. Skag reluctantly agreed. Remus Wolfe smiled at the grim expression on the bogfoke's face. "Probably a raccoon came across it. They're notorious thieves."

"I suppose the bogfoke would have it coming," said Skag as they turned back toward the lake. Then they suddenly heard Stump shouting.

"Remus! Skag! Beware! Come quickly! Beware!"

FOUR

Confrontations And Crows

The man and the bogfoke were nearly clear of the orchard when the sound of more voices drifted to them. These were the voices of men shouting, and the bite of ax on wood. Skag went suddenly still when he saw two burly fellows wrestling with Stump, who was trying to wrest the ax from one of the men who had attacked the raft.

The bogfoke would have rushed to aid the troll, but Remus Wolfe grabbed his shoulder, shaking his head negatively. "They are Yolande's men. It will be no good for you to expose your existence to them. I can handle this."

The words oozed angrily from Remus, and Skag's eyes widened to see the gnarled hand upon his shoulder. In a flash the man-wolf moved across the last stretch between them and the threatening men. A savage snarl trailed in the cold air. The witch's henchmen knew that sound and whirled to face the onslaught. One of them brandished an ax, but went pale upon seeing the long, keen knife in the man-wolf's hand.

"Your steel cannot bite my flesh," laughed Remus. "The curse of your mistress is turned back on you!"

The knife flicked out and a gash of crimson stained the ax-bearer's cheek. Remus Wolfe laughed again. "A mark for your honor, Jake! Now you can run tuck-tailed back to her with a sign of being bested. Now you and she will know whose dominion is this bit of forest."

The two men turned and fled before the wrath of the

man-wolf, sloshing along the edge of the lake. Remus Wolfe pursued them for a short distance. Then he turned and came trudging back, breathing hard at the exertion as his malicious demeanor melted away. By the time he stood near the shaken troll he was completely the human Remus Wolfe with whom they had shared a meal.

Stump was on his knees, shaking his head ruefully. Around the troll were the broken remains of the raft, and pieces of the reed basket stomped into the mud. He turned toward Skag and grumbled, "We have a long walk ahead of us, stump-thumper."

Remus and Skag kicked at the broken lengths of saplings. It was useless, the raft was ruined. Skag helped the troll to his feet. "Come along then, friend Stump. I'll take the lead."

"I can carry your sack, wood-knocker," offered Stump, relieving the bogfoke of the deer hide.

"Farewell, Remus Wolfe. Thank you for your gifts," said Skag with a grateful nod of his head. "You are the only live human I've really known. You make me hope that most are as decent and kind as yourself."

"Many are less so," sighed Remus. "But, many more are better people than am I. Be careful, master bogfoke. You are fortunate those men did not see you. Take care, too, lord of the lake-wood."

Stump bowed low from the waist, like a tree in the wind. The man-wolf smiled and watched as his two guests made off through the forest.

***

The marsh cut a wide wedge into the woodland. The weak predawn light had not reached the western edge of the lake as the two companions sloshed cautiously through the tall grasses. They struggled a difficult and wet mile before coming to the reasonably drier edge of the cypress swamp.

"There is a deer trail," noted Skag, pointing out the way. "It should be solid ground."

They followed this path for a while before forced to abandon it when it angled sharply westward. The mist was rolling off the lake, but the sky was gradually turning blue above them. It was light enough for Stump to take the lead.

They had come to the portion of the forest that Skag could recognize. The barrow was only a little more than a mile away. The tumble of ravines and low ridges were familiar sights. They could have saved time by cutting across the wide finger of marsh, but that place was a favorite haunt of gators and could not be trusted even in the deep winter if the sun was shining upon it.

Stump drew to a sudden halt. Skag's frown of annoyance melted as he followed the troll's gaze into the sky. A dark tendril of smoke rose against the azure and drifted out over the lake. It was thicker and darker than the smoke of any bogfoke fire. For a moment they stood still, with eyes hard upon the sight. Then Skag darted around the troll and began to run for the barrow.

He stumbled, struggling past snaring bramble and thorny vines. He had covered nearly half the distance to the barrow when he realized the smoke came from near the edge of the lake. He cut toward the water, relieved but perplexed.

The ground descended toward the water, becoming spongy beneath his feet. Cypress knees began to rise from the soil on occasion and willows forced their way among the evergreens. The smoke had begun to fade, making it difficult for Skag to follow it through the forest canopy.

He emerged from a copse of willows and stopped. The other bogfoke were clustered along the lake shore. Weart was the first to see him and alerted the rest. They turned in greeting and it was then that Skag saw they were standing near Stump's old cypress. A haze of smoke cut darker through the lake mist, stinging his nose.

Stump was not far behind him and came blundering from the wood. The troll sloshed through the water, darting one way and another to avoid the knobby cypress knees that had once been part of his tree.

"Men came on a boat," explained Gristel. "There were two of them, big fellows. They cut up some fallen branches and some pine saplings. Then they stacked it all around Stump's burrow and set it on fire. After that they left.

"We waited until they were well out of sight, and then we tried to drown the flames. Most of the saplings were still green, so it wasn't too difficult to smother the fire."

While she spoke, Stump had been pulling the last stacks of unburned pine away from his home. The cypress stump was a little blackened by the smoke but otherwise unharmed. A look of relief pried its way onto his face and the pale yellow eyes turned to the clustered bogfoke.

"I thank you my friends. It were the witch's men, stump-thumper. Probably those two that Remus Wolfe chased off came to teach me a lesson. The witch wouldn't take lightly that Remus and I should parley."

"Remus Wolfe?" wondered Gristel.

Skag told them briefly of the meeting with the man-wolf. The bogfoke grew sullen, still not used to taking part in such matters. Kribble was shaking his head slowly, but a slight smile was teasing the corners of his mouth.

"I will have nightmares thinking of the next time you run off with this troll," he complained with a laugh. "Witches, a man-wolf, ax wielding henchmen -- can he not reveal to us something pleasant for a change?"

Slignan was fingering the edge of his hatchet and gazing hard toward the eastern rim of the lake. "I've spent a good deal of time and effort on this barrow. I know that this is the sort of thing we need to consider slow and careful, but I believe it'll take more than a witch-tale and some clumsy half-giants to run me off from this place."

There was a murmur of agreement from Welken and Weart, but argument from the others. It was then that Tegmina moved a little forward. Her glance was furtive, darting first to Skag and then back to the ground.

"What is it, quiet one?" asked Skag.

Tegmina looked up, trying hard to instill a spark of intensity into her gaze. "It's just that during all the time at the cemetery we were always guided by the whims of Father Daugth, and fear of his black heart and that red-eyed crow. Then came Skag, who was more kind, but still with a forceful will and a cedar stave. But, you taught us something.

"When you were ill, Gristel sought out the place for a new barrow. Slignan, Weart and Welken devised the manner of its construction. The Mother taught me about herbs and healing. Kribble learned to work the clay. Robbis wandered the forest, scavenging hides, bones and whatever the sons of Cornbread Jack might have discarded.

"The barrow is not just a shelter from the cold and rain. It *is* our purpose. I think we finally understand that. Our purpose might not be so fine or noble as those professed by Jeremiah Simms, but it is ours. Even as you promised before we passed through the weeping arch, we understand."

She looked down at the ground, made nervous by this flood of words. She missed the smile upon Skag's lips, and the fierce pride in his eyes. Truly, for the first time ever he could remember, Skag was proud to be a bogfoke. The cedar-bearer went to take the hide sack from Stump, and then sloshed back to the lake's edge, slinging the sack over his shoulder.

"Come along," he said to his kith. "We will let the matter rest for a while. We will each mull it over before making a final decision."

They began filing in behind him, heading for the barrow. Stump watched them go, with his long arms folded before his chest. It seemed to him that for good or ill, old wood-knocker and his friends would be staying.

***

Green rose fresh from the earth as spring came to the forest. The winds were sometimes cool and at other times warm as the seasons wrestled for dominion. The bogfoke busied themselves in the midst of this ebb and flow by planting honeysuckle, ivy, Virginia creeper and nameless grasses around and on top of their barrow to conceal it from all but the most interested eyes.

Welken and Weart planted corn and potatoes in scattered and inconspicuous patches. It was painstaking work. They must carefully weed and tend each patch while maintaining the illusion of wildness. The womb brothers had also learned to catch crayfish and crabs. Having themselves become important providers for the clan they lost much of their envy over Slignan and his hatchet.

Skag observed as special talents emerged and were honed by each of the bogfoke. Robbis and Gristel became expert scavengers. Their greatest find was what Gristel excitedly called *a find of finds!* It was a now disused trash dump that had served the sons of Cornbread Jack before they had abandoned the lake-wood all those years ago. It was a treasure heap of useful items for the crafty and clever bogfoke.

A shiver of appreciation would often pass through Skag as he watched the bustle and purposefulness of his kith. He was not without worry, though. Above all was the oppressive realization of living in the long shadow of the witch, Yolande. Because of her presence, they had to be cautious in their movements. They rarely risked a fire in daylight, lest the smoke should draw attention to them.

It gnawed at Skag to think of her amidst all the strivings and contentment the bogfoke were experiencing. Often he felt gloom descend upon him because of this, and he would take himself off to sit alone for a few minutes until the mood passed.

Spring won its battle with winter, but summer came stealing quickly to stake its rule upon the land. The velvet green of spring gave way to the shimmering gold of summer. As the season progressed the heat became as fat and lazy as a sated beast.

Skag stirred from sleep in the cool dark of the

barrow. Light spilled in from the doorway. Though still cautious, the bogfoke had quickly adopted the daylight hours to be as much their own as was the night. It was a necessity if they were to tend their plots strewn throughout the forest. As Skag sat up, scratching his stubbled beard, he saw Welken's face appear in the bright sunlight.

"They're back," muttered Welken.

"Who is back?" asked Skag as he gathered his cedar stave and headed for the open doorway.

The humid summer air squeezed him in an over-friendly embrace. The heat created a golden haze on the water of the lake and rose in a shimmering veil from the hard earth. The air beneath the forest boughs was heavy and still. The trees caught and jealously held any breeze that might stir.

"Those birds," replied Welken as he squinted against the sun.

"Birds," mused Skag as he vaguely remembered Welken and Weart complaining about a flock of birds that seemed to be watching them, waiting patiently for them to leave before swooping in and inflicting damage on the patchwork gardens. "Can you not just run them off?"

Welken shook his tangle-bearded head, "Oh, at first they'd scatter away for a while. We could startle them by mimicking various noises. Now they just flit up into nearby trees and seem to laugh at us."

"I do not think I've ever heard a bird laugh," replied Skag with the pretense of a worried expression on his face. Before Welken could protest, Skag waved it off and gestured for the gardener to lead the way so that he could investigate this strange event.

The corn had been planted in a small clearing. It was scraggly and sparse but ready to yield nonetheless. Welken pointed toward the branches of a tall pine. The birds were watching, occasionally hopping from branch to branch.

"There's more of 'em every day," growled Welken.

Skag rushed toward the tree waving his stave and

shouting. The greater part of the flock rose into the air screeching their indignation. They made a short arc against the azure sky but quickly settled into the branches of another tree. The handful that had not fled at Skag's charge casually drifted in twos and threes to join the others in their new perch.

"It's always the same," Welken glowered. He stomped over to the stand of corn, kicking at the broken and stripped stalks. "See? Eventually they'll ruin the whole lot. Then they'll follow us around to find another. Stupid birds."

Skag scratched at his jaw line while he considered this. The birds were raucously flitting from place to place in the tree. Finally Skag could only shrug, "I can think of nothing. If we build a scarecrow as do the sons of Cornbread Jack, then we may as well trumpet our presence. We may have to abandon these patch gardens of yours, or the witch's men might notice all these birds and come to investigate.

Welken stared grimly at the stand of corn and then back at the birds. The bogfoke ground his teeth in frustration, but could offer no alternative. He angrily began snatching the ears from the remaining stalks while muttering, "At least we shall leave nothing for those wicked, miserable creatures. Birds, pah, whatever use have they ever been to the bogfoke -- excepting the Father?"

"We did steal their eggs, back in the cemetery." Skag reminded him, despite sharing some of Welken's frustration. He also felt sympathy for all the hard work going to waste. He helped gather the remaining corn, but all the while he watched the brooding forms in the tree, even as they watched him.

∗∗∗

"Blackbirds are the most obnoxious birds I've ever seen," grumbled Welken. The bogfoke tended to call every black or dark colored bird a blackbird. He threw a pine cone at a nearby river birch and a small cluster of birds fluttered about. "Well, they're not all blackbirds. It is odd, all these different types flocking together."

The flock had followed the bogfoke to each patch of garden like a turbulent shadow swirling from tree to tree as they went. Then the birds had followed them to the barrow and for three days the flock had squawked and fluttered in the trees nearest the bogfoke dwelling. Welken and Weart had run themselves ragged trying to frighten the birds off. Weart had finally given up and retreated to the lake for some crabbing.

As Welken sat dejectedly in the shade of an oak, Skag came from out of the barrow and sat beside him. The cedar-bearer considered the flock and then said to the gardener, "That is odd. Black birds, sparrows, catbirds, even some doves."

"I was just musing on that," grumbled Welken.

Skag nodded. "It just ain't natural, is it?"

"Are you thinking of the witch?"

"It is difficult to say," said Skag. "Though I think of her often enough. We must consider the possibility. I am made more than a little uneasy with these creatures perching all around our barrow.

"Robbis has said that he might have a way of ridding us of these creatures. He and Kribble have been huddled together since early this morning, with a lot of nodding, whispering and chuckling between them."

Welken snorted, "Those two should be at least a match for the obnoxiousness of these winged devils."

"Be careful how you speak of those who are about to rid you of a great nuisance," called out a voice from near the barrow. It was Robbis. He carried a large, dark object in his arms. Kribble was following with a wide grin on his face and a mischievous glitter in his eyes.

"A great debt of gratitude," replied Welken. "When you have actually done such a thing, muddle-head? What *is* that?"

"*That* is *this*," answered Robbis as he set his load onto the leaf mold. It was strange creation, an oblong basket made of woven willow fronds, and slathered over with now dried clay. A haphazard spray of feathers were affixed to the creation. "I coated it with pine resin and some of the feathers those damnable birds are leaving all over the place."

"And these are the hands that fashioned it," declared Kribble proudly as he extended his hands for all to see.

"It's supposed to be an owl, isn't it?" asked Skag as one finger brushed the sparsely feathered surface.

"Of course, light-head," muttered Kribble. "See, I made his eyes with bits of crab shell."

"The feathers are a nice touch," deadpanned Skag.

Welken burst out with a laugh before seeming to turn serious. "Can owls catch the mange?"

Robbis just rolled his eyes, to which Welken responded, "I hope birds don't see so good."

Robbis kicked a spray of leaves at his amused comrades and then hefted the owl in his arms. "We'll see how funny you think it is once all the birds have flown away"

After that retort he began scrambling up the branches of the oak. The other bogfoke stood back to observe. Robbis made his way slowly into the upper branches until the boughs began to sway beneath his weight. He then wedged the owl securely into a fork. He leaned back to observe how it was situated and then began climbing back down.

"It looks a little more convincing from down here," admitted Welken.

"But the birds won't be down here," noted Skag, and again Welken was wracked with laughter. Kribble merely pursed his lips and helped Robbis from the lowest branch.

"Look," whispered Robbis, pointing as the flock took wing from their feeding ground. A few of them spotted the dark form in the upper branches and dove toward it.

Kribble mimicked the sound of an owl, and suddenly the birds darted noisily away, screeching an alarm that drew the whole flock to them like an enormous black wind. A few birds made as if to harass the owl, but their courage was momentary and they were soon fleeing with the rest of the flock toward the eastern wood.

The bogfoke were so stunned by this spectacular success that Kribble and Robbis forgot to brag or wallow in their victory. They stood with eyes blinking at where the birds had been.

***

Two days passed free of all but the most usual of birds. Then on the third day Skag was helping Kribble gather clay from the lake shore when he caught sight of two large birds soaring over the lake toward them. A chill swept down his spine, and he hissed to his companions, "Crows, big ones."

One hand tensed on the cedar while the other shielded the morning light from his eyes. The birds flew overhead, and then circled wide for another look. Crows were curious creatures, and bold scavengers. Skag hoped they were merely sizing up the chances of stealing a meal from the bogfoke.

"Perhaps they'll go on when they see we're not fishing," suggested Kribble.

The crows circled again, this time sweeping much lower. They came so close Skag could see the glittering black eyes. Against his better judgment he shouted and waved his stave threateningly. A long, trailing caw was the only response. The birds passed over them just above the forest canopy.

"They're going toward the barrow," observed Skag, following the forms with a worried gaze. Suddenly the birds swooped, and then darted high above the wood before swooping again with angry shrieks. Skag realized the crows had spotted the owl, and he started down the forest trail as the sound of the crows mingled with the shouts of bogfoke.

The cedar-bearer burst into the clearing around the barrow and found Welken, Weart and Gristel flinging pine cones at the fluttering dark forms. The birds were ignoring the bogfoke and angrily attacking the clay owl. A few of the owl's feathers were floating through the morning sunlight. The imitation bird had been knocked askew and leaned perilously from its perch. It appeared unlikely to survive another strike.

Welken ran toward the gum and began scaling the trunk. The crows darted in again. Weart flung a pine cone that scored a hit, causing one of the ebony birds to swerve away. The other pressed its attack and gave the sentinel a solid thump. Amid a puff of dislodged feathers, the pride of Kribble's hands fell from its perch. Welken grasped desperately, but he was not even close.

The owl hit another branch five feet below, knocking off the wide-eyed head. The body bounced against the tree trunk and clay broke off in pieces before landing on the leaf mold. The skeletal basket framework collapsed upon itself as it landed atop the shattered clay. The crows had fluttered in pursuit of their enemy. They finally settled in the high boughs of the sweet gum, seeming confused by the magnitude of their success.

Welken let go a sigh that filled the sudden quiet, and began slipping from out of the tree. Kribble came trudging into the glade with his basin of clay. The other bogfoke watched him expectantly. He set down his burden and walked over to his fallen handiwork. Then he looked up to search the canopy of branches until his gaze settled on the crows.

Nodding in a matter of fact manner he asked, "What are crows afraid of?"

"I think they're too stupid to be afraid of anything," replied Weart.

That brought a half-hearted chuckle from Welken. Skag was still watching the crows and thumping his stave against the earth. "They are smart birds, and they don't fear much."

"We have more problems than just the crows," whispered Gristel, pointing toward the tall pine just beyond the barrow. The flock was returning.

Mother Crabba appeared in the doorway of the

barrow. She fretted at the ends of her moss wig as she studied the birds. The flock was maintaining a respectful distance from the crows, but otherwise their raucous behavior was little changed. The Mother gestured suddenly, waving with her hands to encompass both the crows and the garrulous flock.

"This is not natural," she warned with her dry voice. "Something is amiss. Crows are troublemakers, devious and black-hearted. These other birds should be trying to drive them off."

Skag's thoughts were on the witch, Yolande. The other bogfoke shifted uneasily. Weart hurled another pine cone. It clattered against the tree limbs and then fell to the leaf mold. One of the crows cawed loudly, and a number of mockingbirds darted nervously into the air, but soon they settled back into the trees.

This ominous calm was broken when both crows began their hoarse cries. The flock became agitated, with small numbers repeating a high arc into the air before returning to the canopy of branches.

"What can all that be about?" wondered Skag aloud. Before he could go on there came the rustle of underbrush from along the forest aisles. The ragged form of Stump came shambling into the glade. The troll's pale, yellow-brown eyes were squinting hard as he watched the birds. He pulled up in front of the cedar-bearer and gestured back toward the lake with a twisted gray arm.

"Men, the witch's men, there must be a half dozen of them coming across the water," he muttered. He glanced up at the flock. "It's those birds what brung 'em."

"Are they her creatures?" asked Skag.

The troll shrugged his hairy shoulders and replied, "Can't tell for certain. I suspect she'd find such a gathering to be of interest. If they are not truly her creatures, she can still influence them. Something ain't right with all them contrary birds flocking together like that. Now them crows. They'd be in league with her, I'd warrant."

Stump paused to glare angrily at the two black forms before continuing, "You must flee. Hide in the witch's ward. Let her own handiwork protect you from her men."

Skag turned to the other bogfoke. "Quickly, we must remove all traces of our presence."

They began to carry all their equipment into the barrow. The potter's wheel, the tanning basin and racks, the half woven baskets, and the broken owl were spirited from sight. They placed it all in a pit at the back of the barrow and quickly covered it with a reed mat and then loose soil. The entrance of the barrow they covered with clinging vines and dry leaf mold.

Skag turned to Gristel. "Where are Slignan, Robbis and your sister?"

"They went to cut willow fronds near the southern marsh."

The cedar-bearer frowned, staring uneasily along the forest aisles. Finally he took Gristel by the arm. "You take the others into the ward. Take them to the place of the deer bones. I will remain here and lead the other three there when they return. Certainly one bogfoke can evade the eyes of men."

"What about them?" asked Gristel, pointing toward the birds. "They might lead the men right atop our barrow."

Stump smiled darkly. "I can deal this this lot. Perchance you should have come to me in the beginning. Now, off with you!"

While Gristel herded the rest of the bogfoke toward the ward, Skag watched as Stump pulled himself straight and stretched his long gray-brown arms wide. The troll's eyes closed as his toes curved into the soil beneath his feet. The birds had settled down and were tensely quiet, as if in the face of an approaching storm. Skag felt the vague disquiet himself. The trees around them began to tremble though little wind was stirring.

Branches began to whip the air and the trunks shivered. The birds of the flock darted about uncertainly. The crows cocked their heads to glare hard at the troll. Stump's long fingers began to curl away from his palms and his smile became ominous. The sweet gum began to sway and its branches lashed at the ebony birds. The starlings were the first to rise, forming a dark cloud and fleeing from the forest storm. Soon the sparrows, mockingbirds, and black birds followed them in a panic. Finally even the crows had borne all they could and fled squawking into the eastern sky.

The troll's eyes opened and his shoulders sagged as he relaxd, but his smile was self-satisfied. Skag looked from the gray face to the last of the fleeing birds. Despite the impending danger of the witch's men, his bogfoke grin spread wide.

"Perhaps there is more to the lord of the lake-wood remaining in you than you let on," suggested Skag.

Stump shook his head ruefully. "I've kept some of the tree-smarts, but nothing of the real power. This were but a bit of trickery. A touch of what I once knew. Now, I think perhaps I'll go down to the lake and raise a bit more trickery to divert the witch's men."

"Trickery? Well then, I can see why the witch feared you," replied Skag. "I'll come along and see what else you might be up to. Do not worry, I'll be careful enough. You have been a friend to us and I don't know that the bogfoke have ever had friends before. Besides, I would rather stalk the witch's men than to be stalked by them."

Scratching his moss-like hair, Stump nodded to admit the sense in the words. Together they tramped toward the lake. The cloudless sky was reflected on calm waters. A rare breeze would stir the surface for a moment and the image would ripple like an unsteady dream. Then would the stillness return, but haunted by the steady splash of oars in the distance.

A long, badly weathered boat came gliding past a spur of cypress trees. Seven men occupied the vessel. Four of them were rowing. At the back, seeming their leader, and with one hand on the steering oar, was a heavy set fellow with a red scar streaking one cheek. Skag guessed him to be the same man who had felt the anger of Remus Wolfe back on that cold winter night.

The troll motioned for Skag to hide, but it wasn't necessary. The bogfoke had already slid back into a clump of stunted dogwood. The oars dipped into the water and stroked backward to slow the vessel before being raised high. Stump moved toward the water's edge. Scarred-cheek was glaring at the troll as the boat neared the shore.

"Get from here, you toe-lickers!" shouted Stump as he shook a fisted hand at them. A couple of the men chuckled darkly, but Scarred-cheek ground hard on his teeth.

The boat bumped lightly onto the marsh bank, and those men not rowing slipped over the side to tug it ashore. Stump retreated a bit, but his pale eyes were still defiant. Some of that resolve faded, however, as Scarred-cheek and a few others hoisted axs from the bottom of the boat.

"If'n the ax could've done me in, Yolande would have had the job finished long ago," the troll warned.

Scarred-cheek laughed. "It's not for you, Woody. This is for your friends."

Skag's heart twisted and he saw that the troll was startled by those words. Scarred-cheek smirked broadly and gestured toward a stand of cypress near Stump's burrow. "Say good-bye to 'em, Woody."

The trees, Skag thought in a sigh, but then he realized what this might mean to Stump. These were the cypress trees that had been the offspring of the tree he had once been. The most intimate connection the lord of the lake-wood had to the forest, save his own ruined stump of a tree. Stump's demeanor took on that of a pending thunderstorm, with darkness gathering on his brow. One twisted arm shot out as he pointed at the cluster of men.

"Careful, witch's scum," he hissed. "She may feel well and safe back in her village, but beware that she might sacrifice you lot to her ends. This flesh may set uponst me an exile, but I am *still* lord of the lake-wood."

The motion of each man was snagged by hesitation. They looked toward Scarred-cheek, but he could not completely mask his indecision. There was a grim power in the troll's voice. Scarred-cheek's hands tightened on the ax handle, seeking a surrogate for courage. Slowly, fear of the witch was pressing aside fear of the troll.

Scarred-cheek turned the ax in his hands so that the edge glinted in the sun. His smile returned to cling arrogant and cruel upon his lips. He turned toward the stand of cypress, and the troll's hold upon the men was sundered. Together they stalked toward the trees.

Stump glared hard at their backs, and he straightened his own. Skag watched as the troll closed his eyes and curled his toes into the loam. The trees began to quiver, and the witch's men slowed their pace, gazing about suspiciously.

Scarred-cheek turned back to Stump. His face was contorted with fury as he screamed, "I can let you feel the bite of this steel, maggot-wood."

The trees began to whip furiously, pelting the men with cones and dead branches. Scarred-cheek broke toward Stump, but the troll suddenly opened his eyes and grabbed the man's wrist. The troll crouched as he reached out and the impetus of Scarred-cheek's charge carried him over the bending form. The wrist in Stump's grasp made a noise like a snapping twig. The ax landed with a thud upon the leaf mold and a desperate shriek was wrung from the wounded man.

Scarred-cheek struggled to his knees, trying to fight off the troll's clutching hands with his good arm while hugging the grotesquely mangled wrist against his chest. Stump was unwilling to release his hold upon the soil, so the sobbing man was able to wrest free.

The comrades of Scarred-cheek were stunned by the sudden, violent confrontation and stared blankly at their retreating leader. The trees had settled, and for just a moment the struggle was suspended. The quiet was usurped only by Scarred-cheek's ragged moans. But then to Skag's keen ears came another sound, and his stomach constricted anxiously at the footfall of bogfoke running along the lake shore.

He realized that Slignan, Robbis and Tegmina must be returning. They would certainly have heard the uproar and suspected trouble at the barrow. With his mind in a whirl of panic, Skag anticipated them bursting into the midst of the witch's men. He must do something.

Diversion; Skag leaped from his place in the dogwood scrub and scrambled toward the lake shore with the cedar stave waving above his head. His entrance onto the scene stunned even the troll, who loosened his grip upon the forest loam to look back at the commotion. The men all stared wide-eyed, even Scarred-cheek as he sat gasping for air.

"Cornbear," one of them hissed in a tone of superstitious alarm. In all their eyes was the memory of Yolande's hatred for such creatures.

Cornbear! Cornbear!" was repeated in series of shouts as Skag dashed away from the lake-shore clearing. In an instant they bolted toward the cedar-bearer. Even Scarred-cheek came shambling after the fleeing bogfoke.

FIVE

Leaning One Upon The Other Is A Together

Skag made quickly for a clump of shrubby growth.
Behind him came the crackle of branches and a stream of
curses as the witch's men crashed into the thicket. The
bogfoke ran low beneath the thick brush. The men surged
with great ruckus in his wake. A few of them were flailing
away with their axs, but the thick undergrowth rendered their
efforts useless.

Skag emerged onto an old deer trail and he began to
run for the witch's ward. When he heard the men make their
way onto the path he dove into a thicket of thorny vines. He
adroitly wove his way with minimal fuss, but from behind him
came the frustrated shouts of the men as the thorns bit and
stung.

At last the tangle of vines and bramble began to
thicken and Skag knew he was moving into the ward of
Yolande. The curses from behind him became more and
more enraged as the men realized where he was leading them.
He used his mimicry to make it sound as if he might be going
in one direction, then another. The frantic thrashing
diminished until he judged that only one man continued a
ragged pursuit. Skag guessed it to be Scarred-cheek.

There had been no mistaking the insanely fanatical
glint in the man's eyes from the moment he had charged the
troll. Some secret desire or fear must now drive him beyond
his own misery. Yet, the ward of Yolande was a tireless

creation. Over and again Skag could hear his pursuer fall thrashing to the forest floor, only to rise again with screams of pain and anger.

"You cannot run so far, cornbear!" shouted the mad man. "Nor can you run so fast that I shan't have you in the end! Yolande wants you, cornbear! And *I* will bring you to her!"

They were well into the ward and the sting was so fierce that even Skag was reduced to crawling along his belly. With the smell of moist earth in his nostrils the bogfoke forced his leaden limbs to keep moving. The fiery thorns ripped savagely at his ragged shirt and raked crimson streaks along his skin. Still he forced himself onward, becoming only dimly aware of the sound of pursuit in his own fixation on escaping.

With a grim and determined smile Skag turned to move parallel with the ward, knowing that his tortured foe could not suffer much more of this nightmare. Obsession was driving Skag's flight as surely as it did Scarred-cheek's pursuit. Then he suddenly found himself stumbling into open woodland. He fell to the ground beside the trunk of a huge pine.

He turned painfully onto his back gasping for every breath. Above him rose the pine, with its height stabbing into the blue sky. When his own breath was still enough for him to hear beyond it there came to him the distant, tormented advance of Scarred-cheek.

Skag groaned and jabbed the cedar stave into the loam, using it to force himself to his feet. He ran instinctively away from the hunter. His exhausted mind failed to realize that this was taking him from the sanctuary of the ward and into open wood. He was a good way along an open path when he heard the man behind him begin to laugh hysterically, having just won free of the thorny tangle. Skag poured all his remaining strength into flight. Then the blurred canopy disappeared and the azure dome of the sky was open above him, descending unhindered toward the horizon.

Half blinded by sweat and blood, the bogfoke realized that he had stumbled into an open field. It was a fallow farm field covered with grassy growth over the furrowed soil. He closed his eyes a moment, hoping to clear the darkness from the edge of his vision.

He opened them but the shadows were persistent. Exhaustion was a thick fog swirling through his mind. He considered hiding in the nearby corn field, or perhaps turning back into the wood. His feet were rooted by indecision. Amidst the rustle of the corn stalks and the murmur of leaves stirred by the faint breezes, he could hear the steady approach of the maniacal Scarred-cheek. The demented laughter had melted now into anguished sobbing, but still he came.

Skag had hardly the strength to grip his cedar. He wiped the blood from his eyes, cautiously inspecting the forest. His head nodded and he turned back for the shadowed aisles in an angle intended to avoid the mad man.

The first step was hardly taken when a growling howl burst from behind him. Skag whirled with the cedar raised in feeble defense. There was the blur of the largest black dog he could have ever imagined rushing from the cornfield. It occurred to him in his weariness that this was the end. Then from the edge of the forest came the triumphant shout of Scarred-cheek. There was nothing more Skag could do. His strength failed and darkness closed complete upon him. He knew no more as he collapsed to the earth.

***

Slignan, Robbis and Tegmina came stumbling onto the lake shore with indiscreet haste. They froze at the sight of the boat and the dazed figure of the troll. Stump raised his eyes to them and with a furtive gesture motioned them back into the undergrowth.

The bogfoke scrambled back along a shrub-thick gully with the troll following. Slignan turned, with hatchet held defensively. Stump came only so far as the gully mouth, keeping a wary eye on the wood into which Skag and the witch's men had disappeared.

"What is all this?" demanded Slignan.

"The witch's men came," explained Stump. "Gristel took all the others, save Skag, into the ward. Skag was going to wait for you here. The men came. They were going to cut down the cypress grove around my burrow. I had it out with one of 'em. Just about that time you three come unsuspecting up the path. Skag must've heard you and jumped out in plain sight so's to distract the men. They took off after him."

"What?" gasped Slignan. He began to move past the troll, but Stump restrained him with a hand on his shoulder.

"Skag's no idiot. Surely you know that," scolded the troll. "He'll lead them a merry chase, no doubt. He took off toward the witch's ward, but in the opposite direction from where Gristel led the others. Now, if'n you remember how difficult it is for a bogfoke to move in that tangle, you can imagine how it must be for men. That's why you must stay hidden. I reckon they'll be turning back before long."

"But now they know we're here," whispered Robbis.

"They know only of Skag," Stump reminded them. "They thought he were a cornbear. Could be they think he is a cornbear that just slipped from Yolande's net when she was rounding 'em all up. They might think he has escaped from the Weeping Hill, but, if they'd seen the lot of you. . . Well, it's best they didn't."

"How many men?" asked Slignan.

"I didn't count 'em. Half dozen, maybe more..."

"Even if Skag escapes, things will be unsettled for a long while," sighed Tegmina.

Slignan nodded. "Skag'll get by that lot, but I worry about their return. All this should have these men in a foul mood. Had it not, friend Stump?"

The troll nodded his shaggy head, "Gristel and the others went to the place of the deer bones. You know it?"

"Yes, but we cannot leave now. Not without knowing what has happened to Skag."

"Would you rather those men come back and find you?"

"We can hide," insisted Slignan.

The troll shook his head. "One bogfoke can hide easily enough, but three would be a dangerous attempt. We can look for Skag after these men are gone from here. They're chasing after him, so they'll leave a trail that a blind bogfoke could follow on a single leg."

Stump fell silent then, and he turned his head so that his eyes were on ward of Yolande. Slignan had also heard the sounds, and he nodded his head as he spoke, "You're right, friend troll. They're already heading back. But we can't go running off just yet. They'd see us for sure."

Stump set his jaw stubbornly, "That may well be true, but don't be doing nothing rash or thick-headed. Stay in this place and out of sight."

The troll slid from the mouth of the gully, stamping off toward his grove of cypress. The three bogfoke moved deeper into the ravine, beneath a dark shroud of holly. Stump listened until their bustle faded, and then nodded with satisfaction. He rooted his toes into the swampy earth, waiting grimly.

The men came dragging from the deep wood, axs slung over their shoulders. Their feet were noisy on the fallen leaves and their grumbling noisier still. Scarred-cheek was not with them. They pulled up near the boat when they saw the troll. A short man, seeming the leader in Scarred-cheek's absence, motioned to another.

"Fetch the rope out of the boat, Quinn."

A gangly fellow with a stubbled red beard went to fish around inside the vessel, returning with a coil of finger-thick rope. He handed it to the short man. "Here you go, Silas. What you up to?"

The short man smiled, watching Stump and motioning to the other men. "You four take axs to the wood. Quinn and me will take care of old maggot-wood."

Quinn didn't seem so certain, but followed Silas nonetheless. The others moved past them toward the cypress grove. Stump's toes curved hard into the spongy turf.

"Go ahead," chuckled Silas as he fashioned a loop with the rope. "Dig in real good."

When the two men closed in Stump suddenly reached out, coming within a breath of snatching Quinn. The man lurched away and tripped over his own long limbs. Stump glimpsed the dark whirl of the rope as he reached out for the fallen man. He loosened his grip on the soil in an attempt to avoid the lasso, but was too slow and the loop slid around his outstretched arm.

Silas was ready and he jerked hard on the rope, pulling Stump from his feet and down into the mud beside the fallen Quinn. The lanky man scrambled to wrap the rope around the troll's chest and free arm. Then he shouted, "You got 'im, Silas!"

The short man smiled and quickly tossed his end of the rope over the branch of a pine. He motioned urgently to Quinn and shouted, "Give me a hand."

Together they tugged the rope until Stump was hefted nearly a yard off the ground. The troll hung like a side of beef, with the two men considering their handiwork in front of him. From behind them came the sound of axs upon the cypress. All Stump could do was close his eyes as resinous tears rolled down his gray cheeks.

In the thicket, the sound of axs startled Slignan. In the shadows beneath the thick undergrowth, Tegmina and Robbis stared back at him with eyes glittering. They could hear the harsh laughter of the witch's men.

"What has happened to Stump?" whispered Tegmina.

Slignan shrugged and motioned for his companions to remain where they were as he slipped from under the holly. He edged his way along the ravine, finally climbing a low ridge to peer down toward Stump's burrow.

The men were working slowly as their enthusiasm

melted in the growing heat of the day. They were cruel despite their dawdling. They mangled trees so that they were sure to die, rather than expend the energy to bring them down completely.

Slignan saw Stump bundled and hanging from the pine. He looked around to see if there might be a way he could sneak down and free the troll, but the pine was isolated from the other trees, and there was no underbrush to conceal his approach. With the exception of Silas, the men were taking turns using the axs. When they were not working at the trees the men were sitting near the water's edge, or taunting the helpless troll.

Slignan moved further along the ridge. He held the hatchet with a hand made tense by his own helplessness and the dark anger growing in his heart. Sliding down the ridge he drew nearer the men than was wise. Stump had been a friend to the bogfoke and Slignan burned at the suffering and humiliation inflicted upon the troll.

As he watched and brooded, Slignan became aware of another sound from the south. It was the approach of a man moving along the forest trail, and moving quickly. Slignan scrambled as quietly as possible back atop the ridge, hiding in a stand of young oaks.

The bite of steel upon the wood slowed and the men looked up from their work, sensing something ominous in the air. A final tree was hacked nearly in two, leaning against its wounded kindred. The witch's men heard the noise from the forest aisle. Silas began shouting and gesturing for them to follow as he darted for the boat.

Slignan heard the retreat and curiosity dragged him from his hiding place. He looked over the ridge to see the men scrambling into their boat. Just then another man came bursting from the wood. This newcomer was lean and swift, easily catching the last of the men and jerking him from the side of the boat.

Slignan's eyes widened at the flash of a knife and the frightened scream of the witch's man. Quinn swung an oar at the newcomer, causing the man to cease his attack and leap away. The witch's men frantically pulled their wounded companion into the boat as they pushed away from the shore into deeper water.

The newcomer dashed in again, slashing one of the underlings on the thigh. The man shrieked and tumbled into the boat. The knife snaked out again, just missing. The newcomer tried to press his attack, but by now the boat was in water deep enough for the oars to pull it quickly away. Silas stood in the bow, shouting brave insults from a safe distance.

The knife-wielder turned from the routed men and jogged over to Stump. Slignan's hand tensed again on the hatchet, but the knife was used only to sever the troll's bonds. Stump began waving for the bogfoke to join him. Slignan called for his companions and then slid down the mouth of the gully. The newcomer was inspecting him with fierce green eyes. He gestured toward the bogfoke as he turned to Stump. "This isn't Skag."

The troll shook his head, but he could only continue staring at the carnage wrought by the witch's men. Slignan gestured toward the ward of Yolande, "I am Slignan. Skag led those men away so that they wouldn't be here when we came blundering out of the forest. You'd be Remus Wolfe?"

"I would," replied the man-wolf.

Tegmina edged past Slignan, going to stand beside Stump. She brushed away the amber tears that had crystallized on the troll's cheeks and beard. Stump nodded and patted her hand before speaking to Remus Wolfe. "That man you cut last winter, he was after Skag. There was a fierce light in that man's eyes, madness."

"That would be Jake Collanmore," Remus Wolfe sighed. "Yolande will have planted the seed of desperate anger concerning cornbears. Of all her rogues, Jake was the most obsessed with pleasing her. I will go into the ward in case Skag needs help."

"I will go with you," volunteered Robbis. "A bogfoke can go where a man might not."

"Robbis is the best amongst us at tracking," added
Slignan. "Not many signs will escape his eyes. He is the best
at finding things."

"Then come along, tracker Robbis," replied Remus
Wolfe, and the two of them moved quickly off toward the
ward of Yolande.

Stump had walked slowly to the fallen cypress with
Tegmina holding his hand. He swept out a gray arm to
indicate the fallen and dying trees. "These were like children
to me, my garden from the days before my seduction from
the deep soil. I have failed in my dominion. I have failed to
protect and nurture."

Slignan nodded solemnly. He moved amidst the
carnage and began to collect the small round cypress cones.
He glanced back at the troll. "The bogfoke shall plant and
nurture these. So long as we live, we shall honor and
remember the lord of the lake-wood, and his garden of
offspring who died that we might escape."

The hatchet bearer went back to his task and Tegmina
left the troll's side to help. Stump watched them with amber
tears falling fresh from his pale eyes.

***

The heat of the summer day gave way to muggy
night. Slignan went to bring the bogfoke hiding in the ward
back to the barrow. They filed solemnly out of the wood and
sat somberly waiting for Remus Wolfe and Robbis to return
with word of Skag. Every moment that passed weighted them
with worry.

"They should have been back," whispered Welken.
"Something must be wrong."

"That is obvious," grumbled Mother Crabba. The
stern rebuke in her creaking voice silenced any further
revelations of the fear they shared.

Summer haze dimmed the stars, and the moon was a
frail crescent, like a gloomy, lidded eye looking down on the
wood. Gristel ran her hand along her sister's tangled hair.
Slignan fingered the handle of his hatchet. Mother Crabba sat

with eyes closed. Kribble, Welken and Weart all stared into the darkness of the forest aisles as if answers might rise like wraiths beneath the vaulted boughs.

At last there came the sound of someone approaching along the trail from the ward. The footfall was weary -- that of a man and a bogfoke. The clan shifted nervously as another sound joined the procession, the heavy stamp of the troll.

Remus, Robbis and Stump emerged from the darkness with the first two dropping exhausted upon the leaf mold. Stump stood with arms folded and his mouth set grim. Robbis looked at his fellow bogfoke. His dark eyes were wide and his expression dour, "We tracked them through the ward. Skag wove a meandering torture for that scarred mad man. Their trail twisted through the ward until it came to the edge of farmland."

The tracker lowered his dispirited gaze onto the forest floor. "It had to have taken a toll on Skag. I scented his blood along the way, and bits of his clothes were torn from him."

"No sight of Skag or the man?" pushed Gristel.

"We came to the edge of the farm," Remus said. "It looks as if Jake was turned aside by a dog and fled back to the east. From what we saw of the wake he'd cut through the ward, I wonder if he'll survive. Any sign of Skag was muddled at that point, at the place of the dog. It was dark, so perhaps we misread, but I doubt it.

"It looked as if Jake and the dog had a brief confrontation that Jake lost. Then it seems the victorious dog dragged Skag away as his prize. I could not follow further. There are old wards against the witch's magic set at the edge of the fields. I believe I know who once lived there, but that was long ago. The warding held and I could not pass because of the curse upon me. It was too dangerous to allow Robbis to go alone."

"There was blood," said Robbis in the barest whisper. "Where the dog was draggin' something. By the signs it would be as big a dog as ever I have seen. I scented Skag, but also that crazed fellow."

Silence draped over them now like a shroud. Remus Wolfe rose. He looked at the gathered bogfoke. His lean features were softened by sympathy. "He was a special one, your Skag. I haven't known any other bogfoke, but by the standards of men he was brave and determined."

"Gentle," whispered Gristel. "In ways we had never before known."

"Yet, we must go on," rasped the Mother. The others nodded. Suddenly Tegmina lifted her face to the sky and a long keening wail rose from her throat. Gristel pulled her sister close, but her own face contorted with despair and her voice joined that of   Tegmina. Each of the bogfoke was overwhelmed by the pain and their voices joined into the keening wail that flowed into the rhythm of a mournful chant.

The sound of it made the hair stand on Remus Wolfe's neck. The sound of the bogfoke was like the chant of human voices, but also with sounds resembling flutes and a soft thrumming like distant drums. That communion of voices made him realize how *not* human these creatures were. He tugged at Stump's arm and they edged away from the cluster of bogfoke. When they had retreated a little along the path, Stump turned to stare at the barrow. "It would seem the bogfoke learned something of sorrow."

Remus nodded. "They have learned that there are things and persons in this world worth sorrow. It may have come too late for Skag to appreciate, but I believe he would have been proud. And, I tell you my friend, Stump, there is something more to those creatures than one would suspect. I could just *feel* it when their song began."

He took the troll's arm again and they left the bogfoke to mourn.

***

A week passed with hope fading like wildflowers beneath a withering summer sun. A week passed with the bogfoke hiding and sneaking about the wood as cautiously as they ever had in the cemetery, waiting the return of the witch's men.

Into the second week the bogfoke began to ease out of their fear. Slowly their foraging grew bolder, though still only in the cloak of darkness. During the sunlit hours they sat near their barrow tending whatever tasks they dared. Mother Crabba wove for them tales of courage and strength. From these they gathered their own determination to continue in their purpose.

In the shade of the sweet gum they gathered. Gristel sat with her back to the trunk, gazing at the blue firmament above the wood. She saw them first, two dark forms descending toward the tall pine. When she tensed, the other bogfoke followed her gaze.

The two crows were silent. There was only the whisper of air passing beneath their wings as they swept to perch in the tree. Two heads cocked so that glittering black eyes stared at the bogfoke. Welken reached for a pine cone, but a glint in those dark eyes stayed his hand.

"An ill omen," hissed Mother Crabba.

Slignan grasped his hatchet and rose to his feet. He moved as if through syrup. Struggling with nearly forgotten fears he could go no further than a quarter of the way to the pine. His feet slowed to a halt as his courage failed.

Gristel had managed to rise onto her knees. A movement in the sky caught her eye. Another crow, far larger than any she'd ever seen or thought possible. It moved in a wide circle and the huge wings spread to slow its descent and engulf the sunlight. It landed above the first two crows. The tree branch barely trembled despite the great size. Black feathers ruffled and the head cocked. Gristel closed her eyes, shutting out the red glare that had met her gaze.

When she'd gained the courage to look again the crow was gone. As if tugged by unseen hands her gaze was pulled down along the trunk. Finally it settled in the gloom below. She would have closed her eyes again, but she hadn't the courage. She had known before seeing. She had known even as she heard the rattle of skulls. Like a nightmare that wouldn't be quieted, he had returned.

Father Daugth moved a little from the gloom with eyes squinting against the daylight. In one hand he bore an iron rod and with the other he stroked the white swirl of his beard as he observed the bogfoke before him.

"Have you no greeting?" he whispered.

Slignan took a step back toward the others, Father Daugth smiled and spoke, "Where is your courage? Where is the dreamer, Skag?"

"He was taken by a dog," murmured Mother Crabba.

Father Daugth studied her as if to seek the truth of her words. Then the intensity of his gazed dimmed. He seemed disappointed as he shrugged. "That is unfortunate. I have looked forward to dealing with him. Are there any here to challenge me?"

Silence and then a faint shuffling as the bogfoke shifted and stared at each other before letting their gazes fall to the ground. The Father stepped closer.

"Are there any to challenge me?" he whispered again in a voice that was like a snake sliding on dried leaves.

For a moment there was nothing. Then, to the amazement of the others, Tegmina rose slowly to her feet. She lifted her gaze to the face of the Father. She sighed long and sad, but her jaw was firmly set by the ending of it.

"There are all of us to challenge you," she said quietly. Slignan nodded and moved closer to her side. Gristel took her sister's hand and stood beside her. Then Kribble rose, and then the womb-brothers Welken and Weart. Robbis watched them for a moment more before joining them. Mother Crabba hesitated, haunted by the long knowledge of the Father's ruthless wrath. Finally she struggled to her feet and stepped toward the others.

Again the Father smiled darkly as he spoke, "He has left you something, your fallen Skag. Yet, you are like children standing in the ruins of those who have gone before. It is your foolish dreams that support you. They delude you with false strength. I do not think it will serve you at all when the witch's men come again. I shall return. We will see then who is to challenge me."

Stepping back into the forest gloom he raised his arms. Amidst the clatter of skulls the form of the Father was altered. A huge crow stroked the summer air with its wings and rose into the sky. Behind it fluttered the two lesser birds. The three streaked eastward over the lake.

Mother Crabba sat down with a weary huff. She didn't bother to straighten her mossy wig and only stared at the empty gloom beneath the pine. The rest of the bogfoke dropped to their knees or lay on their backs as if released from an unrelenting burden.

"The world is a grim and hopeless place," muttered Slignan.

"Nothing could be as grim and hopeless as was the cemetery," replied Gristel. She was glaring hard at each of them. "We haven't Skag to defend us, and we haven't Skag to lead us. We must defend ourselves, and we must lead ourselves."

They were quiet, absorbing this when suddenly Weart asked, "Do you think he has a pocket in his crow costume for that iron rod? What *does* he do with it, I wonder?"

Like the water of a brook winding over a rocky bed, laughter filtered from among the bogfoke, an unlikely laughter glinting from amidst their despair. Even Mother Crabba laughed, though she also shook her head ruefully, "Illusion, but not just. There is some power at work in him, something darker even than Daugth or the witch."

"Well," sighed Welken as the laughter faded. "What are we to do?"

Gristel's lips pursed uncertainly. She was finally forced to shrug and said, "We must be alert."

Slignan nodded. "We must find some sanctuary other than the barrow."

Tegmina shook her head. "We cannot give up the barrow. However, we could store supplies within the witch's ward. If necessary we could live there for many weeks."

"That is true," remarked Kribble with sudden enthusiasm. "Mightn't we set this in the thickest, most vile part of the ward? Indeed, a place where even a bogfoke can barely pass and no kith of Cornbread jack would dare follow."

Skeptically watching the nodding heads and chin rubbing from the others, Mother Crabba set her wig straight and began to shake her head. "You speak of many things, but not of solutions. The Father has returned and our hiding in the ward will not drive him from us. The witch still rules this wood and our hiding in the ward will not overcome her."

"But it will give us time to think," insisted Gristel. "It will give us safety until perhaps we can solve these problems. There must be some answer. There must be something that contests the Father and the witch, else why would he have left just now?"

"Perhaps," whispered Mother Crabba. She knew of no other action they could take. "Perhaps it is Stump and Remus that causes Daugth to be cautious. He might be waiting for the witch's men to return and deal with them. But we must think on it. We must prepare as we are able."

Welken began to chuckle lightly and the Mother turned a stern glare upon him. He shrugged. "I cannot help it. There is some good fortune in the Father's return. No, truly. Now each of us knows that whatever else may be, we are not the ugliest of all bogfoke."

Weart laughed out loud and excepting Mother Crabba the others had to suppress the urge to do so. But even the Mother seemed less dour. She looked at all these younger bogfoke and understood that they did not know of the great powers in the world. Powers so formidable that even the Father could not contest them. These young bogfoke did not know of the great dark ones. But whatever darkness they might have known, or might ever know, they were bogfoke.

They were bogfoke still, with all the mischievous and resilient nature of their kind.

She smiled then, not at Weart's simple jest, but at something else. It was a sad smile, but she thought that even if Skag and the words of Jeremiah Simms had brought false hope among them, at least they would bring also a final release.

But, what now? She looked into the blue sky. What is there we can do now, at this time? She felt a hand on her shoulder. Gristel's gentle fingers squeezed lightly. A smile found its way again to Mother Crabba's ancient lips. "I will raise a tale. I will raise the tale of Skag Cedar-bearer. I will raise the tale of the battle of the dais. I will tell how Skag showed us the fruit of courage. I will tell how he revealed the strength in purpose. We have much to learn from such things, I think. We have much need to learn such things."

***

Slignan and Robbis crouched beneath the canopy of thorny vines. Robbis was tugging gingerly at the tangle of briars facing them and he finally pulled away a small section. A trough-like depression snaked further beneath the thicket.

"I spent a good deal of time digging this out," Robbis explained. "It leads to a pit where a tree once cast its roots."

Slignan stretched onto his belly and followed Robbis. They squirmed beneath the vines, emerging into a pit formed when the root ball of a tree had been torn from the soil. The roots of the fallen tree still slanted over a portion of the pit. The tree itself had long since been smothered by vines and shrouded by shrubby growth.

Robbis scrambled to the back of the cave formed by the tree roots. He gestured toward a cluster of hides, earthenware vessels and reed baskets. "I've stored supplies back there. Ain't nothing likely to get at them. I suppose the only things we need worry about are snakes."

Slignan ruefully massaged the many scratches on his arm. "Snakes might be able to get in, but they'd be a good sight more stupid than bogfoke for wanting to. Only trouble I see is that it'll take us near a half hour to work our way this far into the ward."

"That is true, but consider how difficult it would be for the witch's men," replied Robbis.

Slignan frowned and looked about as if someone might be eavesdropping. "There is something I've thought of, but didn't want to alarm the others. What if the witch's men were to figure that we were hiding in the ward? Mightn't they burn us out?"

"You weren't alone in pondering on that," conceded Robbis. "Gristel was musing on the possibility. She mentioned it to the troll and he said it weren't likely. Stump says that fire would attract the sort of attention that the witch don't want, and that it would destroy the ward she had created to keep other folk out of her wood."

Slignan nodded at the sense in those words. "You know, it looks to hardly matter if the witch's men know where we are."

Robbis chuckled. "It *is* a tight squeeze, and of the witch's own doing. The world is an ironic place."

"Indeed," agreed Slignan. "Whatever ironic means. Still, it is a grim place, but maybe not hopeless."

***

The bogfoke stocked their hiding place well, and spent several days devising a meandering route into it. They enjoyed the prospect of the witch's men floundering in the unforgiving thickets. Everything was done to hinder pursuit. They planted sharpened stakes beneath the vines and placed rotten logs over snake pits. They dug holes and covered them with vines or light mats of woven reeds beneath strewn leaves. They cleared narrow trails that led nowhere. This sort of thing came naturally to the mischievous bogfoke, but it was no game.

When the preparations were complete they tried to return to a normal existence around the barrow, but always a shadowy tension was woven through the fabric of their lives. A fortnight had passed since the Father's return, days of anxious waiting, with one bogfoke or Stump always watching the lake and the sky. So it was that they weren't surprised when they heard the stamp of the troll approaching their barrow. He came blundering into the clearing, waving his arms.

"They've come again. All of 'em except Scarred-cheek," he shouted. The bogfoke set about removing the signs of their presence from the clearing, and doing their best to mask the barrow. Stump helped them by sending a quiver through the nearby trees that blanketed the area with fallen leaves and needles.

"Will you come with us?" asked Gristel when all was ready for flight.

Stump shook his shaggy head. "No, I could scarcely pass the ward any better than the men. The further I wander from my burrow and this portion of wood, the more diminished I am. They ain't likely to mess with me none. I expect they remember the look of Scarred-cheek's wrist and I shalln't fall again for their rope tricks. Besides, if that old Father Daugth told 'em where you are, I think they'll be looking hard to find you before the man-wolf can set onto them again."

"Will Remus come?"

Stump shrugged again. "Depends on if he saw their boat. He seems to have a feel for their movements. Maybe that's because of the curse. He's also taken a peculiar interest in you lot. I think he was taken with Skag for some reason. Course, it weren't hard to admire the little stump-thumper. He were more warrior for his size than any legend I think I ever heard tell."

Gristel nodded and squeezed the troll's hand. "You've been a friend to the bogfoke."

Stump pursed his lips and gazed off toward the swampy woodlands along the southern stretch of the lake, to a secret place wherein the bogfoke had planted and nurtured the children of his garden. "You've been friends to me. I had my troubles with the witch long before you came. Had I not failed and fallen, you would not be having to deal with such dark things. But it is good to share the struggle."

"Allies," smiled Gristel.

"Friends and allies," agreed Stump.

Gristel reluctantly let go his hand and turned toward the witch's ward. Robbis had waited for her. He nodded toward the troll. "Will Stump be all right?"

"He thinks so. But, it is difficult to know anything for sure," said Gristel. "Still, he was lord of the lake-wood and should be as safe as anyone can be."

They wove their way through the twisting wooded aisles, swinging well out of their way in an attempt to foil any pursuit. The vegetation thickened unnaturally and thorns snagged at their legs and thistles pricked their feet. They moved in an erratic pattern, and made their way cautiously over the rotten logs covering the pit in which agitated copperheads writhed. Finally the bramble and fire-thorn forced them close to the ground.

They were nearly exhausted by the time they reached the sanctuary pit, but were confident that following them would prove a nearly impossible task. Welken and Weart helped them to their feet and offered a drink of blackberry brandy.

"Had they come ashore yet?" asked Slignan as Gristel took a long draught and passed the jug to Robbis.

"I don't think so, but they couldn't have been far off."

"Then there is nothing for it but to wait," said the hatchet-bearer. He sat against an exposed root, but his expression melted into a frown as he looked into the sky. Dark forms flew high to the south, spreading in wide spirals, "Birds."

"Quickly," snapped Mother Crabba, gesturing into the back of the root-walled recess. "We must hide. We can take no chances that those birds might spy us out and reveal us to the witch's men."

"Could they find us, even so?" asked Weart as he

scrambled into the shallow cave. "Knowing our *where* is not the same as reaching us."

"Have you forgotten the Father?" asked Slignan in return.

The bogfoke crowded at the back of the cave. Slignan ventured a look and saw the birds almost overhead. Some flew high above the ward while others swooped and glided low. He pulled back and motioned for silence.

A mockingbird flitted into the branches of a nearby tree. It cocked its head and looked up at the birds flying above. It ruffled its feathers and let go a shrill, angry whistle. Then it looked around with curiosity and flitted to another branch when it spied the bogfoke. The head cocked to one side, considering as its glittering eyes looked them over.

Welken picked up shard of clay, but before he could sling it Mother Crabba stayed his hand. The bird sat for a few moments more and then flew off into the forest.

"That is not one of hers," whispered the Mother. "I could sense it. I could feel its anger at those others invading the wood."

They sat quiet and tense in the moist gloom of the cave. Above them came the occasional sound of wings, but luckily none of the creatures alighted nearby. The afternoon was deepening into evening before Slignan again ventured a look. The graying auburn sky was clear of the birds.

Stiffly the bogfoke spread into the pit, but were silent still. They looked at one another nervously. Above the noise of crickets and frogs came another sound. It drifted over the wood and echoed along the aisles.

"Dogs," hissed Slignan as the howls faded and rose anew, "They are sending dogs to track us."

"Can they get through the ward?" wondered Gristel.

"It depends. We are not their usual quarry, so perhaps their desire will not be so strong."

Mother Crabba hissed for silence and the other bogfoke sat down, attentive of the approaching pack. A few satisfied smiles spread when they realized the dogs were following the meandering trail woven by the bogfoke, a less than merry chase that should be. Soon the baying became yelps of pain and howls of frustration. The voice of the men carried curses through the deepening gloom.

Finally the men began to call the hounds back from the ward. All the bogfoke smiled when they heard the clamor begin to fade. Welken could stand it no more and elbowed Weart and whispered. "The witch did a good job with this warding, wouldn't you say?"

"How long are we to stay here?" wondered Kribble aloud.

"Through the night, anyway," replied Gristel.

Robbis nodded. "In the morning I can scout around the edges of the ward and make sure the men are gone."

"There is a chill on the air this evening," Tegmina said.

"Like a touch of early autumn," whispered Mother Crabba. "It is not natural. I will raise a tale to warm you."

"Tell us again of the battle upon the dais," suggested Slignan. "The tale of when Father Daugth was bested."

They carried the images of desperate courage and hope into their dreams. The night passed free of the wings of birds, the baying of hounds or the voices of men. Robbis woke in the gray light of pre-dawn, while the darkness was still heavy beneath the trees.

The tracker made his laborious way through Yolande's nightmare garden. In time he came upon signs of the previous day's search. Dog hair clung to bramble and thorns. Dried blood stained the forest floor in places.

When Robbis emerged from the ward he saw signs of the witch's men. They had trampled all along the edge of the tangled vegetation, like wild dogs worrying at a treed possum. Robbis made his way toward the barrow with ears alert. He stopped abruptly, as he came to the clearing. The men had found the barrow.

Everything had been dragged from within and then scattered over the clearing. The potter's wheel was smashed to pieces. The washbasins were crumpled and punctured. The tanning racks were broken and scattered. A heap of broken earthenware was already covered with flies feasting upon the spilled contents.

With leaden feet Robbis turned to make his way back into the ward. When he had gone a ways, he called for his comrades to join him. They came quickly but their relieved expressions faded at the look on his face.

"They found the barrow," explained the tracker.

"Is it destroyed?" asked Gristel.

"No, but they have ruined nearly all else."

"Let us have a look," said the Mother.

They hastened into the clearing. Each of them slowed upon catching sight of the destruction. Kribble picked up pieces of his potter's wheel and then let them fall back onto the leaf mold. "Why? What does it all mean?"

Slignan's brow furrowed with angry determination. "To frighten us, perhaps, because of their frustration at not being able to reach us."

"Then perhaps we should build the barrow within the ward itself," suggested Tegmina as she crouched amidst the shredded hides.

"That shall not be necessary," replied a voice from within the barrow. The bogfoke started at the sound of it and moved quickly to group together. The darkness within the barrow shifted and became the form of Father Daugth. The skulls rattled as he moved into the dim morning light. A crow perched upon either shoulder. "You may remain within the barrow with me."

His voice was like noxious smoke choking the bogfoke into silence. "The witch has shown me many things, and within the barrow we can have a place free of the kith of Cornbread Jack."

"Like the cornbears bound up within the Weeping

Hill?" retorted Slignan when he'd finally found his voice.

"Even so," replied the Father, slowly turning. The two crows took wing, moving like shadows into the tall pine. Father Daugth tapped his iron bar against the palm of his hand, "I am your only choice. Skag is gone and you are mine again. Who can challenge me?"

The words wove around them like snaking bonds. The Father's eyes glowed and the slap of iron against skin was like a rhythm of death. The other bogfoke shifted nervously from foot to foot. Father Daugth moved closer to emphasize both warning and threat.

Silence was heavy with fear for a long moment. Courage was wilting beneath the venom of Father Daugth's hatred. Slignan closed his eyes, summoning the memory: The vision of a sweet gum staff twisted from ancient hands by a stave of cedar. He remembered also that the hard earned hatchet had been entrusted to him.

He opened his eyes and sighed softly. Then he hefted his hatchet. "I have learned, Daugth, that there are worse things in this world than you or the fear of you. It is possible to live in misery that must be greater than anything death might bring. We haven't Skag anymore, but we each bear his gift within us."

A smile came to the hatchet-bearer's face. A sad and resigned smile, but filled as well with defiance. So it was that he stepped with uncertain courage toward the undying nightmare of Father Daugth.

SIX

Nannela Walker

One eye managed to half open. It focused on a distant grove of pecan trees. The slightest wind would send a spray of falling leaves. Between two of the trees burned the golden orb of the sun. The eye blinked weakly at the light spilling onto the shadowed world. After an effort of concentration the other eye managed to open in a small slit.

A rooster crowed. Not the resigned crow that heralded a sunset, but the robust and eager crow that greeted a new day. Without the rooster's greeting there would have been no way of knowing if the sun were rising or setting. A noise stirred somewhere near. Again the effort must be summoned and the gaze shifted in that direction.

Framed against a doorway was an elderly lady with skin the color of pecan shells and dark hair pulled into a tight bun. She was stooped by the years and despite the muggy warmth she wore a tattered shawl. The brown eyes were steady and a smile twitched at the corners of her mouth.

"Well, master cornbear," she said softly. "You have had quite a nap. It is a fine thing for you, though. You have healed faster than anyone I have ever seen. But it has taken more than two weeks."

Cornbear? The eyes could see much better now, but there should be more. No sense of body, or of feeling. It was like existing only with mind and sight. The old woman's smile was an attempt at reassurance.

"You'll feel a bit groggy. Put out as it were. I've been pouring herbal tea and such into you to help the healing. It'll take your head a bit to get reacquainted with the rest of your body."

The eyes closed. Why am I here? I remember only the dog and the darkness. The eyes opened again. What am I doing in this dwelling of men?

The dark skinned woman edged close to the bed, offering a cup of broth. The brown eyes that looked up at her were filled with worried questions, but she shook her head and put the cup to the lips set amidst stubbled whiskers.

"Drink up, master cornbear. I mean no harm. When your strength has returned you can go back into the wood."

Skag swallowed and the warm trace of the liquid brought feeling back into his limbs. Slowly he drained the cup before resting his head on the pillow again. He looked down at himself and saw that he was wearing a soft, clean but strange looking gown, with human writing on it. Even his feet had been washed.

"Aren't many people know the truth about cornbears," the old woman informed him. "They think you're just beasts. But beasts don't wear clothes, or carry a cedar staff. My father was Cherokee and his folk knew something of your kind.

"Still, don't your folk ever wash? You were filthy, and your clothes had nearly rotted from off your back. I stitched you up a sleeping gown from out of old flour sacks. I've managed to mend and patch those ragged trousers you were wearing, but that tattered thing you wore as a shirt wouldn't even hold the thread."

Skag had to digest this. His folk? His kind? Memories came creeping back, but mostly he remembered the dog, the great, black dog. He looked at the old woman and managed whisper, "What happened. . .the dog?"

"I expect he saved you, did ol' Ralph," she replied with a chuckle, and then her expression changed to a bemused frown. "Why, you thought he was after you, didn't you? Lord knows, master cornbear, old Ralph thought you were the grandest creation this side of a Sunday ham bone. Of course, he had to drive off that no good for nothing, Jake Collanmore."

"He drove away the witch's man?" wondered Skag. The old woman's face softened into an expression of sadness. She nodded as her gaze drifted to the horizon beyond the open window.

Skag could only shake his head and stare at the slatted boards of the ceiling, "What am I doing here? I thought at first *you* might be the witch."

"No, I am not the witch," replied the woman with a slow shake of her head. "I was in this very room. I saw you come running out of the wood. I knew you weren't an animal, nor yet a man or child. But, I knew too that you were no conjuring of Yolande's or you'd not be able to step foot in the field. Then I saw her good for nothing scoundrel come chasing behind you. Ol' Ralph, he's bounding out all worked up in joy to meet this creature such as he's never seen before. Then he sees Jake, and he knows the dark ones, that dog does. He tore into Jake and it might have been the end of that bit of evil except he managed to make it back into the warding and Ralph would not go there."

The old woman paused for a light laugh. "Between following you through that ward, and having tangled with ol' Ralph, I suspect Collanmore has never been so battered and beaten.

"Well, by then you had passed out cold. Ralph starts dragging you home. I met him half way. I fetched your stick, the cedar. The way you were clutching it, I figured it to be important to you."

"You know the man who was chasing me?" asked Skag.

"I knew him. Haven't seen him in near a dozen years, nor talked to him in more than a dozen. But I knew him. I could go two dozen more without seeing or speaking to him ever again, master cornbear."

"I'm not a cornbear," sighed Skag, fighting the drooping of his eyelids. "I am a bogfoke."

"Bog folk?" the old woman mused. "I think maybe I've heard of such in some old tale or the other. Well, I am pleased to have helped you, but even as you might not call yourself a cornbear, but that is what you are all the same.

"My name is Nannela Walker. Most folk just call me Nanna. So, you can see that I'm used to names not always sticking. In fact, I'm used to things not always being what they seem. That's for sure the way it was and is with the cornbears."

"We don't even look like bears," said Skag as his eyes softly closed.

"No, no you do not," agreed the woman named Nannela Walker. "I reckon you could have been called marsh monkeys. I figure your kind probably have been called goblins, bogey men, and perhaps by names beyond numbering in the many languages of men. Well, now to think of it, a monkey would have a tail, and seeing as I washed you, I know you don't have one, and do not seem to ever have had."

Skag tried to smile, but he could not. He tried to raise his head, but he could not. His heavy lidded eyes turned toward the woman named Nanna. Her smile was reassuring and she patted his arm. "It's just the herbs. Sleep seems to do wonders for cornbears, and bog folk. Now, do bog folk have names? You haven't told me your own."

"We're *bogfoke*, and my name is Skag," he managed before sleep stole over him. Nanna nodded to herself, lifting her gaze to the window and the forest beyond. She stared for some time before looking back to the sleeping bogfoke.

"Skag, a strange name for a strange creature," she murmured. "Not the prettiest of names, to be sure. I doubt that is your truest name, master bogfoke. I doubt you even know your truest name. But, rest easy, Skag. For a time you are safe from Yolande, and those who serve her. Even from the one *she* serves."

***

The morning light poured through the windows. It pried open Skag's eyelids and filled his vision with golden haze. He sensed that this was a different day. The air was cooler, and the wind stronger. He flexed his toes, and they wriggled back at him. He could feel the length of himself. It was indeed a different day.

He looked around the room. The walls were of slatted boards only a little wider than those of the ceiling. The whole lot had been whitewashed. There was only one picture on the wall, a bearded man who seemed to be exposing his heart which was wreathed in flames. There was an old chest of drawers with one leg replaced by a brick. The curtains on the windows were of bleached burlap. The bedding was worn but clean.

He pulled himself up to sit cross-legged on the fresh linen. The morning air washed through the windows with the sunshine. He squinted and looked down at the patch of garden below. The woman, Nanna, was picking from what the earth would yield.

He thought of fleeing but it was a mercurial consideration and soon abandoned. He saw the dog resting in the sunshine near the edge of the garden. That alone was reason enough to reconsider. He would never be able to out run the animal. Besides, the old woman had been kind and she seemed unfriendly to the witch. More importantly, she seemed not to be intimidated by the witch.

He squinted harder and stared over the field of corn to the wood beyond. Were the others safe? Had he drawn the witch's men away from them? Certainly he had drawn away Scarred-cheek.

His thoughts were disrupted by the clap of the screen door. He heard the sounds of busy-work from below. After a few minutes there came the sound of footsteps along the stairway. The door opened and Nanna came tip-toeing in as if she expected him to be asleep. Her smile spread wide when she saw him sitting up on the bed.

"Well, you look fit and ready," she remarked. "But, I have to declare that it is odd seeing you there, like that. You look like one of those old Negro men white folk used to draw for their picture books."

Skag frowned, not understanding. She waved her hand good-naturedly to dismiss the notion all together. "Don't pay me any attention. I would guess the affairs and slights of mankind do not mean much to you."

She sat on the edge of the bed, with her eyes fixed on something outside the window as her hand reflexively smoothed the old quilt. "Where are your folk from, Skag?"

"The city," he replied, before continuing in response to her arched eyebrows. "Oh, we kept well away from the eyes of men. We lived in the cemetery."

"Which one?"

"There is more than one? Yes, I suppose there are. Well, this one had many cedars and a gray stone wall. And it had an arch that wept."

Nanna nodded, "They call it Cedar Dale, but when I was a girl the really old folk still called it Cedar Bog, on account that it was started at the edge of a bit of useless swamp land. Eventually they even filled in the swampy portion to use it. That's why there are so many above ground tombs and mausoleums. Many of those became useless from leaning to one side or the other, or even collapsing because of the soft earth."

"They were not useless to the bogfoke," interjected Skag with a smile.

Nanna laughed softly in return before continuing, "Excepting a few church cemeteries, it is the oldest in the area. One of the biggest, that's for sure."

"Did you know Cornbread Jack?" asked Skag with a surge of wonder. But Nanna looked at him as if she didn't understand the question. "He was the one who built the wall. He was dark skinned like you."

"Lord no," she replied with a laugh. "I am not all that

old! But I know who you must be talking about. His name was John Elisha. He was a slave belonging to Captain Benjamin Merrill. The captain was a good enough master. He fought in the revolutionary war. A stone mason, he was. He taught John how to work the stone and treated him more as an apprentice than a slave. In his will he set John and his few other slaves free. John finished the wall around the cemetery after his master's death, and then he went up north."

"He liked cornbread," replied Skag with a shrug. "Some say his spirit lingers at the wall because of a curse he wove, though he may be gone now that we are free of it. Have you heard of Jeremiah Simms?"

Nanna leaned back, pursing her lips thoughtfully. "I don't know. A whole lot of white Simms from up the river, and a handful of black Simms further to the south. Who is he?"

Again Skag shrugged, "I don't know, exactly. He drowned trying to save some children. I only talked to his ghost, but I think he might have been white."

Nanna looked at him, but not in disbelief. "It is no small wonder Yolande fears your folk. You talk to ghosts?"

Skag shifted nervously, but felt a strange and compelling trust in this woman. "Only this one, though I've seen a good many. It was the city who let him speak to me. She held him as if he was a dream. I've seen many of her dreams. They are like the shadows of an evening, as if you were standing between two worlds."

Nanna smiled understandingly, "I know what you mean, master bogfoke. I know that feeling. The city is just a construct of men, but there about dwells an ancient spirit. A guardian spirit, a guiding spirit, like unto an angel, I reckon. I think the good Lord cast them about to help heal this Creation that my folk caused to go askew. Or, rather, they help to heal us so that we may make atonement, and they work against the wiles of the dark spirits."

The old woman smiled at herself, giving Skag a never-mind shake of her head before continuing, "I don't know about the rest of your folk, but at least *you* have been touched. Oh yes, Yolande has much to fear."

Skag looked out toward the distant wood at the mention of his comrades, "I don't know that they ever saw the dreams of the city. Not as I did, anyway. But I know they've seen the ghosts before. And there have been other bogfoke who have seen the dreams, my mother, for one, so the tales say."

Nanna considered this, and looked down at the bogfoke with her eyes reflecting the earnestness of her question, "Do *you* remember Cornbread Jack?"

Skag looked up, and then shifted his eyes as he thought about it. "I don't know. Maybe, or it could just be the remembering of tales raised by Mother Crabba. She has a powerful ability to bring up images. Seems I can remember the cemetery before the raising of the wall, but not clearly. I know a troll who would say it is like peeking into someone else's dream."

"Curious," whispered the old woman. "You know a troll. You talk to ghosts. You might be hundreds of years old. Yet, you have no firm memory of such a life."

"I am only a young bogfoke," said Skag as he scratched his belly and shrugged at her musings. It was his turn to ask a question, "Do you know the witch of the wood?"

Again the sad expression, and the eyes drifting to the eastern rim of the world as if chasing an elusive memory. The nod was slow and uncertain. "I knew her since she was but a child. I am not sure I know her still."

"Why does she hate cornbears? Why did she seduce the lord of the lake-wood from the deep soil?"

"I don't know," sighed Nanna, smoothing her dress as if wiping away the crumbs of memory. "She's not the Yolande I knew, though I should have seen it coming."

The old woman stood suddenly and looked out the window. "We'll talk of such things another time. It's going to warm up directly, as the sun rises. It will be seasonable at least. This cold has come premature upon us.

"Now, it wouldn't be wise for you to go outside. *The forest has eyes and Yolande has spies*, that's what folk say. Still, you need to stretch your legs, got to get yourself used to moving about again. Come along to the kitchen. I could use some help snapping beans."

She helped Skag to stand, and he did indeed find his legs to be wobbly. He stood for a moment, slowly bending each knee in turn and flexing his legs. When he nodded that he was ready, Nanna helped him into the hall and down the narrow stairwell.

He grinned sheepishly when forced to rest at the end of the steps. The staircase faced the front doorway. Skag looked past the screen door, down a long winding drive with huge pecan trees along either side. The road that passed by was narrow and unpaved.

"How far to the next dwelling of men?" he asked.

"*Ttch*, nearly five miles," replied Nanna, but she fixed Skag with a curious stare. "Why do bogfoke hide from men?"

Skag's brow furrowed and he finally shrugged as he replied, "Why indeed? I don't know. We just always have, since I can remember, even from the oldest tales raised by Mother Crabba. Seems you lot have been dangerous to us for some reason. Like a poison. Of course, there have been times when we have had dealings with men. Cornbread Jack, for one, and now yourself for another."

"Accidents, it would seem," mused the old woman as she took his arms and urged him to his feet. "Maybe that it has to do with our souring of Creation. Who can say?"

She led him to the back of the first floor hall. The kitchen was a bright room with two windows on the north wall and two windows on the south wall. A wood burning stove dominated the east wall and a sink cabinet with a hand pump was set against the west wall. A table with an oilcloth covering sat against the south wall beneath the windows.

Nanna guided the bogfoke to a chair next to the table. Skag scrambled onto the oversized seat, flexing his legs ruefully as he told her, "They feel about as sturdy as willow fronds."

"They'll soon recover," she assured him. "Sit here in the sunshine. You can see out the windows a bit, past the curtains, but they should shield you from prying eyes."

The old woman then got up and retrieved a basket full of beans. She dumped them onto the table cloth before picking one of them up to show to Skag. "What you need do is snap it on the ends and pull away this string that runs along the spine. If it is a long bean, and most of 'em are because I tend to them myself, then you snap it in the middle, like this. After that, throw the strings and caps back into the straw basket. The beans you toss into that basin sitting on the floor there. I can rinse them in that."

Skag took a bean, snapped it as she instructed and then tossed it into the enameled basin on the floor. He saw that it had many holes along its bottom and sides. Very clever, he thought it, and thought how useful the others back at the barrow would find it. For a brief moment he pondered the possibility of stealing it, being a bogfoke, but quickly put it out of mind because Nannela Walker was not like most of her kith.

Nanna nodded with satisfaction, but her smile was cautioning as she spoke, "The first dozen or two are easy enough."

Skag watched her for a moment, and then adopted her rhythm. They soon filled the room with the fresh green odor and the sound of their snapping. Skag's fingers were long and clever, and he became better at snapping beans until his pace eventually exceeded that of Nannela Walker.

"*Gracious,* you learn fast," she chuckled.

"Bogfoke have always been clever with their hands," replied Skag, but that made him think of the others and he continued, "I must return before long to my friends."

"You will need to gain strength before you challenge the warding again," she warned him. "It might not be as difficult as it was with Collanmore chasing you, but it is designed to keep *out* rather than in."

"You know a lot about Yolande it would seem," observed Skag. "Yet, Remus Wolfe told me most folk don't know what goes on within her wood."

"Remus Wolfe," replied the old woman with a raised eyebrow and a snort. "If he'd tried to make a decent living instead of piddling with them nets. . . Well, Yolande couldn't be satisfied with that. Now, she has to bear responsibility for what she has done, but if he'd used that brain of his and moved them away from that place, maybe she would have escaped the darkness."

Then she just shook her head ruefully. "I don't know. I reckon the dark might have found her elsewhere. No way of knowing. Maybe they deserve one another, Yolande and Remus."

Skag paused for a moment to take all that in, and then replied, "But, they're enemies. She's set a fearful curse on him and he cannot leave the wood."

Nanna's expression betrayed surprise, but she never broke the rhythm of her fingers snapping the beans. "Things must be grim indeed beyond that girdle of thorns. The poor children."

"I do not understand."

"I can see that you don't," Nanna said with a sigh. "The woman you know as the witch of the wood was once known as Yolande Wolfe. They are, or were, married."

"Is that possible?" he mused. The intricacies of human relationships escaped him. He began snapping beans again, but Nanna shooed him away from the last handful.

"I'll finish these," she said.

"Who would marry a witch?" Skag wondered aloud as he watched Nanna's fingers snapping the remaining beans. He leaned forward a little, trying to see into her eyes. "Why have you not answered me? How is it you know so much of this witch, Yolande?"

There was a long moment of silence, and now

Nanna's gaze was fixed on the enameled basin filled with snapped beans. Finally she looked up at the bogfoke. Her eyes were filled with determination and no hint of apology as she spoke, "Yolande is my granddaughter."

Skag felt his heart skip, but he calmed himself as he realized there was no threat in her tone. "Then why is it that you have helped me?"

"You haven't listened well," chided the old woman. "I told you that this is not the Yolande that I remembered. But, as I said, I should have seen it coming. The witch's sight has long been in my family. You must understand, my mother was a slave and my father was Cherokee. He was what white men would have called a medicine man, a shaman. My oldest brother was born into slavery. There were eight of us altogether, but he was born a little before the war ended. I was the youngest, and the war had been long over before I was born.

"My father tried to help her escape, but was captured himself. He managed to slip from the gray coats, but then he fled into the mountains, into the Cherokee lands. After the day of jubilation, when the blue coats freed the slaves, my father returned for my mother. They went to live for a while with my father's people.

"I was born there. I was the youngest of the eight children. We just didn't fit in it seems. My father took to the drinking. He was shot over a poker game. So it was that my mother took me back here, to the plantation where she'd been a slave.

"The master's widow—he was killed in the war—took me on as kitchen help, but only for my room and board. My mother made arrangements like that for all of us who were still living at home. My mother went away, trying to find work, went up north. I never did see her again. Word came eventually that she took sick and died."

"There is pain in your eyes," noted Skag.

"Yes, there always shall be," said the woman. "At least in this life, but, I did eventually get a job working in the kitchen at an orphanage run by some missionary nuns who came down after the war. They also gave me an education.

"In time, I caught the eye of Nathan Walker; he was an iron smith, a good man. We were married and had a daughter, Cassie. She was as wild as the wind, and she resented that her parents should be working folk. Imagined herself too good for such things and she seemed to resent that ever her family should have let themselves be slaves.

"It is hard to know what gets into a child's head, but I think now that it was the same darkness that would haunt her daughter, Yolande. Anyways, she ran off with a Yankee peddler. Worse, they never made it right in the eyes of the Lord or the law. They lived up north and that's where little Yolande was born, into a world where she was hated or envied by black folk and white."

"Why?" asked Skag.

"Because her mother was black and her father was white," Nanna explained patiently. She smiled when she saw that Skag still did not completely understand. "Eventually the peddler makes it rich, but dies soon after. He didn't leave Cassie anything in his will. He left nothing to the child either. In fact, turns out he had a wife already, a white woman."

Nanna released a long, sad sigh. "She killed herself, my Cassie. So close to everything she wanted in this world, and then it was snatched from her. She couldn't bear to come back home defeated, I guess. It broke my Nathan's heart. We both wrestled with wondering what we might have done or not done, that Cassie should come to such an end. I went up north to fetch Yolande from the orphanage and brought her home."

The old woman shook her head as she stared into the distance as if watching memories only she could see. "Poor Nathan. He died within a year. The doctor said he'd had a bad heart all along, but I know it was what happened to Cassie that killed him."

She bent to pick up the basin of beans and take it to the sink. She pushed and pulled at the pump handle until a gush of rust tinged water turned clear and clean. She put the basin in the sink, letting the water flow over the beans, and then she swished them around with her free hand.

"That is why you should've known?" asked Skag, "about Yolande."

"She never complained," replied Nanna as she shook the basin to hasten the water draining. "I knew the other young'uns would tease her. But she never said nothing of it. I guess she was saving it up. But what I *did* notice was the light in her eyes. The witch light was on her for sure, just as it had been upon my mother and my father."

Nanna stopped to wipe her hands on a towel. Her head tilted as she drifted in the memories. "If only Remus had made a decent living, maybe things would have been all right. I shouldn't say that. I blame him o'er much. He was a smart man, but he was a white man. It must have been difficult, with his wife being nearly half black and raised by colored folk. "

She returned to sit near Skag and leaned forward to look at him with earnest intensity. "She couldn't take it no more. They were different than everyone else. They were poor, not hungry, but poor enough. How much humiliation could a child suffer? And there was foolish Remus, thinking love was enough all by itself."

Skag tried to imagine what it must be like. The ways of humankind were difficult for him to grasp, but what the bogfoke did know something of was despair. That must be what this Yolande had felt. He knew something, too, of humiliation. He nodded to himself. He'd felt humiliation when cowed by the fear of Father Daugth for all those years. He looked up at the old woman, beginning to understand, but still grasping for more as he asked, "She was a child no longer, was she?"

Nanna smiled sadly. "In most ways, no. But we human folk carry something of the child we were forever within us, Skag. Certainly she had the body and mind of a grown woman, and a fine woman at that, educated by the nuns at the mission school. But there was something in her that could never grow. It was suffocated by all the hate, all the fear and all the humiliation she'd ever known. I should have seen it more clearly."

Understanding came to Skag. "Now it is Yolande who is feared. Yolande who humiliates those she fears or hates."

The old woman nodded softly. Skag sighed at the revelation, thinking he liked it better when he need feel no sympathy for the witch at all. Still, this brought him no solutions. In some ways it tainted his trust of Remus Wolfe. Why hadn't the man-wolf told him of this? Then again, hadn't Remus turned against the woman he loved after the cruelty and folly of her deeds exceeded his sense of honor and decency? This was an act of courage akin to revolting against the life of despair behind coquina walls.

"You have the look of someone who has much to think over," said Nanna. "Let me help you back to the bedroom. Later I'll fix you something solid to eat."

She helped Skag to his feet, but he managed to wobble along on his own. The steps were a trial, but each one strengthened the sense of feeling in his legs, even if it was an ache. The room was dimmer now that the sun was reaching midday and no longer angling its rays through the windows.

"You have been kind to me," said Skag as Nanna turned to go.

"Some part of your troubles is my fault," replied the woman without turning around. "I should have known. It seems that my people, we children of Adam, are destined to always taint the great promise of this world."

***

Skag rested and watched the day pass beyond the window. Without the canopy of leaves that veiled it in the forest, the sun was fiercely bright. His conversation with Nannela Walker had created a tumble of thoughts in his head. Men were not so much unlike bogfoke. The weight of fear, degradation and sorrow that each individual can bear is different. What bows one mayhap is of little hindrance to another.

He did not want to feel sorry for the witch, but now it seemed at least in some part to be inevitable. Still, fear and instinct for survival were not likely to be subservient to empathy. Skag sighed and decided that knowledge and time made any life bittersweet.

Sleep drifted over him like clouds scurrying across the sun of his consciousness. The day slid steadily into twilight, and the world changed from golden haze into a moist, shadowed green. Skag was hungry, and got from the bed to make his way down the steps. He smiled at the steadiness of his legs.

A soft glow of light came from the kitchen and he heard Nanna's feet shuffling across the floor. She was at the sink when he entered the room in triumph. A single kerosene lamp sat on the table. The dim, golden light made everything seem as if in a dream. Nanna was humming softly. It was a tune Skag had heard before, sung by mourners at the cemetery.

"What is that you are humming?" he asked.

Nanna raised her eyebrow as if wondering to herself and then understanding lit in her eyes. "I didn't even realize I was humming. It's just a hymn. Of course, you would have heard it before. It's often sung at funerals."

"Why?"

She moved over to the stove as she pondered the simple question. She lifted the lid of a pan and poked with a long fork amidst the roll of steam before turning back to Skag. His question was still weighing in her mind and finally she shrugged. "I don't rightly know how to explain it to you, master bogfoke. It makes us feel better, in general. Singing, rocking and swinging are a comfort to us.

"Hymns in particular are a promise to us. They are filled with the possibility that all will be made right. When things get real bad, and when it seems as if my head is unraveling like worn burlap, I can go sit on the porch-swing and sing to myself. It's like darning the material, so to speak."

She dipped a ladle of green beans onto a plate upon which there was already a fried chicken leg, some boiled red potatoes and a biscuit. "Eat lightly now. This is your first real meal in a long while."

The bogfoke started with the chicken while butter melted in the biscuit and over the potatoes. It was better than any meal that ever he'd had. He told her so while chewing a mouthful of the biscuit. She smiled. Then she watched him for a long moment, considering some thought before she spoke, "Skag, it seems likely you'll be heading back into the wood soon. I have never seen anyone rebound from about dead the way you have. But there is something I must tell you, though I can't be completely sure of what I say."

Skag looked up, chewing slowly and waiting. The old woman gazed past him into the gathering dark beyond the windows. "I told you that my folk have carried the witch light for a long while. So they have. But with Yolande, it is different. I'll tell you that I have never seen nor heard of anything like it. There is something more than frightening in all this, Skag. I don't know what, but I'll tell you that *something* has given her more power than I've ever heard tell.

"Now, folk talk about deals with the devil and what not. I don't know about that. But, I do know there are spirits about in the world. Like your lord of the lake-wood, or even more powerful, like that of the city. But not all of them are guardians and tenders. Some are dark, very dark and destructive."

"What is the witch light?" asked Skag.

Nanna replied, "Those who are touched by it can sometimes see things that have yet to happen. They can see things that others cannot. Things like the dreams of the city. They have unusual skills with herbs and healing. I've even seen folk who could pray the fire out from a burn. Some can divine water. Some can cast a curse. It is a thing that can be as fine or as evil as the person who holds it. But, Yolande is far beyond such things, more so than I had even guessed until I heard your tale."

The heat of the cook stove had made the room grow very warm. Nanna wiped a bit of sweat from off her brow upon the edge of her apron. Skag had finished the last of his meal. The old woman motioned for him to follow her, "Come along onto the porch."

She led him to the front porch and sat in the porch swing while Skag sat cross-legged on the floor with his back against the wall. The old dog, Ralph, came trotting up the porch steps. All the tail wagging and lolling tongue couldn't wipe away Skag's trepidation. The very size of the dog was intimidating even if he seemed an overgrown pup.

When Nanna saw the bogfoke's unease, she clucked her tongue in a mildly scolding manner. Ralph turned reluctantly away from Skag and went to plop himself down at the porch edge with a long sigh, but he couldn't seem to remove the gaze of eager eyes from the bogfoke.

The porch swing creaked in counter rhythm to the slight moan of the floorboards beneath Nanna's feet. The slightly chilly breeze was pleasant after the moist heat of the kitchen, and Skag relaxd as he gradually came to accept that the dog meant no harm.

"I think I shall return to the wood tomorrow," he said quietly.

"I wouldn't think you quite fit as yet."

Skag shrugged. "I'm well enough, and I've been gone for too long. I must see what has happened while I've been away. Things were looking grim. Besides which, if I stay much longer I'll be so fat I could never waddle through the ward."

The old woman chuckled lightly for a moment before turning serious. "I can understand your concern for you kith and kin. But the ward will take right much out of you. I would reckon you would do better to go up along the edge of Stone's creek, where Taterbarge creek joins into it. From what I've heard tell, the ward doesn't extend into the marsh. Though the marsh land has its own travails."

"That's the creek that runs into Yolande's village,"

noted Skag, remembering the words of Remus Wolfe.

"Yes, but you need not go that far along. Just go until you've passed most of the warding. From what you have said, I think you can cut westward and you'll come to the lake sooner or later. Then you can reckon yourself home without too much fuss."

"That makes good sense," replied Skag, who had dreaded the fury of the ward. "Thank you, Nannela Walker, for all you have done."

There was no reply except for the creak of the swing, but Skag could see the soft, sad smile and weary eyes. He looked back along the drive and then up at the stars. He'd sometimes liked to gaze at the stars on moonless nights in the cemetery. It was a peculiarity of his among the bogfoke. He stared at the points of light and wondered. Such a large world, he realized, and he wondered if there was to be a place in it for the bogfoke.

***

Skag rested through the night and well into the following afternoon. Nanna returned the cedar stave to him when he came down from the bedroom. Skag smiled upon having the cedar in his hands again, holding it close to his nose so he could breathe in the scent of it.

"This is more than just a tool or a weapon to you, I would guess," observed the old woman. "It is a portent. It is a symbol of some importance to you."

Skag regarded the modest length of wood in his hands. He had never thought of it that way, but she had hit upon the truth of it. Whenever this wood was in his hand, and whenever he smelled the sharp scent of the cedar, he could feel the rush of memories and a surge of confidence. He could remember the fall of Father Daugth and the blood of a demon crow.

"Yes, it is like a finger tapping my shoulder and reminding me of the purpose I have chosen. It also reminds me of my duty to those who have trusted me."

"It'll be dark soon," said Nanna. "You may as well eat a good meal to tide you over. I'll let old Ralph follow you a ways, until you're into the ward. He insists on it. I'd guess he is aiming to keep any other dogs or men from messing with you. He's taken a liking to you."

"I'm glad he didn't take a disliking to me," replied Skag with his mouth in a skeptical twist.

Nanna smiled and motioned him to his meal. The bogfoke happily ate as the sun continued her steady course toward the western rim of the world.

***

With the gloaming there returned an unseasonable chill. Nanna led Skag toward a field of tall corn. Ralph plodded along behind them.

"I suppose it's just as well you are going," sighed the old woman. "I'm expecting Mr. Parker to come harvest these fields. I lease them out to him. He pays me with a portion of the harvest. He's late already, so I expect him any day.

"In the meantime, they'll do nicely to hide you while you make your way to the forest. If eyes are watching for you, they would see you all too plainly if you went across the fallow fields, just stay between the rows. When you get to the forest, move eastward until you come to the creek."

"Again, I thank you Nannela Walker," offered Skag solemnly. "I thank you for everything. Perhaps there will come a day when I can repay your kindness. Farewell."

"Good-bye, Skag," replied the woman softly. "My Nathan would have said that you've got a sack of smarts, a gallon of guts, and a spark in your eye that suggests you mean to use them. Good-bye and may the good Lord be with you."

With old Ralph following him, Skag turned and walked down one of the aisles between the corn. A slight breeze rustled the stalks and stirred dust from the thirsty earth. Skag counted paces before crossing over to the row on his left. Then he counted paces again before crossing to the left once again. This would keep him beneath the shelter of the corn while making his way to the eastern edge of the field. To have just cut straight eastward would have mean fighting the rows and causing a bustle in the field that might have attracted attention.

Gradually he could see trees above and beyond the corn. Ralph had followed him faithfully, and when they'd reached the edge of the field, Skag dredged up the courage to scratch the beast behind its ears. It was a strange thing, this bond between the kith of Cornbread Jack and dogs. They could both grovel in weak-hearted treachery, or stand courageous and loyal.

"Well, Ralph, now it's time to skirt the edge of the forest and make my way to the creek. It still gives me shivers, friend dog, to venture so near the witch's own lair, but I think your mistress is right. It is the easiest path both to make and find my way."

The dog was painfully unconcerned with stealth and made so much noise that Skag cringed at each snapped twig or crackling rustle of brush. Ralph must be plenty sure of himself, decided Skag. He found himself wishing he could be so unafraid.

As they moved through the boundary of the forest Skag was comforted by the familiar smell of pine needles and loamy soil. After a bit he turned deeper into the wood until confronted by the ragged edge of Yolande's ward. Now he just followed the ward eastward.

Darkness was gathering beneath the trees, and Ralph moved like a shadow of night. Whenever Skag turned to look he could see the eyes of the dog glowing nearly like those of a cat. Ralph sensed something dire about the nature of the ward and had become stealthier in his movement than his bulk would have suggested possible. Whenever Skag stopped, the dog stopped. Whenever Skag quickened his pace, the dog quickened. It was as if they were attached by an invisible cord.

They were very near the creek when Skag decided to rest. He found a patch of dry forest floor to settle upon. He could feel the moist breeze blowing over a northwestern curve of the creek. It brought with it the stagnant odor of the marsh. He massaged his legs as he looked at the dog. "I feel silly, being tuckered out like this from such a bitty little jaunt. Well, anyways, I reckon you can turn back now, Ralph. I'll be going into the ward. I ain't got nerve enough to go one step further east."

The animal just sat on its haunches, panting and unconcerned. When Skag rose, Ralph remained seated. The bogfoke smiled and ventured another scratch behind the dog's ear, which Ralph accepted with a grateful thumping of his tail. Skag chuckled and turned toward the ward. Ralph sat contentedly watching as the bogfoke disappeared into the tangle of vines and bramble.

The wicked bite of thorns reminded Skag of where he'd ventured. He wasn't in a particular hurry, and didn't intend to challenge or force his will upon the ward. He let the tangled vegetation herd him this way or that as it would, only being careful to maintain a generally south by southwesterly bearing.

Cresting a low ridge he saw the dark water of the creek across a quarter mile of marsh. The ward of Yolande stretched into the tall, waving grasses, easily defined but greatly diminished. He glanced up at the sky, fixing his gaze on the pattern of stars that would be his guide. He would keep it relative to his position and push on to the southwest.

The sodden ground of the marsh was cool. He was glad for this unusual chill because it would make sluggish any alligators or snakes he might chance upon. The slight wind caused the grasses to whisper, masking the faint noise of his hurried passage. More than once he was suddenly knee deep in the water of a washout.

His legs grew wobbly from the exertion and he pulled himself to rest on a slight rise dominated by a lonely cedar and a few scraggy wax myrtle shrubs. He sat with his back against the cedar, considering it a good omen. His eyebrows arched as he looked back across the marsh. He'd covered a half mile, far better than expected. His legs could tell the entire tale, however.

Looking southward he figured less than a quarter mile remained before he would be clear of the ward. It was a grim looking stretch, filled with scum covered pools and tendrils of dark water spreading like a web. He smiled, realizing that what lay before him was a bog.

"Well," he mused aloud. "Let us see how aptly Cornbread Jack named those who tormented him."

He eased down from the firm soil around the cedar onto what most resembled some sort of path through the bog. He poked ahead cautiously with the cedar stave, feeling out any uncertain ground before advancing. It made sense to him that his folk might have once lived in such a place. Certainly it would be nearly impenetrable to humans.

The unstable ground made it difficult for him to maintain a steady course and he meandered for over a mile before nearing a spur of wood cut into the marsh. The way was barred by several wide, shallow ditches, the remnants of a long neglected drainage system. The stumps of drowned trees attested to the bog's re-conquest of its ancient holdings. He remembered that boats as large as trawlers had once maneuvered along Stone's creek, but now the water was silted and spread out shallow over the bog.

Finally Skag struggled onto the needle covered floor beneath the pines. Nettles were stinging at his feet and thorns plucked at the fabric of the trousers Nannela Walker had patched for him. He found a place free of tormenting plants and sat with his back against a dying oak. The ground beneath the leaf mold was soggy with water backing in from the creek.

A breeze ruffled Skag's bristled hair, as if apologizing for his tribulations. He was tired and depression squeezed his heart until it felt leaden in his chest. He rubbed his aching legs, trying to ease the cramping muscles.

He stretched his legs out and looked across the marsh. His eyes narrowed. Something was moving out there. A dark form shambled recklessly through the tall grasses. Was it a bear? It seemed too tall and thin, but darkness distorted any real perspective. Whatever it was, it caused Skag to feel uneasy. The dark smudge against the grass was weaving erratically, but it seemed to the bogfoke that it was coming toward the spur of wood where he had found shelter.

It might well be his imagination abdicating to his fears, but Skag had no intention of chancing that whatever was on the marsh might be benign. He dropped to his knees and began to crawl southward through the tangled warding. This portion of the ward was not so fierce as that near the barrow and he made good time despite the weariness of arms and legs. After a while he found he could actually stand and trot along if he stooped and watched his step. The tangle of vines had climbed over fallen trees, leaving the area near the ground relatively free.

The dark beneath the wood had become nearly absolute, but Skag was able to distinguish the trees and undergrowth as darker shadows against the night. He was moving as quickly as possible, desperately driven by noises from within the ward that suggested he was being pursued. Beneath his feet the ground became soggy and Skag realized that he was moving too far to the east. He tried to alter his course, but the tangled growth seemed determined to drive him toward the creek.

The wood began to thin and allowed him to force his way westward. It was a hard earned progress, with the ward thickening as he went. The sluggish advance closed the gap between Skag and whatever was following him.

A tendril of fire-thorn caught at his trousers and tumbled him onto the marshy soil. In the darkness behind him the pursuer was closing fast. Skag rolled to his feet and began to climb into a young cypress. He climbed until the branches bent and swayed dangerously beneath his weight. If it was a bear chasing him it would not be able to follow him this far.

He saw a smudge of darkness staggering through the vines below. There was a pause, as if waiting to catch the sound of the prey. When only the sounds of the forest drifted in the night air, the dark form began to move cautiously forward. Then it stopped again.

"I can see you now," cried a hoarse voice that was certainly not that of a bear, but it seemed hardly human either. It cracked and rumbled like a falling tree.

Skag clung tight to both his cedar stave and the branch upon which he was perched. The sound of ragged breathing came from below, and he could hear feet dragging across the ground. It was beneath him. Suddenly the tree was violently shaken.

"Cornbear, cornbear, come on down! I'm getting tired of chasing you 'round!"

Skag's heart twisted. He recognized the voice that was like a corpse beneath a shroud of crackling and rumbling, Scarred-cheek. The tree shook again and a rasping laughter was spat from below. He could make out the form of the man, stooped and cringing with one arm held tightly to his ribcage.

"I'm tired of foolin' around! I'll come up for you my ugly little pest!"

There was the sound of scraping and the snapping of branches as Scarred-cheek tried to climb into the tree. His efforts with only one useful arm were futile. Finally he slid back to the ground, whimpering as he went. Then he sprawled onto his back and began to laugh.

"I'll wait! I'll wait! That's what I'll do! You ain't going no place at all!"

Skag wedged himself into a position that wouldn't strain his arms. The limb dipped and swayed, but it held. He saw Scarred-cheek still spread on the ground. He could hear the man talking to himself, sometimes with sobs and other times with laughter. There was nothing the bogfoke could do but wait and keep trying to figure a way out of this mess.

For three hours Skag clung to his perch, occasionally shifting to relieve the stiffness in his arms and legs. Scarred-cheek lay as if dead, but let loose sporadic volleys of curses and dry laughter. Finally the man rose to his knees and turned his face toward his prey.

"I'm tired of waiting. Here I come!"

Again the frantic scrambling at the tree branches, but this time he managed to gain a few feet and his erratic laughter echoed in wicked delight. There was a pause and then he struggled a few more feet. The young cypress began to curve beneath the man's weight.

Scarred-cheek painstakingly made his one-handed way up the trunk. The tree was bent so severely that Skag was closer to the ground than was the man. Scarred-cheek made another advance of a few feet and the tree dipped even further.

Suddenly Skag moved from his place between the two branches. He slid off the tree limb and dangled by one arm. With a deep breath he let go and dropped to the ground below. The air was pushed from his lungs but he never paused as he rolled to his feet and fled.

From behind there exploded an anguished roar and the sound of branches snapping. Then there was a heavy thud behind him as Skag ran along the barest trace of a path. The ward was fading and he had to make full use of his speed.

The sound of the pursuit was slow in coming, but eventually he heard the sobbing and faint curses as Scarred-cheek lumbered doggedly after him. The ground turned to bog beneath his feet as he drew nearer the creek. He dove into the darkness beneath wild privet. The uncertain tramping of Scarred-cheek sounded far behind, granting the bogfoke a moment to muster his strength.

When he was ready to move on, he decided to try and curve his path westward. A narrow rabbit run afforded him a passage that Scarred-cheek would find less welcoming. It opened after a bit onto a wider deer trail. As he paused for a gulp of air Skag heard the sounds of the man's confused and tortured pursuit.

Skag pushed on, coming finally onto a wide glade.

Just as he was about to step into the open a sudden blur of motion swept past his eyes. He tried to whirl in retreat but was too late. A net flashed up around him from beneath the cover of the pine needles. He was jerked from his feet and bundled into the air four feet or more above the ground. Two pie pans tied to the webbing clanged against one another in makeshift alarm.

Skag twisted and pried at the hemp with his stave, but it was useless. He calmed himself, realizing that his struggles just made the pans clang all the louder. He listened intently and knew that it was too late, someone was coming.

A short man came stumbling into the glade, rubbing the sleep from his eyes. Skag recognized him as one of those who had come with Scarred-cheek from over the lake. The man put his hands on his hips as his eyes grew wide. A wicked grin formed on the face. He jabbed at the net with a forefinger, chuckling as he said, "Well, my ugly little cornbear, imagine this! My great fortune and your misfortune that I should have set this trap not ten minutes ago! Yolande will be mightily pleased with what I have netted."

SEVEN

What The Witch Wants

The short man was happy with the quarry his trap
had bagged. He whistled contentedly while cutting the ropes
and then retied them to bundle Skag firmly in the net. He
slipped a bit of rope through the top-knot of the bundle so
that he could pull it along. Skag couldn't resist trying to bite
the fingers as they looped the rope, but the man only
chuckled.

With the end of the rope tightly wrapped around one
hand the man began dragging Skag across the forest clearing.
They had not gone far when a ruckus from the wood caused
the man to stop. He turned, frowning as he searched the dark
beneath the trees. From out of the inky black shuffled
Scarred-cheek with fiercely glaring eyes.

"Where are you going with my cornbear?" he hissed
at the shorter man.

"Is that you Jake?" asked the man holding Skag.
"Look at yourself. You're an awful mess. Stand downwind.
You smell worse'n a pig sty. What happened to you? Where
you been all this time?"

"Where you going with my cornbear?"

"I'm taking this fellow to Yolande."

"My cornbear, that is, Silas," snapped Scarred-cheek
with choking rage. He moved threateningly but was halted by
the flash of the knife in the short man's hand.

"Now stand back, Jake," warned Silas. "You look like you done been messed up enough, but I can fix you good if I got to. You know it wouldn't bother me none to cut you right proper. What's the matter? You afraid Yolande might snuggle up to ol' Silas for bringing her this present?"

Scarred-cheek snarled and moved forward a little but couldn't overcome his fear of the knife. Silas grinned wickedly and taunted, "Look at yourself. She ain't likely to want what's left of you. You come any closer and there won't be nothing left to tumble with anyway."

The scorn hung sharp as the knife blade. Scarred-cheek drew himself up a bit but backed a little away. His eyes were clearer and focused on the shorter man. "Take him then, Silas. But you know this, that sooner or later I'll settle things with you. That is my cornbear. I have been tracking him for weeks. You take him, but you can number your days."

The cold threat bit, and caused Silas to shift uncertainly. With a final rasping chuckle, Scarred-cheek melted into the gloom of the forest. Silas stood watching the empty path for a long moment, and then tugged on the rope to drag his bundled prize along.

"I guess you'll have to watch your back now," smirked Skag.

Silas was startled because he had not known that cornbears could talk. He kicked at the net. "Shut up, or Yolande will get a cornbear without a tongue."

The bogfoke admonished himself for the impulsive words. He twisted to keep his face out of the leaf mold as he was dragged along in silence.

***

Silas tossed the bundle into a clapboard shed. The place smelled of mildew, dust, grease and the cloying sweet scent from rotting sacks of feed grain. The bags of feed were stacked in the middle of the hard, earthen floor. Dusty canning jars and a rusted assortment of gears and tools had waited for many years untouched on the shelves lining one of the walls. There was a lone window, boarded up and with most of the yellowed glass broken or missing.

The door was closed with a thud, and Skag heard a heavy bar dropped across to secure it. He twisted against the restraining net but could not reach the top-knot to free himself. He managed to slip his cedar stave through the webbing and tried to knock down a shovel or hoe leaning against the pile of sacks so he could work the strands of netting against the blade. The stave came frustratingly short of reaching any of the tools. It occurred to him that they would eventually take the stave away from him, so he shoved it beneath the molding pile of feed sacks for safe keeping.

There was little else to do except wait. Time slipped into the gray light of dawn, outlining the rotten and jagged lower edge of the clapboard. Suddenly he saw a shadow, and then a face. It was a child's face peering curiously through the gap between the earth and the back wall.

It was a girl. Best Skag could tell she was perhaps eleven years of age. She lowered herself to the earth and squirmed under the wall. She rose, brushed off her shift-like dress and then reached under the clapboard for an outstretched hand. With a few encouraging tugs a boy of maybe eight years popped into the interior of the shed. The girl looked around the building and as her eyes adjusted to the dark she spotted the bundled netting that contained Skag.

The bogfoke reckoned that the kith of Cornbread Jack would think her pretty, with thick black hair and almond shaped green eyes. The boy was slender, with dark brown hair and eyes. His features were much leaner than those of the girl. They dropped to their knees beside Skag, looking him over with unmasked curiosity.

Finally the girl nudged the boy with an elbow and jerked her head toward the window. "Keep a look out."

It seemed he was used to following her orders and dutifully rose to stand as sentry, but he kept glancing back at the girl and the bogfoke. The girl turned back to Skag, sizing him up. "So, you're a cornbear. You look like a little bristly troll to me."

"Or a dirty leprechaun," offered the boy. "Though, I don't think leprechauns are so big as that."

"I am neither of those," replied Skag, smiling at the surprise his words registered on their faces. "I am a bogfoke, and my name is Skag."

The girl recovered from the shock of hearing him speak and crossed her arms confidently in front of her chest as she said, "I am Nan, and that's my brother, Owen."

"You shouldn't tell it our names," protested the boy in a whisper.

"I suppose it would be nice to meet you, excepting the circumstance," explained Skag. "I don't suppose you could let me loose from this net?"

The girl gave the appearance of considering it, but decided quickly enough that the trouble it would bring upon her would not be worth whatever statement of defiance it might make. She shook her head. Owen was obviously relieved, which revealed to Skag that Nan was given to willful actions. The boy's demeanor suggested a more reserved disposition. He kept glancing furtively through the gaps in the window boards as worry and curiosity tugged him back and forth.

"I can't imagine why everyone is fussing so much about you. You are kind of cute, like a skinny bush baby," decided Nan as she assessed the round face and large round eyes.

"What is a bush baby?"

"Bog folk aren't so smart, are they?"

Skag shrugged within the tight confine of the net. "About some things, no. About others, yes. And, it's *bogfoke*."

"That sounds like country talk," Nan informed him. "My mother does not like country talk. Anyway, what are you smart about?"

A smiled cracked the bogfoke's expression. He knew it was ridiculous to banter with the child, but he was a bogfoke and badinage was part of his nature. "We know how to steal, beg and borrow. We forgot more tales than most men ever hear. I know something of the languages of red, white, black and yellow men. And, we must have something that the witch of the wood wants?"

"You must," Nan mused, nodding her head at the wonder of it. She was interrupted before she could continue by her brother's urgent hissing.

"They're coming."

"Good-bye, mister bogfoke," whispered Nan as she and her brother hurried to disappear through the gap at the bottom of the clapboard. They were gone much more quickly than first they had appeared.

The sound of the children retreating had barely faded when Skag heard the heavy footfall and voices of grown men. The bar was thrust aside and the door opened with a flood of weak light. A stout man with black beard and shaggy hair was the first through the door, nearly stepping atop the bogfoke. Silas followed and shoved the first man roughly away from his prized catch.

"Be careful you oaf. You'll damage the goods. Get that old shovel handle and slip it through the net," snapped Silas. The big man nodded slowly and fetched the spade-less handle. They used it like a litter to lift Skag from the floor and carry him along.

In the faint light of dawn Skag could see the creek about a hundred yards to his right. A few houses stood clustered about. The people were easing into the first stirrings of the day. If this was Stone's Creek not much remained of it. Many of the houses were empty and derelict.

As the men turned down alongside a ramshackle picket fence, Skag caught sight of a squat steeple against the gray sky. Beneath it was what had been a church. The windows were boarded and the churchyard was overgrown with weeds. Wooden tombstones stood weathered and askew in forlorn memorial.

They were heading toward a small but well-kept

house. Skag saw Nan and Owen peeking from behind a nearby tree. They seemed dismayed at the treatment he was receiving, but their good natured concern was of no help to him. The men carried him up the steps and opened the front door. He was deposited onto the floor.

The room was larger than seemed likely from the size of the house. It was like a meeting room, with chairs and benches. With a huff each man sat in a chair as if having lugged twice their own weight for miles. There was the sound of a door and light footsteps. Both men were quickly to their feet.

Their reaction made evident who had entered the room. Skag squirmed around for a look. At first there was only the hem of a long, plain gray dress. He looked up and found himself staring into deep, velvet-brown eyes. The intensity in those eyes caused him to shift his gaze away and collect himself before venturing another look.

She was beautiful, this witch of the wood, a tall woman, nearly as tall as Remus Wolfe. Her thick black hair spilled like a shadow of night around her shoulders, making her tawny skin seem lighter. Her features were rather leaner than Nannela Walker's, but he could see some resemblance. Her almond shaped eyes spoke of her Cherokee heritage, as did the high cheek bones.

Her smile flashed white and reassuring. It was an easy smile. It seemed devoid of malice. This worried Skag and he wondered if it was a smile of good intentions, or a smile without conscience.

"Good day, master bogfoke," she said quietly before motioning to her men. It was the voice of a young Nannela Walker, but colder despite its pleasantries. "Release him from the net, but for his own safety bind his hands and feet. Not too tightly now."

The men rushed to do her bidding and when they were finished she dismissed them with a slight inclination of her head toward the door. Their hasty exit would have been comical had it not been so wretched. Her eyes glinted at the humiliation inflicted upon her underlings.

Skag shifted himself into a sitting position. He was surprised at his own lack of fear. There had stolen upon him a resigned courage. Yolande looked back down at him. Her smile was diminished by just a bit as she sat on one of the benches.

"Why didn't you call me a cornbear?" asked Skag, suspicious of her knowledge.

"Not too long ago I would have," replied Yolande. "I have learned otherwise. Though, in fact, bogfoke and cornbears are essentially one and the same."

"The same?"

"White men, red men, yellow men and black men are nearly the same. So it is with the two small folk. I doubt that even that much difference exists."

She stood and moved to a large piece of paper tacked to the wall. Her eyes roved over the patchwork of colors and she moved her hand to a place just off center of the bottom. "This is Africa. It is said that on the eastern rim of this place man began his rise toward becoming masters of the Earth."

She turned to look at Skag before continuing, "In nearly all cultures and folklore there are the little people, leprechauns, bogies, goblins, trolls, sprites, gnomes, the yunwi-tsundi of the Cherokee, the nimerigar of the Shoshone. And, of course, there are the cornbears and the bogfoke.

"I wondered about that, master bogfoke. Why so pervasive a belief? Then I saw a cornbear. It was obvious then, it was believed because it was the truth. The descriptions of the little people varied from culture to culture, but less than the cultures themselves differed. These little people always seemed to have certain characteristics in common. All were quick witted, sharp of tongue, given to capricious behavior, tricksters, mischievous, and possessing an unrelenting and often cruel sense of humor. Also, they seemed diminished by contact with mankind, seeking shelter under the earth in hills, burrows, and tunnels."

She smiled again. "That would be a fair assessment of your folk?"

Skag felt the urge to reply that she had forgotten to mention their stunning beauty, but feared she might think he was trying to be unrelentingly humorous. Instead he said nothing. The witch smiled before turning back to the map. "But why no bones? No fossils? True, this is a new science, but still, no physical hint of their existence other than possibly a few standing stones and legends of hauntings?"

She laughed. "Well, it was foolish of me, especially of *me*. I had not considered the one other thing held in common by the little folk in all the tales ever told of them, *magic*."

Yolande paused as if to let her words sink in before tracing her finger up the paper from the splotch of color she had called Africa. "Man spread, encountering the little people wherever he ventured. Then, suddenly, the little people began to diminish at an astonishing rate. Why? Well, I had already missed the answer once. I wouldn't again. Magic.

"In myth and reality, there are two elements particularly troublesome to magic, water and iron. It is probably no coincidence that electricity is also affected by these things. Both are energies. Energy is the very flesh of magic. Man has little ability with magic, but he forged weapons of iron and the little people slipped into the shadows and under hills. The dominion of the Earth was now uncontested. Mankind was master of the Earth."

Skag glanced down at the rope binding his wrists and ankles, "If that is so, perhaps I could just be on my way?"

"You are not thinking," retorted the witch. "Magic."

"I am quick witted, but not a particularly deep thinker," explained Skag. "Though I do wonder at the rate the masters of the Earth fill up cemeteries, but what magic have I?"

Yolande smiled, but it was bitter thing, "You have the sight, have you not?"

The bogfoke sighed. "I have seen the dreams of the

city, but what of that? If it is magic, then it is feeble and of little use."

"City? That wretched little town? No, I have seen true cities. Cities where people number in many hundreds of thousands," replied Yolande with her beauty clouded by a mocking expression. "But your vision of those dreams is indeed magic. Feeble? Perhaps, but it may only be nascent. It may be but a scratch upon the surface of something more."

The witch turned and in a swirl of gray sat upon the bench again. "The Indians believed that everything, every rock, tree and stream had a spirit. Animism is what such beliefs are called. It was not so far-fetched. Energy and matter are the stuff of our universe it seems. Yet, sometimes these spirits are more than just forces of nature. Your city of dreams is one, a sentient existence that predates the arrival even of the red men. Your *city* dreamed long before it was even a city."

She paused a moment and studied the bogfoke. "Look at you. You understand a great deal of what I say. Even though I know of things that even the great men of science in our age can scarcely reckon. Yet, you can hold the notion in your head. You ask why I bind you? You wonder why I fear you and your cornbear kindred?

"The city revealed to you a way out of the cemetery. It revealed to you a passage into the Great Wood. It is a sentient existence and it has contrived to place you within my domain. I do not trust your city. I do not trust you.

Yolande looked to an illustration pinned to the wall near the map. "I have had opportunity to study your kind. You look somewhat like us, but you are *not* human. Your bones are different. Your muscles are different. Your joints and sinew are different. Your knees and elbows have nearly as much articulation in reverse as they have forward. You are stronger than your size would indicate. Your skin instinctively mottles to camouflage you in the shadows. It's just part of your ability to mimic."

Skag felt a deep dread when he realized the depictions

on the wall were of bogfoke anatomy; the segmented anatomy of bogfoke.

Yolande fixed her gaze upon him again. "I wonder why you even bother with clothing, but that brings me to another point. While you look something like diminutive humans, I think that is itself an adaptation and mimicry. Who can know what the original form of your folk might have been? I would theorize that you mimicked humans, learning languages, somehow altering your original appearance, and even adopting aspects of our cultures. Maybe we learned from your folk as well, but you are the great mimics"

"Unfortunately," sighed the witch, turning her hands up at the perceived futility, "The nature of what your folk are and the way your bodies turn swiftly into nothing prevented me from learning as much about what you are and what you will become as I desired. But I know this, I do not trust you."

There was an angry glare in her eyes now as they bore into Skag, "I shall tell you of an ancient people, they were red men who came from the north. They were an enlightened tribe knowledgeable in matters of magic and skilled builders. They were envied by my Cherokee ancestors who set upon them in a battle for dominion of the mountain lands. Of course the enlightened tribe was triumphant in one clash after another. But then there came from under the hills a host of magical beings who joined with the Cherokee to crush the enlightened tribe, to utterly destroy them until they were nothing more than a nameless legend."

Her head bowed as if greatly distressed at the vanquishing of these folk she obviously considered more noble and worthy than her own ancestors. "Think of it, master bogfoke. There came from *under the hills*, a host of magical beings. That is the legend told by the Cherokee themselves. So, you would wonder why I fear you, your cornbear cousins, and that interfering city of dreams?"

"The red men did not have iron," Skag noted.

Yolande's eyebrow arched and she nodded slowly. "So it was. That is why some of your folk linger still."

"How is it that you know so much of these things?" asked Skag.

"You will see before the ending of the day. But, there is much more I can learn," said the witch as she rose. "You will need rest and food. I shall have you taken to a secure room so that you can be free of the bonds. You must be strong for our endeavors."

She turned then and left through the room. Shortly after, Silas and the black bearded man entered and dragged Skag to another room. There was a cot and thin mattress, but nothing else. The window was barred with iron rods. The black bearded man left but soon returned holding a plate of sliced, smoked ham, cold fried potatoes and a stale biscuit in one hand, and a jug of water in the other. He placed these on the floor.

Silas bent and cut the bonds from Skag's wrist and ankles. He gave the bogfoke a warning prick with the knife point; causing Skag to feel a slight wave of sickness, before moving to the door. "Now, don't do anything stupid. We got hounds that'd have your scruffy hide before you got fifty yards."

The door slammed shut and there was the sound of a lock clicking. Skag sat on the floor stretching and rubbing his arms and legs. He ate some of the food and washed it down with a few gulps of water. He was heeding well the warning about needing his strength.

When he had finished Skag moved over to the window and peered beyond the glass. There was nothing much to see, just a long finger of marsh stretching between a bit of yard and the forest beyond. A hound sniffed half-heartedly at something in the grass. The dog was a grizzled animal with a lean, nasty look about it.

Skag finally threw himself onto the cot but could manage only a light and inconsistent dozing. He wondered about the witch's words. He understood fewer of them than she had thought. He suspected she might be daft. If he had some power that she feared, he wished he knew what it was.

How had she known so much about the bogfoke? The escape from the cemetery included?

Whenever sleep stole upon him it was disturbed by vague dreams. No distinct images formed, though it seemed as if he was being summoned by mournful, disembodied voices. He woke each time with the hair standing on the back of his neck. Finally he sat up, rubbing away the sleep from his eyes and the voices from his mind.

Morning stretched into afternoon, and the afternoon descended into twilight. The fading sun angled away from the window and room was grayed. Skag was bored beyond apprehension of what lay before him. He tensed a little at the sound of the lock and the creak of the door opening, and yet was nearly relieved that it was being gotten on with.

Yolande stepped over the threshold. She pushed the door to open wider, "I have brought you a visitor."

Skag craned his neck to look around the witch. Before his eyes could register anything he heard a sound that echoed like a nightmare in his head. He heard the clattering of skulls. Father Daugth stepped past the door and stood beside the witch.

"Now you know the secret of my knowledge of the bogfoke," whispered Yolande. She only smiled at the dark scowl crossing Skag's face. Father Daugth raised an iron bar in one of his hands and slapped it against the open palm of the other. Skag's hands clenched reflexively.

"Where is your cedar?" hissed Father Daugth, but his voice faded as the witch placed a hand upon his shoulder.

"Not yet old one. Skag has much to teach us."

The witch sat on one end of the cot. Father Daugth remained standing near the door. Yolande swept dark hair from her face with an impatient hand. There was a smile on her lips, but the edge of it was cruel.

"My men found Father Daugth washed up on the shore of the lake after the hurricane. I . . . *persuaded* . . . from him the story of what he was and from where he had come. I also discovered much about the nature of your kind. I was able to dissect his physical being, but when I severed his spirit from his flesh, his body swiftly turned to only a trace of powdered dust."

Skag looked confused as his dark eyes gazed at the Father. Yolande nodded to indicate that she had anticipated his confusion. "Certainly you see him here. I severed his spirit from his flesh, but I did not set it loose. You see, with your folk the spirit is much less dependent upon the body than it is with my people."

"What are you prattling on about?" asked Skag. For a brief instant the witch lost her composure and a wave of ill temper passed across her face. Then she recovered.

"I have made a pact with this old one. He is now bound to this world by the rod that he holds. No weapon can harm him. He can take upon himself the illusion of various forms. He prefers that of a crow most often."

"He would," snorted Skag. "Though, perhaps he should remember the stone bayonet of a gray-cloaked warrior. But, why is it that you chose to bargain with him? I wouldn't have thought you interested in compromise."

"Oh, we had mutual interest," replied the witch. "I learned much from him, more even than he intended to reveal. There was a delirium upon him when he was brought to me. Amidst his mumblings I recognized a few words of an Iroquoian dialect belonging to the Tuscarora people, then words from the Algonquin people. This intrigued me. I delved deeper, and deeper. Finally I unveiled a great secret."

She looked now at the Father. "Your patriarch remembered the realms of the red men. Indeed, your Father Daugth had lived for nearly ten centuries. Even he did not realize this. I have discerned that the bogfoke simply forget what they must. When your memories become overwhelming they are simply moved from the conscious mind. It is much like how my people forget the memories of earliest childhood. Of course, forget is not the best word. The memories are in storage."

She waved her hand lightly then to dismiss that line

of discussion and said, "I would suspect that even you, Skag, have breathed the air of this world for several centuries. Bogfoke do not, I believe, relate to time in the manner of my people. It is as if the bogfoke have an infancy of decades and a childhood of centuries."

Skag shrugged. "That is a lot of forgetting."

"Oh, remember I told you, not forgotten," reiterated the witch. "It is stored, saved like the earliest memories of men. I considered these things, the irrepressible curiosity, the irrepressible humor, and the mercurial whims. All are common to the little people, and to the children of men. That was my realization. The bogfoke are naught but children."

Skag frowned skeptically. He observed his own hands. "I do not feel like a child."

"Understandable. While your state of being resembles that of human childhood, you are an entirely different sort of creature. I suspect that a human being is more akin to an elephant, or even a duck than to a bogfoke. It is as if you were awaiting a metamorphosis. Like a caterpillar poised to turn into a butterfly."

"What is it we would turn into?"

Yolande glanced at the Father again. "What indeed? He was terrified of whatever it was, this old one. I suspect that his initial failure to do so was intentional. Now, well, he is a lost soul, trapped as a bogfoke. I could not take him to that point where the change might occur, but I believe I can take *you* there."

"Why?"

"Magic, real, deep and true magic, which is something beyond our material world. It is possible that even immortality might be captured. In Cherokee legends it is the little people who hid beneath the hills, but it was a host of majestic, shining beings who came from under the hills to aid the tribe against their enemies."

"If it's all the same," explained Skag. "I would just as soon not go to that place the Father missed. It occurs to me that if it was my time to do so, then I should have some sense of what you are babbling about."

Yolande's face darkened a moment and her lips formed an irritated frown. Skag had realized even as the words left his mouth that it was an ill-conceived notion to mock the witch. She rose and moved toward the door before turning back to Skag. Her features managed to mask her displeasure but Skag could still see it smoldering in her eyes. "I will leave you with the Father for a moment. He will bring no harm to you. Perhaps he can convince you that your fate is out of your hands and that it will be easier for you to co-operate."

She disappeared beyond the door. Father Daugth and Skag faced one another in a long moment of silence. Finally the Father moved a little closer. His eyes seemed dull and unfocused as he locked his gaze on Skag. "The others think you are dead, taken by a dog."

"Are they well? Are they safe?"

The Father shrugged as his eyes cut toward the door. "They are well enough. Safe? They think you are gone. I am returning to claim them. I will take them beyond the reach of the witch. They are mine."

"And you are hers," accused Skag.

Father Daugth drew to his full height and the iron rod in his hand raised a little. Some of the dark glitter was restored to his eyes. His free hand disappeared into his robe before reappearing. He opened the hand and on the palm was a leaf wrapped around a grayish powder.

"Take this, Skag. There is nothing I can do to save you, but this will be of use to you. I have been where she will take you. She may deaden the pain as she takes you apart piece by piece, but she cannot eliminate your awareness of it, nor what comes looming from beyond. It will make you scream for the darkness of your barrow in the cemetery. This will make you sleep. A sleep she will not be able to manipulate. It may be the death of you, but she will kill you anyway. This will deny her what she seeks."

Skag was unsure but took the leaf from the Father's hand. The touch of that palm was ice cold. "Why are you doing this?"

The Father's eyes narrowed. "You are a fool, Skag. You have made yourself my enemy. For all of that, you are a bogfoke still, and I would not see you dancing at the end of the witch's string. You are as good as dead and I would have it the witch gains nothing from your undoing. I believe that you would have it thus as well."

"You said it will make me sleep," observed Skag.

"So it shall. When you have reached that place the witch seeks, you will be beyond her grasp. If she does not kill you in her anger, the powder may well do so, but she will have gained nothing."

"What *does* the witch seek? What is it she wants?"

The Father seemed to sink into himself. For a long while he was silent. When he did speak he looked not at Skag but at some distant point as if seeking a lost memory. "She wants power. She desires not to die. I know where she seeks to take you. You do not want to go there. It is a fire that devours who you are. Perhaps some part of you survives this change. What she calls a metamorphosis. Others of her kind speak of a purifying flame. But, on the whole you will not be Skag. It is better to die."

"Or live on as some puppet of the witch?"

"I know things she cannot guess at," grated the Father's voice. "I did what I must to survive. Now she will pay the price for her error in judgment."

Father Daugth turned and walked toward the door. He paused at the threshold and said, "Put the leaf in your mouth now. It works slowly."

Skag hesitated for only a moment and then did as instructed. The Father disappeared beyond the door. The powder was bitter, causing Skag to grimace. He had to look away as the witch entered the room.

"Tonight, Skag, we shall begin our work together,"

she said firmly. "Perhaps you will not survive, but perhaps you will. Whatever may come, we shall unlock secrets together."

"What is it you seek from this?" asked the weary bogfoke. "Power? Wealth? Love?"

The witch laughed. "Power and wealth are but the residue of what I seek. Love? Love is but a weakness that can be used against you."

"What of your children?" asked Skag.

A darkness passed over Yolande and her eyes glared at the bogfoke. "Never speak of my children, you wretched creature."

Then Yolande seemed surprised, confused even, by what had swept over her. She gathered herself and looked dispassionately at the bogfoke. "Rest. Then we begin."

Skag nodded his head in resignation and Yolande left the room. The lock clicked with a grim finality. He felt dead inside; with hopelessness filling him like shadows filled the night.

***

The last red glow of the sun had faded beyond the western world when the witch's men came for Skag. The black-bearded fellow made another appearance, but not with Silas. After they had bound him hands and wrist, Black-beard hefted him like a sack of potatoes and carried him outside.

The powder was causing a heavy drowsiness to creep over Skag. His sense of awareness was skewed. His sense of touch was numbed but his hearing was made sharper. As they passed outside, the din of crickets and frogs was so heightened and distinct that he felt as if he could pick out each individual creature. Vaguely he was aware that as his physical sense of being was deadened, the strength of his spirit was flooding into his mind.

They were inside again and Black-beard shoved the bogfoke atop a large table. The bonds were removed for a moment before being replaced by others that drew Skag spread eagle upon the table top. The tall fellow had lit a kerosene lantern. It glowed bright for a moment until he trimmed down the wick. Now the room was cast in a weak yellow light.

If there was a chill this night, Skag could not feel it. He tried to remain wide eyed so the witch would not become suspicious. He should have been frightened, but after a few minutes where his breath was short and fast he felt a sense of fatigue wash away the fear.

The door to the room opened. Skag cut his eyes and caught sight of Yolande standing just beyond the circle of light. Her dress was black. A black, shawl-like cloth was draped over her shoulders. Skag could see symbols and patterns embroidered upon it with silver thread, but they were meaningless to him.

The witch moved closer to him. She held a small, smoking brazier that she placed beside Skag's head. The pungent smoke drifted over him and into his nostrils. She crumbled a handful of dried leaves into the brazier. The flame spit, flared and the smoke grew more acrid.

Yolande began a soft chant. Skag thought she had a beautiful voice and felt immediately foolish at the notion. He strained to understand the words, but they were elusive and floated away from him. The more he tried to grasp the meaning of the words, the more he was drawn into the hypnotic rhythm.

Finally he began to comprehend the intent, if not the meaning. They were seductive, inviting him into the shadows. They urged him to meander through his memories, and to gather them like possessions long lost. The memories, a long line of memories stretching behind him. The beauty and terror that he had forgotten.

As he rummaged through these images, sounds and smells, he wondered why the Father should find them so terrible. They made Skag feel a bit anxious and uncertain, but he felt as if he were returning home after a long voyage. There were so very many. How could his feeble consciousness order such a flood of memories and the knowledge they held?

If only he could expand. If only he could stretch his mind to encompass them. If only every fragment of his existence could be saturated with them. There was triggered in him some instinct and he suddenly felt as if there might be a way. Yes! There was a way. He could do it. He could see the pattern now. He could become that which would hold this enormity of who he truly was!

That is what the witch wants, he realized. No, he did not want to surrender it to her. Instead he surrendered to a great weariness that crept through his mind. So tired. A wave of unfeeling swept him. His heart slowing. His lungs growing still. Even his thoughts fading.

What is this?

The witch's thoughts burned into his brain. Her hold upon him had slipped and now he was hurtling into oblivion.

What treachery is this? That black-hearted shaman. Oh no, my dear Daugth, you cannot cheat me so easily.

Her voice rose into a beautiful song filled with life and sunshine. Skag saw her face floating above him and her hands upon his forehead. They were cool and moist, driving back the lazy grasp of sleep and sucking the numbness from him. He marveled at what a healer she could have been had she poured herself into that instead of what she had become. A netherworld balance settled upon him. He was conscious but unable to speak or move.

"I will hold you here until I can master this," whispered the witch pleasantly, but then her expression became grim. "In the meantime I shall deal with that dark, little lordling, Daugth."

Her hands disappeared. They reappeared holding a small vial she placed against his lips. A small amount of fluid was poured into his mouth and he swallowed reflexively, only vaguely aware of a bitter taste upon his tongue.

"This will help revive you," cooed the witch before disappearing from his vision.

He was aware of the door opening and then closing. His vision was swirling as if from utter exhaustion, but sleep was denied. In this mental gloaming he waited. He would have wept but even that required a physical effort he could not muster.

A gust of air washed over him, filling his lungs with the cool of the evening. The weight seemed lessened upon his chest and he drew a deep breath. He wasn't sure if it was the fresh air, the witch's potion, or both, but he found himself able to stare at the raftered ceiling above. The door had been opened and he heard the scruff of feet upon the floor. With an effort he managed to tilt his head toward the doorway.

His eyes focused on a face pressing near his. It was a girl, Nan. Her eyes were wide, glittering with apprehension. She placed a finger to her lips, cautioning him to silence. There was a pair of scissors in her hand and she began sawing frantically at the bonds on Skag's wrists and ankles. They gave way reluctantly, strand by strand.

Skag could barely lift his arms. Nan leaned forward and pulled him into a sitting position. With her help he stumbled into the night beyond the door. She steered him into a thick clump of azaleas and dropped beside him with a relieved sigh.

The night air restored some presence of mind to the bogfoke, but his muscles were rubbery and his joints stiff. Nan helped him to his knees. As he surveyed his surroundings he saw that they had come from a small barn near the house.

"Where is that storage shed I was in earlier?" asked Skag in a low whisper. Nan pointed to the southeast.

"You will have to follow the picket fence. I will help you. The dogs will do as I say."

"Why are you doing this?" asked Skag.

The child's eyes were touched with fear and misted with tears. "They were going to kill you. Silas has taken some men over the lake to fetch that dark one that's been around here. They say that he betrayed them and they want him dead. They said the only good cornbear was a dead one and that included you. They act as if children can't hear them talk or understand what they are talking about, but this one can. You ain't done nothing wrong. Why should they kill you? It ain't right."

Skag shook his head, wanting to answer, to make it clear for both of them. "I just don't know, Nan. There is something darkly amiss in all this."

The girl nodded her head emphatically. "There is something wrong here. My Granny would call it the devil's work. There's something bad behind all this, Mr. Skag. But right now, we must get you out of here."

"I must get to the shed. There is something I must retrieve."

"Come along then," replied Nan. She took his arm and helped him stumble across the yard and along the fence.

They were on the opposite side of the picket alongside of which Skag had been carried earlier. Moving in a low crouch they made their way behind a tree and paused. The night was quiet except for crickets and the occasional bellow of a bullfrog.

Nan let the bogfoke catch his breath a moment before urging him to his feet again. Her eyes were cat-like as they studied the last stretch between them and the tool shed. They covered this distance in a quickened pace, gliding from the dark of one night shadow to another.

The girl guided Skag to the back of the building, gesturing at the jagged edge between earth and wall. The bogfoke slid underneath. He crawled quickly to the grain sacks and pulled his stave from under the moldy pile. A smile touched his lips at having the cedar in his hands again. He held it for a moment so he could pull in that sharp, sweet scent.

Nan grabbed his arm and helped pull him back through the gap. "For that? We risked coming here for a stick?"

"For this," smiled Skag. "It is a magic stick. It is filled with dreams of wonder and hope. It gives me strength."

The girl shrugged skeptically. "Well, I can take you to the edge of the wood. Birdy Coster's old hound will be between us and the trees. You let me go first and I'll shush him up. He likes me 'cause I bring him treats and brush him sometimes. Birdy is terrible to the dogs, but he's got some hunting dogs he'll set after you eventually. They're half wild and I can't do anything with them."

Skag nodded wearily, but his gaze looked deep into the child's green eyes. "I must thank you. I will worry about you. Certainly you must know they'll figure out that you've helped me."

"They might," shrugged the girl. "Owen might tell. He can't face up to our mother without going all soft. I might be in for a lot of trouble, but I couldn't let them kill you. Some things just are not right."

Skag closed his eyes at the girl's naiveté. "They are dangerous folk. They might hurt you."

Nan frowned. "I'll be punished, maybe more than I ever have, but my mother won't let them hurt me. I'm not *crazy*. Besides, none of them would lay a hand on me for fear of my father coming out of the woods for 'em."

"Your mother. . . "began Skag, but the words faded as it became obvious to him. It was a frustrating thing to be so addled when he needed his wits most. And this was something that should have been as plain as the nose on his face. He chuckled lightly, looking down at the patched trousers he was wearing. "Very well, lead on, Nannela Wolfe."

The child nodded and darted off toward the southwestern boundary of the village. Skag let her get almost beyond the range of his vision before he followed. They were moving through the tall grasses of unkempt, abandoned lawns and encroaching marsh. The bogfoke heard a dog growl and flattened himself beneath a stunted magnolia.

After a moment he ventured a peek and saw Nan with one arm draped around a battered old hound. Her free hand was clasping the dog's muzzle. Using his stave for support Skag moved along as swiftly as he was able. Two lofty pines stood as sentinels for the forest, spreading their limbs as if in welcome.

He turned beneath the pines and waved farewell to the daughter of the witch of the wood. She couldn't return the wave without relinquishing her hold on the hound, but Skag sensed a smile on those young lips. As he disappeared into the sheltering dark of the forest he whispered to himself, "My debt to you has grown, Nannela Walker."

***

Skag suspected they would look for him along the paths leading to the lake and the barrow. Instead, he swung in a wide arc to the southeast. He sloshed through a stretch of standing water hoping to throw the dogs off his trail. In the back of his mind he was considering the possibility of following the edge of the lake wood toward the dwelling of Remus Wolfe. He knew the witch's men, and perhaps Yolande herself feared the man-wolf.

An hour into his flight he heard the distant baying of hounds, but it came from far to the northeast. The dogs had lost his fresh scent and quite possibly picked up the trail along which Silas had dragged him. While it offered him a bit more time, the men would sort out what was happening before long and pick up his trail again.

His desperation could not drive him any faster. His feet felt weighted and the anxiety of an escape so teasingly near robbed him of breath. With his mind still reeling from the images of the witch song, it was all he could do to gather his determination and push forward.

The land began to rise into rolling ridges and made progress a torture for his sorely tested body. He made token efforts at masking his scent by treading through puddles of water or sloshing down a rivulet that wound toward the lake. He was lost in the concentrated effort of keeping one foot stepping before the other. Then he suddenly looked up and saw the night-black water of the lake spreading before him, an impassable obstacle between him and the barrow.

Stars glittered high overhead and were reflected back up by the calm waters. Skag shrugged and began to slosh southward along the lake shore. He was intent on making his way to Remus Wolfe. The witch's men knew the barrow's location and even if they lost his trail would simply lie in wait for him. He must take sanctuary with the man-wolf. He needed time to clear his head and consider his limited options.

It was a long way to stomp, and this portion of the wood was such a tumble of hillocks and low ridges. He tried to hug the lake shore but was soon driven inland by tall bluffs. The sound of pursuit had first grown distant, but now had shifted southward and was drawing nearer. The dogs had found his trail, and despite all his precautions would surely close the gap faster than he could flee.

After a half hour of struggling over the rugged terrain Skag finally cast himself down upon the leaf mold. His eyelids had grown so heavy that he could no longer see the stars. He feared some enchantment of the witch. He was so tired, but he knew he must not give way to sleep. It was death if those hounds caught him on the ground.

His mind spun in the dark like a raft caught in a whirlpool. At least death would bring peace. He wanted peace. All those memories rushed to fill the darkness until he thought he would scream at the agony of trying to hold them all in his poor, inadequate brain, every memory so lucid and real. Every joy and every pain made fresh.

He wanted oblivion, but the memories were unrelenting. The din of night noises in the waking world of the forest crowded upon him. He wanted quiet but all he got were crickets and voices.

Voices.

He half opened his eyes. *I am not asleep, and yet I hear those dream voices pleading from the dark. Why do they weep?*

It should have been such a simple thing to rise, but it was like a long climb from the bottom of a shadowed pit, with each muscle defying his will. He managed to shift onto his stomach. Then he got to his knees. He jabbed the cedar into the loam and pulled himself erect.

Voices. Not the voices of men. Not the voices of pursuit. Something in the bittersweet song touched him. Their fears were his fear and their joys his joy. He began to stumble into the wake of that song. *I am dying and they have come to console me.*

Suddenly he was on his knees again. The voices were still all around. He forced his eyes open and his vision was engulfed by the broad mound of a grass covered hill. Wild roses grew in a tumult at the base of the hill, defying the autumn chill and even the threat of winter. The voices were all around him, with songs of sorrow and songs of joy.

Then there was a dark scar upon the hill where before there had been only grass. Skag looked upon it with confusion. It was like the mouth of a cave. Even as he stared, there came from within a glowing light. It was faint but warm, like the promise of home and shelter.

He hesitated, wondering if this was some witch magic. He wondered if all had been a long nightmare and he would wake to the living nightmare of finding himself still bound by the gray coquina walls of the cemetery.

No. He remembered the dreams of the city. Now he understood, the Weeping Hill. The cornbears were within. Bound within? Hiding? It mattered not, for they were safe. Perhaps Yolande would not have him after all.

Leaning heavily upon his stave, Skag limped into the opening upon the side of the hill. With unsteady gait he moved hopefully toward the light beyond the threshold. The warm light and the voices, like lost memories regained.

Then there was only a grassy hill. Skag and the opening had both disappeared from the night of the forest. There was only a fading echo of sing-song voices in the empty dark.

EIGHT

Standings

"All we want is to be left alone."

Slignan knew his appeal to be futile. The Father answered with a crackling chuckle and stepped forward as he growled, "I grow tired of words."

He pushed at Slignan with the iron rod. The younger bogfoke slapped the hand away. Father Daugth scowled and shrugged his massive shoulders. "Then you must die."

The old bogfoke's hand darted out with unnatural speed. The iron rod slammed against Slignan's shoulder. The hatchet-bearer slipped as he tried to twist away from the blow, but he managed to roll again to his feet and swing out with the hatchet. Father Daugth's rod met the effort with shriek of metal against metal. Slignan grabbed at the Father's ankle, but again Father Daugth showed unlikely agility as he backed smoothly away.

Slignan sprang from his crouch, flailing the hatchet wildly before him. Father Daugth parried once and then struck Slignan a glancing blow to the chest. The elder bogfoke moved in quickly but Slignan desperately kicked out at the patriarch and knocked him from his feet.

They rolled away from one another to scramble to their feet. Slignan's breath was ragged, but the Father was unaffected by his exertion. The hatchet-bearer frowned, with eyes glaring suspiciously. His foot still burned from the winter cold touch of the Father's skin.

"*What* are you?" spat Slignan.

"You cannot kill that which is not truly alive," Daugth

sneered. He paused to let the words settle into the younger bogfoke's brain. "You are mine now. You have spirit, but no real strength, Slignan. Submit to me and I will give you strength. No witch, no other kith of Cornbread Jack shall stand before us."

Slignan snarled. "I have seen that death is preferable to a life in bondage."

The younger bogfoke leapt at the patriarch. Father Daugth swung and the rod cracked against the handle of the hatchet. Slignan screamed as the iron smashed against his fingers. The hatchet was flung to the sod, but Slignan surged forward still, driving his shoulder into the skull adorned chest. The charge forced the elder bogfoke against the side of the barrow as Slignan reached with his good hand to stay the strike of the iron rod.

For a moment Slignan held the balance, but the ice chill of the Father's flesh numbed his grasping hand. Father Daugth was untiring and relentless. Inch by agonized inch Slignan felt his arm being forced down. The Father's dark eyes bore into him, eager for his pain and humiliation. With a final effort Slignan pushed himself away from the ancient one, rolling across the leaf mold.

Slignan scrambled frantically toward his weapon. He expected to feel the crushing blow of the iron rod, but from the corner of his eye he caught a turmoil of action. Welken jumped forward, wrapping his arms around the Father's chest in an effort to pin him against the barrow. Weart followed his womb brother into the fray, grabbing at the dark arm that raised the iron rod. His fingers brushed only the Father's dark robe and the rod came smashing down upon Welken.

There was a grunt of air expelled from Welken and his knees buckled, but from within sprang a grim tenacity and he stayed upon his feet, holding the Father against the barrow. Weart managed to grasp the Father's wrist, though a howl of pain was torn from him at the burning cold beneath his palm.

Now Robbis came charging forward with a length of

firewood in his hands. The tracker swung at the iron in the Father's hand. There was a roar of anger from Daugth as he clenched ever tighter to the rod and tried to bring his other hand around to grasp it as well. But now Weart was fierce and wrenched the Father's arm further away.

Again Robbis swung with all his strength. The iron rod was ripped free and clattered against the side of the barrow. Gristel rushed in to kick it away.

Welken collapsed, but the others barely noticed as they clasped their ears to shut out the shriek torn from Father Daugth. Slignan hurled the hatchet at the Father, but it passed through the form as though he were only a dark mist. The blade affixed the hatchet to the side of the barrow. Father Daugth reached out with hands like shadow.

"I am one of your own. Do not let me fall into the darkness! You need me to protect you from the witch!" he pleaded. His dark eyes were wide and burning with overwhelming fear. Almost his desperation touched the hearts of the other bogfoke, but Mother Crabba quickly shuffled to scoop up the iron rod. She shoved it into Tegmina's hands.

"Hurl this cursed thing into the lake, be quick!" she hissed. Tegmina reacted to the urgency in the Mother's voice and sped swiftly into the forest toward the lake. As the Father roared his anger and fear, they heard Tegmina splashing into the water.

After the barest moment of silence there came the distant splash. Again the patriarch screamed as the final dark devoured him. His voice became a thin, fading wail. Then the shadow of him was gone from their presence. For a moment all the bogfoke stood in stunned disbelief that it was over. Then a moan from Welken wrenched their attention from the void where once had stood Father Daugth.

Weart dropped to his knees beside the stricken form of Welken. He took his womb-brother in his arms and rocked him gently. Mother Crabba waddled past the other bogfoke and knelt beside Weart. She put her ear gingerly to

Welken's chest. Sorrow shadowed her eyes as she straightened and put her fingers to the fallen bogfoke's bloodied scalp. The iron had struck a swiping blow against his skull and then crashed onto his shoulder. Mother Crabba closed her eyes as she slowly shook her head.

Tegmina came stumbling back into the clearing. In a tumult of revelation she knew both joy and sorrow. The Mother spoke quietly to them all, "The blow has broken his skull. I do not understand how he could have stood for so long. There is nothing I can do."

Weart looked up into the morning sun as his eyes filled with tears. In a quavering voice he wailed aloud his sorrow and his pain. He held tight his fallen brother, as if to keep him from sliding into the darkness. The Mother took the dying bogfoke's hand into her own. She sighed in grieving wonder. "It was a death blow, and still he stood. Still he held. If some portion of whatever steeled his will is within each of us. . . "

Tegmina moved to kneel behind Weart, resting her head against his shoulder. The other bogfoke were stunned, but moved hesitatingly toward their fallen comrade. Except for Slignan, who stood with fierce eyes as his chest heaved in pent anger.

Mother Crabba gave the limp hand over to the hand of Gristel. She went for a moment to scavenge in the ruins of their possessions and found a half emptied sack of dried herbs. She poured the herbs onto a piece of cloth and sorted them. Gathering those she needed, she quickly ground them between two stones and scraped the resulting powder into the palm of her hand.

"This will ease some of whatever pain he may feel," she said, returning to Welken's side. Her voice was tinged with the frustration of a healer confronting that which could not be cured. She pried open Welken's mouth and poured in the herb-dust. Gristel brought a gourd of water and let it slowly dribble past the whiskered lips. The Mother nodded, but when their eyes met Gristel knew the loss they faced.

There was a nearly imperceptible swallow, but most of the mixture spilled from the corners of Welken's mouth. Weart had bowed his head against his womb-brother's chest, leaning also against Tegmina for support. Kribble had taken Welken's hand in his own and rocked on his heels as his voice droned in quiet mourning.

Robbis stood now near the group but suddenly stiffened. His eyes glared hard along the forest aisles as he hissed, "Someone is coming."

The sound of hurried thrashing and stomping came from the east. Slignan pulled his hatchet from the barrow wall and moved to the eastern edge of the clearing. Then his grip relaxd on the handle as he turned back to the others and said, "I recognize that racket. It is the troll."

Stump came trampling into the clearing. His yellow-brown eyes were clouded beneath a furrowed brow and his twisted arm brushed impatiently at clinging vines and saplings. He stopped when he saw Slignan and then the cluster of other bogfoke around Welken. The frown melted into an expression of comprehension and sorrow.

"What dark thing is this?" he wondered aloud.

"Father Daugth returned," growled Slignan. "He was different, like a walking shadow, but cold like the coldest winter wind."

"The witch's magic," hissed Stump, but then the light of urgency returned to him. "Her men are returning from over the lake."

"So soon," moaned Gristel.

Slignan sneered angrily, with one finger tracing along the edge of his hatchet. "Let them. I am finished with running and hiding."

"We cannot leave Welken," added Tegmina firmly.

Stump looked down at the wounded bogfoke. "He were a good 'un. I could tell by the way he loved the green growing things. How he loved life coming up from the soil. But, he looks done for, and the witch's men are returning.

You must flee into the ward again."

"We will go into the ward," muttered Slignan as he gazed into the eastern wood. "But we shall not flee. No more shall we flee."

He turned to the others. "We must make a litter to carry Welken. Mother Crabba and Weart can do that. The rest of you must come with me. We have guest soon to arrive."

A cruel smile creased Slignan's face beneath his crooked nose. He had found a vent for his frustration and anger. Let the witch's men come.

***

Slignan sent Tegmina, Mother Crabba and Weart into the ward with Welken. Hampered by Welken's litter they could not go as deeply into the tangle as they wanted. Finally they settled in a thicket of fire-thorn and waited, forced to trust that Stump and Slignan could turn aside the witch's men.

Robbis, Kribble and Gristel remained with Slignan at the barrow. The hatchet-bearer instructed them to gather up and bundle together various items from out of the shelter, "Tie a rope to each piece. Now, Gristel and Robbis, each of you head down to the lake. When you get there you must drag the bundles along the shore. Then you must head in different directions, but most especially *away* from where the others are hiding. Drag the bundles along the ground so that the dogs will follow your scent."

"We will lead them a merry chase," said Robbis with a dark grin Gristel only gazed absently. Her thoughts were weighted by worry and sorrow. Together they headed off toward the lake.

Slignan called after them, "Give it about a half hour or so and then circle back. But be careful, the men most likely will have landed by then."

He turned to Kribble and said, "Now, let us see what mischief our bogfoke hearts can devise."

Kribble smiled at the possibilities. Woe to the witch's

men, thought the potter, when Slignan's thoughts run dark.

***

Kribble and Slignan stood on a low rise that ran along the lake shore. They were in plain sight to the men in the boat as it glided over the water. The bogfoke showed no signs of fear as they laughed and gestured derisively at the approaching vessel. Four hounds were crowded into the boat and they howled in frustration at the sight and scent of their prey.

The sound of curses and the quickened dip of the oars competed with the fury of the dogs. The boat was near enough for the bogfoke to see the angry faces of the witch's men. Kribble looked at Slignan with eyebrows raised in question. A smile twitched beneath the hatchet-bearer's crooked nose and he nodded.

Kribble picked up a reed basket and loosened the bindings that held its top in place. Holding it by those bindings he began to swing it to and fro. With each swing it gained momentum until he let go. In a high arc it flew out over the water. The top was flung off and from within the basket came a cascade of very angry snakes. Snakes fell writhing into the water. Snakes rained upon the terrified men. Snakes dropped into the boat in a vengeful tangle.

Chaos erupted within the vessel. Two men leapt into the water. One man, who held a shotgun, panicked and fired at the basket. Two of the others wrested the weapon from him but it was too late and the boat began to list as water surged through the punctured bottom. The men and their dogs jumped into the lake and sloshed toward shore.

Both bogfoke were doubled with laughter, but Kribble suddenly nudged the hatchet-bearer and pointed out over the lake. In the hazy distance they could make out the approach of another boat. Slignan's laughter faded to a determined grin.

"More guest. Good, we have surprises yet. I would hate to waste them," he whispered. Then he motioned to Kribble and the two bogfoke slipped into the forest. They retreated to a ridge jutting between the lake and the southwestern arc of the marsh. From their vantage they could see the second boat gliding closer toward the shore. Gristel joined them, followed by Robbis.

"I followed the northeastern rim of the lake," reported Gristel. "I wove in and out of the ward. That should keep the dogs occupied and make them earn their way."

Robbis was grinning with wicked delight. His smile was infectious and Slignan looked at him in anticipation, "What have you been up to?"

"I went into the marsh."

"But dogs will have a difficult time following the scent."

Robbis shook his head. "I made sure to keep the bundle dry and to drag it through the grass and reeds. I only went a half mile or so. I thought the men and their dogs might enjoy a jaunt into the gator bog. Why, one of the gators was so fond of our bundle that he relieved me of it. Last I saw he was dragging it further into the bog."

The bogfoke were trembling with dark laughter. Slignan managed to get to his knees, wiping tears from his eyes. He scrambled into the low branches of a scraggy oak. As he peered toward the lake his grin vanished.

"The witch," he hissed, immediately sliding to the ground and silencing the others. She stood in another approaching boat among men and dogs. It had taken only one glimpse of the woman. Only one look at the deference made to her by the men, and Slignan knew she had to be Yolande.

The other bogfoke crawled to the top of the ridge. The second boat had grounded. Yolande and four of her men were standing on the shore. A couple of the men went to the assistance of their comrades sloshing in the water. Two men from the first boat had been bitten by snakes. One of the dogs was also limping.

The witch began tending to the bitten men after gesturing for the others to begin the search. Her quick, agitated motions were a beacon of her anger and the men hurried off with the dogs. They let the animals roam a bit to pick up the scent. The strong trail provided by Gristel and Robbis caused them to split into two groups. One headed along the northern shoreline, and the other into the southern marsh.

Slignan nodded grimly. So far all was going well, but he hadn't been prepared for the presence of the witch. All he could think about were those birds, the seduction of the troll, and the shadow that had been Father Daugth. How could the bogfoke contend with such power? He felt a hand on his shoulder. It was Gristel.

"We faced the Father," she whispered.

The hatchet-bearer turned to look again at the witch. She was finished with the first man and working on the second. Her healing prowess was potent, but both men were badly shaken and were not likely to be of any use to her on this day. Slignan could sense her frustration and growing anger. With any luck she had more troubles coming.

He motioned the others to follow him as he slid back down the ridge. They sat beneath a fountain of privet. Slignan crossed his arms and sighed, "Now we wait."

A half hour passed before shouting erupted from the southern marsh. Eventually the witch's men came sloshing through the tall grasses. Two of them were helping a third, while a fourth brought the dogs. Three dogs had gone into the marsh, only two returned. The urgent shouts of her men had brought the witch to meet them at the edge of the marsh.

Slignan crawled to the crest of the ridge. He saw the men throw themselves with frightened exhaustion onto the soggy turf. Only the one with the dogs remained standing to meet the witch. He was shifting from foot to foot, and looking anywhere save into Yolande's eyes.

The witch calmly waited for the man to gather his wits. Slight breezes ruffled her dark hair as she stared past her underlings and into the tall grasses of the marsh. Even the dogs were cowed by her presence and sat hunched at the man's feet.

"The dogs got hold of a strong scent," he began to explain. "We followed it into the marsh, down to a little black water bog. Then, I don't know. We stumbled into a bed of gators. One of them popped Toby with its tail and broke his leg. An' that old hound, Whiteback, craziest mean dog that has ever lived. He bounded right into the middle of 'em. Well, ma'am, he finally met his match. So I gathered up the other dogs to keep them from doing anything as stupid as ol' Whiteback done. If any of them cornbears ran into them gators, well, ain't gonna be nothing left to find."

The witch glowered at him for a moment. "There are no cornbears in that bog. It was a ruse, you imbecile."

She whirled away from the quaking man. Slignan pressed himself so close to the ground that the moist soil filled his nostrils. He kept half an eye on Yolande. She strode away from her men with her hands clenched in frustration.

The bogfoke smiled. Even the witch must lose some of her smarts as she lost her composure. He figured that things were not going at all according to her plans. He motioned for the other bogfoke to remain where they were while he slid over the ridge and into the cypress wood.

He followed a faint rabbit run that snaked through the swamp, finally coming to dry land near the witch's grounded boat. He smiled when he saw the group of men who had taken the northern trail come staggering back toward the lake shore. They were tattered and exhausted.

"What is this?" demanded the witch. Her words stopped the men like a slap in the face. The one Slignan remembered as Silas shifted a bit and then moved forward.

"We followed them until the dogs lost the scent at the lake shore," he reported. "The trail went in and out of the ward, and around in circles. We passed some places two or three times. It near 'bout killed us. It was a plain trail. Too plain if you take my meaning, ma'am."

"At least there weren't no gators," muttered the leader

of the southern group.

"Silence," hissed the witch. Her angry glare enforced her order. Both men stood as if poised on the edge of an abyss. Yolande looked off into the wood, almost directly at Slignan who dared not move even to press further into the soil.

"Enough of this you fools. You've said you saw them on that rise. You should have picked up the scent from there, not by the shore," she scolded "But first, take me to their barrow."

The chance to redeem themselves moved the men into a frenzy of head nodding and gesturing. Yolande stood still for a moment with her irritation rooting her to the soil. At last the men calmed themselves and she followed them as they lead the way into the wood.

Slignan slid back through the swamp to rejoin the other bogfoke. Their eyes glittered with impatience as he rushed into the clump of privet. He motioned for them to follow him. "They are heading for the barrow."

Robbis led the way, angling into the forest so that they could reach the barrow before the witch and her men. They positioned themselves behind a low growth of shrubby dogwood. The mid-morning breeze played at the loosely woven reeds draped over the door of the barrow.

The witch and her men came struggling through the undergrowth, seeming almost thrown by the forest into the clearing. They had brought two dogs but the beasts were cowed by the presence of the witch. Robbis had been careful to position the bogfoke's hiding place up wind of the barrow. The dogs just sat stupid and mute at the feet of the men. Then a shuffling from inside the barrow caused them to bristle and growl.

"Listen," snapped Silas, gesturing toward the barrow. "Must be some of them hiding in there. Come on, Birdy."

The man named Birdy nodded and took an ax from one of his comrades. "Just in case they're thinking of any more surprises."

Birdy and Silas approached the barrow cautiously at first. Then Silas seemed to remember what pitiful little things the bogfoke appeared to be, and perhaps aware of the sort of impression his over-wrought caution must be making upon the witch, he surged ahead to tear off the reed curtain from over the opening.

"Welcome!" boomed a voice that trailed into laughter. Two wicker baskets came whirling from inside the barrow. The air was filled with buzzing and darting black flecks. Silas screamed and covered his eyes with one hand while the other swatted the air around his head. Desperately he bolted for the lake.

Birdy was swinging his ax like a madman, but it only served to draw the agitated bees upon him. The hounds broke away from the man who held them as he swatted at the frenzied insects. The two remaining men were about to flee when Yolande suddenly held out her hand and shouted, "*Stop!*"

Her fist clenched tight and a bright light flashed over the clearing, followed by a clap like thunder. The bees dropped dazed from the air, with only a few buzzing in flight away from the clearing.

"Well done," Stump smirked as he emerged from within the barrow. He watched idly for a moment as the stunned bees rose from the leaf mold and flew drunkenly into the forest. "Of course, the bees couldn't hurt me none. Why, I've got hide like wood! But, you'd know that, wouldn't you?"

He urged the last few groggy insects into the air with his long, hoary toes. All the while he was nodding his shaggy head. Then he looked back at the witch. His pale eyes locked on her gaze and a smile twisted upon his lips as he said, "You've gained some power since last we met. Still, are you ready to confront Remus Wolfe this far removed from your potions and hex castings? He's almost for sure on the way, seeing as how he's got this inhuman sense for your doings."

"I can stop his heart as easily as I felled these bees,"

she replied quietly, but her demeanor was betrayed by the hatred burning in her eyes and a hint of uncertainty. She made a gesture with her hands, whispering something the bogfoke could not hear.

The hounds came slinking back out of the wood. Their tails were tucked and they cringed close to the earth. Yolande turned to Birdy Coster, "Let one of the dogs track the cornbears from here. Take the other one to that ridge and start from there."

Birdy motioned to the other two men and they took one of the dogs and let it pick up the trail near the edge of the clearing. It suddenly lifted its head and bayed before trotting into the wood.

"They're heading toward that damnable ward," muttered one of the men. "Haven't we had enough of that place? It got us nowhere last time."

"You follow them," ordered the witch. The unhappy fellow swallowed any argument and took off after the hound. The other fellow quickly led the other hound toward the ridge.

Behind the screen of dogwood Slignan felt Gristel take hold of his arm. Her eyes were urgent as she whispered, "The dog is following the trail the others took into the ward. They can't have gotten very far with Welken's litter."

Slignan gestured toward the south, "I want all of you to take off. Cut toward the marsh. That is your best chance to escape. Perhaps you'll meet Remus Wolfe if he is truly on his way."

They hesitated for a moment, but he gestured again in adamant fashion, "Now. Go. I'll divert them from the others."

Reluctantly they turned to scramble away through the undergrowth. Slignan turned toward the clearing, wondering just what sort of diversion he might make. He saw Stump standing with his hands upon what might be his hips as he addressed the witch, "Yes, dear Yolande, you have grown into your power. Nice trick, beckoning those dogs and all. But, I too have grown into this existence you have cast upon me. I mayn't be the lord of the lake-wood, but neither am I a mere troll-creature any longer."

"I thought when I sensed the Father's fall that you might be behind it," replied the witch. "But I am no bogfoke lordling."

"Ah, well, I can't take credit for that," Stump chuckled. "Them little folk took care of your puppet themselves."

This wouldn't do, Slignan moaned to himself. Keeping the witch occupied with banter wouldn't turn those dogs. There was only one thing to be done. The hatchet-bearer suddenly shouted aloud and charged into the clearing. All eyes turned upon him as he scrambled back down the forest aisle.

"What are you doing?" shouted Stump. He saw the bogfoke disappear into the brush but knew the poor fellow would never escape the dogs now. The troll thrust out his arms, closed his eyelids and sent his toes curling into the soil. His call went out to the forest and the trees began to quiver.

"I've seen this act before," snarled Birdy as he hefted the ax. "I don't mean to take no more of it."

Turned by the troll's shout, Slignan saw the man closing upon Stump with the ax held high. He tried to call in warning, but the witch's shout came first, "No! You fool, not the ax! Do *not* set blade to the troll!"

As the agitated forest knocked him from his feet Slignan saw only the tossing branches, but heard the sickening bite of the ax and a furious shriek torn from Yolande's lips. The forest exploded into a maelstrom of twisting and whipping tree limbs. Undergrowth snaked across the aisles and tree roots writhed beneath the loam. The ground beneath him trembled and the terrifying chaos usurped Slignan's fear of the witch. He struggled through the nightmare of the lake-wood. As he burst onto the lake shore he saw Gristel, Kribble and Robbis huddled in the swamp around the troll's burrow.

All around the felled cypress a relative calm held sway.

Slignan stumbled into the refuge and fell to his knees on the patch of dry ground near the burrow. Gristle grabbed at his arm as she shoved her face before him. "What about the others? They are still in the wood. This madness will destroy them."

Her words drove the hatchet-bearer to his feet. He twisted around, following the lake shore with his eyes. Like demented phantasms the whole of the wood seethed in an impossible dance, but he saw that the further from this burrow he looked, the less frenzied was the wood.

"Stump was master of the lake-wood. I do not believe that his domain extended into the ward. Not far into it. That is the witch's domain," he reasoned aloud.

"Stump is doing all this?" asked Robbis skeptically.

Slignan cast a wistful glance at the stump of the cypress. "One of the men attacked him with an ax. I heard the witch try to stop him, but it was too late. I doubt that she did that from some whim of mercy. No, I believe that the ax released him from his binding. He is a troll no more. He is lord of the lake-wood again."

"I should not want to be the target of his undiminished strength," replied Gristel as she watched the wood-storm raging around them. They stood there, uncertain, as debris was hurled in a swirl around them.

"Get down," hissed Kribble.

They all fell quickly to their knees. From the north came the witch and her men bursting from the wood. The witch gestured angrily, driving the men before her as if they were sheep. With great strain she was holding back the worst of the fury, but the bogfoke could see it was a tenuous shielding.

Birdy Coster, still holding the ax in his hand, ran wild eyed for the boat but exceeded the reach of Yolande's power. Immediately tree roots spiraled up from the earth to wrap around his legs, causing him to fall face first into the water. He struggled to his knees, screaming in terror and chopping frantically at the roots. A sapling leaned as if in some unseen wind to slap him back into the water. Roots sprang over him to pin him beneath the frothing surface.

Into this gruesome fray came Silas. His face was bleeding and he surged past everyone to leap at the boat. He managed to grasp the side but as he was pulling himself up a cypress root wrapped around his ankle and dragged him into the water. Behind him Birdy had managed to raise his head above the roiling water but had barely time to gasp a breath before the roots dragged him under once again.

The witch sloshed into the water now, with the other men forming a cowed crescent around her. With her arrival the frenzy eased enough that they managed to push Silas into the boat and pull Birdy from the water. The troll slayer was screaming in agony and the bogfoke saw that both his ankles were grotesquely swollen. As all the men and the witch crowded into the one usable boat, oars began to bite the water. Slowly it drew away from the raging lake-wood.

With each length the boat withdrew the forest grew calmer. The bogfoke all stood now beside Stump's burrow. The witch was in the stern of the boat. The bogfoke could sense her gaze upon them. Slignan hefted his hatchet so that the sunlight glinted from it. He was smiling grimly.

"We haven't seen the last of her," warned Gristel.

"Nor she of us," replied the defiant hatchet-bearer. He turned to consider the lake-wood as it grew placid. "I don't know if Stump is gone for good. I do not know if his spirit can be of any more use to us. I do not know if Remus Wolfe will help us. But I do know that I will not go without struggle into any misery she might try to send upon us."

The other bogfoke nodded, and Gristel laid a gentle hand upon Slignan's shoulder. "We should go now. We must see how the others have fared in all this."

Together they sloshed through the swamp toward the forest. They thought of Skag, Welken and Stump, those who had fallen. How many more? It did not matter. They would fall one by one until they were all gone, or until free of the witch.

NINE

Ahkomaic And The Nunnehi

Skag stumbled in the dark. He turned back, but could see nothing from where he had come. Is this better than the witch, he wondered? Darkness was so absolute he could not see his hand even as he passed it before his face. Not an empty dark, though. He could still hear voices.

What was that light he had seen? Illusion? There was nothing he could do if it had not been real. He calmed himself and tried to pick out the direction from which the singing originated. Without anything to orientate himself this proved difficult. Finally he made his best guess and began feeling along with the stave.

The footing beneath him was as hard and smooth as polished granite. Then he thought he saw the light again, reflected from the surface ahead. He peered hard. There *was* light, glowing softly against the dark. The singing was suddenly stilled.

He heard a voice call out and stopped at the sound of demand he sensed in it. He did not understand the words. Then it called out again, the words were only vaguely familiar to the bogfoke. Then at last the voice called out, "Who are you and what are you doing here?"

"I am Skag," he replied softly. He could see no one within the glow of the light. He moved cautiously ahead, but the voice spoke again.

"Come no closer. What are you doing here?"

"I am a bogfoke," replied Skag. He saw no point in

being evasive. "I am fleeing from the witch, Yolande."

"Come forward five paces," commanded the voice.

The bogfoke did as directed. He could see the soft light settling around him, illuminating him to whatever hid in the dark. Skag held the cedar stave close to him but in a submissive manner to keep from alarming whatever was looking him over.

"Why, you're a cornbear!" exclaimed the voice, now light and filled with surprise.

"He is indeed," replied another voice.

Three forms moved into the light. They were smiling broadly through shaggy whiskers. Skag could barely believe his eyes. He knew them for what they must be, cornbears. It was no wonder that the kith of Cornbread Jack confused them with bogfoke. Certainly they were a bit taller and more stout, and their whiskers rather thick, but overall they were much less unlike Skag than he was unlike Father Daugth.

"My name is Skag, and I'm not quite a cornbear," replied the bogfoke.

"Then what are you?" asked the foremost cornbear as suspicion replaced his smile.

"I told you, a bogfoke. I'm told that we must have once been the same folk. There's scarcely any difference that I can see. Now I am trapped here just as you are."

"Trapped?" chuckled one of the cornbears in reply. He seemed older and probably the leader. His had been the voice in the dark. He stepped past the others, moving close to Skag. "We can leave anytime, but why would we, with the witch waiting?"

Skag nodded. "I see. But, I must leave eventually. There are others of my folk who are in danger."

One of the cornbears nudged the leader. "He can't just walk off, Nammais. We must take him to the founding spirit."

The older cornbear turned and quietly asked, "You are telling me what must be done, Suquahan?"

The second cornbear smiled sheepishly and stepped back a bit. Nammais turned again to Skag. "We must take you to the spirit-father. This is his dominion. If you fear the witch, then it is possible you will find him to be a friend."

Skag realized he had no other option, so he nodded. Nammais motioned to the other cornbears and they began leading the way. Nammais took Skag by the elbow, smiling to relieve the bogfoke's fear. "Come, Skag Bogfoke."

The first two cornbears walked straight into the glowing light. Skag hesitated, but the hand on his arm was insistent. The light washed over him, forcing him to close his eyes. The white-gold glow faded from his eyelids and he ventured a look after Nammais let go of his elbow.

It was daylight. Nammais and Suquahan were standing nearby, but the third cornbear was not in sight. Skag looked back and saw a hill that looked vaguely like the Weeping Hill, except that it held a doorway framed by stone. The doorway was filled with light.

The land around was not heavily wooded. Meadows and scattered clusters of trees spread alongside the path as it reached into the distance. Birds raced against a blue sky, or flitted from tree to tree. Skag looked upon it in wonder as he asked, "What is this place?"

Nammais looked around. He nodded as he realized how confusing this must be for the bogfoke. Still, he hesitated a moment, as if his reply was weighted with suspicion, before replying, "We call this Ahkomaic. That would be *land beyond*, or perhaps *land on the other side* in your language."

"You name it in the language of the red men," noted Skag, not liking the condescension in the cornbear's tone. He gestured around as he gazed into the blue dome of the sky. "*How* is all this?"

Nammais frowned. "You ask many questions. This is the dominion of the founder, the spirit-father. We will let him answer what he will."

Skag nodded and, with Nammais urging him on, followed Suquahan along the path. The bogfoke took time to notice the cornbear's clothing. It was certainly cleaner and in better repair than what the bogfoke had ever worn. Yet, it was primitive and scant. Suquahan wore a vest woven of some course material, linen made of flax, guessed Skag. Nammais wore a tunic of a slightly finer fabric, cotton most likely. They both wore loose trousers from the same cotton material.

They had not gone very far when Skag's legs began to betray him. Nammais steadied the bogfoke and he raised his bushy eyebrows in question. Skag took a deep breath and nodded that he could go on. "But please, a little slower."

His experience under the hill, and especially the passage through the light, had renewed his energy, but now all he had been through was once again sapping his strength. Suquahan continued to range ahead, though never out of sight. Nammais patiently allowed Skag to set the pace. The path wound through low, mostly treeless hills. Skag felt exposed in such openness, but could see that the trail eventually passed into a more thickly wooded region.

After some distance, with the sun approaching noon, Nammais motioned for Skag to sit and rest beneath a chestnut tree. Skag eased himself thankfully onto the grass beneath the shade. They were on a low hill and the path forked at this point. The narrower trail headed north. Skag followed it with his eyes.

He saw a dozen or more goats ambling along the grassy meadows. A few bowl-like huts of sod, sapling and bark stood beneath the spreading limbs of fruit trees. Skag saw movements amidst those huts and instinctively shrank closer to the ground.

"What is that place?" he asked in a whisper.

Nammais chuckled. "It is home. You have nothing to fear in this place if your intentions are good."

Skag got to his knees and studied the cluster of huts. There were indeed cornbears moving about. He saw others that were herding goats. There were more than two dozen huts. Many of them were small, but several were much larger than the bogfoke's barrow.

"How many of your kind are there?" asked Skag.

"You ask so many questions. I suppose that alone speaks surely of your relationship to my folk," chuckled Nammais. He stood up, gesturing to the bogfoke that it was time to resume the journey.

"Are we going to your home?" asked Skag as he fell into place beside the cornbear.

Nammais shook his head and pointed to the wood lying along the southeasterly path, "We are going to the spirit-father. This is his dominion."

"This area?"

"This *everything*,"

The cornbear who had disappeared rejoined them at the fork in the path. He had a water skin. Skag was allowed a long swallow, and then cupped some of the water in his hands which he splashed over his face. He was also given a peach to eat as they walked on. The water-bearer turned away again, taking the northern trail to the cornbear's hamlet.

The peach and the water gave new strength to the bogfoke's considerable endurance. Nammais was happy with the increased pace and they were soon not too far behind the ever restless Suquahan. Skag felt himself smiling and was lost in thought. This was a strange place and he felt as though he had stumbled into someone else's dream, as Stump would have said. It was not that he was unwelcome, but he sensed that no lack of animosity could make this place his.

As they neared the forest Skag saw a herd of deer watching them with mild curiosity. There was no indication of fear. The animals had kept the undergrowth down and the trees grew strong and tall without interference from choking shrubs and weeds.

Suquahan was walking abreast of them now, seeming intimidated by the forest. The expression borne by Nammais hinted at reverence. All this contributed to a sense of unease rising in Skag.

The sun had descended past noon and the rays cut

through the canopy in haphazard patches. This forest was much more open than the Great Wood of the bogfoke. There was something encompassing about it, however, making Skag feel closed in somehow, though he did not feel overtly threatened.

The path wound between ridges where the roots of the towering trees bound the soil on either side making it feel as though they were passing between two walls. The hills were steeper than those around the bogfoke's barrow. He saw many stones and boulders, but no sight of swamp or pocosin bogs. The woodland finally began to thicken, with saplings crowding in competition for sunlight. The bogfoke smiled at the familiar sight of dogwood in bloom, though he was confused that they should be in flower when peach and apple were in fruit.

The wood suddenly opened again with huge oaks towering above the other trees. Skag had never seen such huge oaks before. Grass spread beneath these giants, but nothing else ventured into their realm. The cornbears were walking as if pushing against some obstacle. Finally they stopped. Suquahan sat down with his back against an oak trunk and from his lips passed a long and contented sigh.

Nammais tugged on Skag's arm, leading him off the path and across the grassy aisle beneath the trees. They came to an ancient oak. It wasn't so tall as the others but none could come close to matching its girth. Roots tumbled everywhere, rising above and diving beneath the grassy surface. The branches twisted as if holding at bay any intrusion. Skag frowned.

"Why are dogwoods blooming at the same time that peaches are ripe?" asked the bogfoke.

"It is the spirit-father's dominion," whispered Nammais. "Time is different here."

"Then, why is there no leaf mold beneath these trees?" persisted Skag. Nammais nudged him for silence.

A new voice replied to his question, "Because the trees know no winter. It might be cold. It might even snow, but they will not have to submit to it,"

The sound of the voice was smooth and gentle. Skag whirled around trying to place it. Finally his gaze settled on the tree. The tree was talking to him?

No, not the tree, but someone, or something, sitting beneath it. Skag clenched his cedar defensively. At first he thought it might be a man, but it was much more slender than any man. It had a beard as gray and coarse as Spanish moss. The eyes that stared back at the bogfoke were mottled like green sea-foam. It was much taller than a bogfoke, but peculiarly thin.

"Are you a troll?" asked Skag.

The creature smiled and shook his head. "No, I am not a troll. I am what you see, but I am much more as well, as are we all. In time I will become something else. None of the created are unchanging until the time of the timeless comes upon us. Sit, Skag."

The bogfoke sank reluctantly to the grass. He saw the creature a bit more clearly now. It was clothed in a robe of the same cotton material as the cornbear's trousers. A thin hand rested on knobby knees while the other gestured at the forest, and perhaps the world around them. "This is my dream. I am one of the founders. If they weren't so secretive, the cornbears would tell you that we created all this by reflecting the Song of Getchemandou."

"Who is Getchemandou?"

The creature smiled, wistfully. "Who, indeed? What, indeed? The Great Spirit. The being that is *being* itself."

Skag frowned, trying to encompass with his mind such a notion. The spirit-father smiled for the bogfoke to be patient and continued, "The founders have many names, because the humans have many languages. The cornbears called us *nunnehi*, which they borrowed from the Cherokee. Most of the cornbear language is borrowed from the many tribes of their memory."

"They spoke the tongue of the white men to me," replied Skag. The creature nodded.

"English, yes, but very few of the cornbears speak it. They have not had much contact with the men from over the sea. These you have met are the *coquanon*, the translators. They are very skilled in language, and they guard the door between the worlds," explained the creature that called itself a nunnehi.

"What are you?" asked Skag.

"You would do better to ask what we *were*," answered the spirit-father. "In the beginning we were much like you and the cornbears. All of us were once of the same folk. But, what you see before you is only a reflection of my spirit."

Skag wrapped his thoughts around this, feeling the hair stand on the back of his neck. He leaned forward and asked, "You are what the witch sought to find in me?"

The nunnehi nodded slowly, with those green eyes bright as they studied the bogfoke. "You are swift of thought. We are indeed that which you may become."

Skag sat back as he consider those words. "I thought we mightn't be so ugly."

The bogfoke heard a choking sound beside him and saw Nammais staring wide eyed. The nunnehi chuckled, "You have startled poor Nammais. You must understand, the cornbears feel we are their protectors. They venerate us overmuch, no matter how we protest it. I find your irreverence refreshing, but Nammais finds it disquieting."

"Why does the witch hunt cornbears and bogfoke? What is it to her what we are to become? And why are cornbears safe within this place?"

"They are safe because within this world we are more powerful than Yolande. We are more powerful even than that which she serves. She hunts you because of that. She seeks the power of what you are to be. Yet, though she should hex, enchant, and slay a thousand bogfoke or cornbears, her efforts would be futile. The power she seeks cannot be traded or stolen. It exists as it is and cannot be transformed into something it is not."

"Why can she not be made aware of this fact?"

demanded Skag. He looked around at this place, at this *land beyond.* "With your power such a revelation should be possible."

The nunnehi rubbed its long beard. "She would not believe us. She *has* been told such a thing. The lord of the lake-wood himself told her. But there is more to your difficulty than just the witch."

Skag's worried frown deepened. "Ah. You see, we find her difficulty enough."

The nunnehi smiled. "I should imagine that you do. It is not easy to know where one story begins and another ends. Let me say to you that this place is not meant to be the true home of cornbears or bogfoke. Whatever our kinship, there is too much difference of experience between us for you to remain here. Neither you nor the cornbears can grow whilst you hide in the Weeping Hill. The presence of my own kith would hinder your growth, like a tall oak blocks the sun from a sapling."

"We won't do much growing with the witch chasing us," noted Skag. "It is very tiring, being chased."

"Actually, you have grown because of that very thing," replied the spirit-father. "But you are correct in assuming that ultimately such a confrontation is not advantageous to you. That is why you are here. The spirit of the city has sent you to us. You will lead the cornbears from this place. If you fail, then they may perish, but you are their best hope."

"I am not so quick witted as you might think," murmured Skag.

The nunnehi crossed its skeletal arms. The smile was insistent, hinting at the truth in some distant relationship to the bogfoke. "There are places in the world, Skag, that are held by spirits. What the cornbears would call a manitoh. The city is such a spirit. She gathers to her the dreams and aspirations of men. She is fascinated with such things, but she existed long before the men came to her. She existed even before the great river flowed, even when the deep sea covered the land."

The nunnehi's face drew into a more serious expression. "There are many such spirits, some great and some small. They guide, they nurture they reflect the will of Getchemandou. But, not all such spirits are benign. There is one such existence that the cornbears call Machamanitoh, the dark spirit. It gathers the nightmares and despair of men. It gathers such things from our own folk as well. Any such evil or misfortune *feeds* this spirit.

"It wants to be *all*. It despises what it thinks to be the chaos of life and wants everything to be brought into the empty singularity of its own will. Such a thing it cannot do.

"The Song of Getchemandou, what others might express as the weaving of the Great Spirit, is a union of complexity, a paradox. The dark spirit would have all reality submit to its will, though it cannot possibly sustain such a thing. It seduces life itself into a destructive menace. In the end would be only madness. The red men named it Amhomag, after the black cherry blossom which is beautiful but poisonous."

Skag caught the direction taken by the nunnehi. "This is the source of the witch's power, is it not? Nannela Walker suspected something of the sort."

"It is," replied the Nunnehi. "Amhomag is ancient beyond the memories of men. When first it seduced men to its power none can remember. It was not the first, nor the most powerful of such dark powers, but the power of the witch is as nothing in comparison. It was brought from the north by one tribe many centuries now passed. The dark spirit molded them into a degenerate and secretive people who sacrificed their captives and practiced cannibalism in rituals designed to draw power into Amhomag because they believed he would raise them to be a mighty people.

"They destroyed an ancient civilization in their greed and power lust. Such violence sapped them of their strength and it was many generations before they were again powerful enough to challenge other tribes. They moved into the mountains where they eventually confronted the first fathers of the Cherokee. It was a bitter struggle and the stalemate ended only when nunnehi came from the hills and checked the strength of Amhomag. In the end, the tribe was obliterated."

"Excepting?" interjected Skag.

"Excepting a few of the highest shamans who fled east into the very wood you have called home. There they tried to revive the strength of Amhomag. The shamans of the woodland tribes were warned of this by the nunnehi. They cast down the priests of Amhomag, but they hadn't the power to destroy the dark spirit itself."

"So it exists still today" sighed the bogfoke.

"Its lair is within the Great Wood. The tribal shamans knew of this place. They avoided it, and they placed a taboo against it upon their people. They venerated the guiding spirits in the hope that they might contain the darkness of Amhomag. Their honoring strengthened the spirits, especially the one you know as the lord of the lake-wood. It was ever an impulsive but powerful elemental whose song was woven through the forest, forming a nearly impenetrable barrier against the dark one."

The nunnehi stroked its beard, pausing for a moment so that ancient memories could be revived. "White men came. They did not know the haunt of Amhomag, nor did they believe in what they saw as the superstitions of the tribes. The clash of the two people was inevitable. With each dark thought or deed the black spirit grew in strength. It nurtured the unworthy thoughts of the white men, and stirred the fears and indignation of the tribes."

"I've never thought men needed much meddling to stir up their darker side," noted Skag.

The nunnehi smiled patiently. "It was inevitable as I have said. Yet, the fury that was unleashed descended like a nightmare upon the land. White men took for themselves the place that is now the city of dreams. The spirit of that place had long countered the darkness of Amhomag, but now it could no longer influence the minds of the red men.

"The tribes had given to the place of dreams the name, Chautaugua, because they thought the waters enchanted. They grieved at losing the sacred place. Anger burned in their hearts, fanned by Amhomag.

"There were wise men on both sides. They tried to reason with their people. Pestilence had weakened the ranks of the shamans. Their efforts were in vain. There was war. The settlements of the white men were burned. An army of white men and their tribal allies came from the southeast to retaliate. That was the beginning of what the tribes would later call the time of the black moon."

The nunnehi paused, gazing into the air as if the memories danced around him like moths before a flame. His words had woven those images before the eyes of the bogfoke with a clarity even Mother Crabba could have never mustered. The nunnehi looked at Skag, smiling to dispel the intensity of those memories. He was unwilling to reveal in total the evil upon the land in the time of the black moon.

"Only at Chautaugua was the fury abated. Men, women and children of both sides took shelter there. The wise men among all the people wept at the darkness that had descended upon their people. Amhomag grew powerful, bloated by the evil."

"But it could not have succeeded," insisted Skag. "Even now it is not so powerful."

The nunnehi nodded. "To which much debt is owed to many. A short lived alliance of red and white men managed to quell the violence and bring a fragile peace."

"And the manitoh named Amhomag?" asked Skag.

"It has brooded, gaining substance from whatever evil it can. There is a paradox in that spirit, as there is in much of this creation. Its power is mostly through illusion and the weakness of others more than anything it possesses itself. What it does possess is a writhing ability to persuade, to delude. It needs others to exercise its will."

"And that would be Yolande," sighed Skag, thinking

of all the fear and humiliation borne by the witch.

The nunnehi nodded again, looking sorrowful and grim. "She gains her power from it, and it gains its substance from her. They have been growing stronger."

Skag swallowed hard, "You have called me the best hope, but here I am, hiding from the witch while my own folk are in danger."

"Your comrades are resourceful. That is a trait of our kind," replied the nunnehi. "But you, Skag, challenge yourself. Push yourself. That is why the city has sent you. We will unlock these secrets and unveil the power. Not *your* power, but the power that will defend you. Come."

The nunnehi rose. Nammais helped Skag to his feet. They followed the founding-spirit through the grove. They came to a willow that was nearly as wide as the ancient oak. Its fronds swept low to the earth, forming a golden-green veil around the trunk. The nunnehi swept this aside with a thin arm. Skag and Nammais stepped past the leafy wall.

A pool of water spread on the other side of the willow trunk. The water glittered in the patches of sunlight. Another nunnehi sat between the willow and the pool. This one seemed vaguely female. It was beardless, but its hair swept long and coarse like that of the founding-spirit.

The willow-nunnehi was holding a goblet of fired clay. The founding-spirit turned to Skag. "Remove your clothing, and then you may bathe in the pool."

Skag hesitated, but Nammais gave him a nudge and a slight nod. "Do not fear, Skag Bogfoke. This is a sacred place. The waters can heal and refresh."

The bogfoke shrugged and did as told. At a gesture from the nunnehi he eased into the water. He had expected it to be cold, but it was surprisingly warm. He squinted his eyes against the dazzling sunlight that reflected from the surface of the water. The light lingered on his limbs as he bathed. He cupped the water in his hands and splashed it on his face. The water cascaded over him like red-gold liquid.

He was much revitalized as he waded from the pool.

Nammais handed him a towel, and then a shirt and trousers of the same forest green material that the cornbears wore. It was light and comfortable clothing.

The founding-spirit went to the willow-nunnehi and lifted the cup from the slender hands. Skag saw the willow-nunnehi turn its golden eyes to him. The founding-spirit brought the goblet to the bogfoke, delivering it gently into his hands.

"Drink but a sip of this, Skag," he instructed.

The bogfoke put it to his lips, tilting the cup until it barely wet his lips. The liquid was warm but flavorless. It smelled slightly like the air after a thunderstorm. The fluid spread a glowing freshness through him and he would have instinctively taken a deeper draught but the spirit-father gently pried the cup from his hands and returned it to the willow-nunnehi.

The air around Skag seemed to go hazy and his eyelids hung heavy. He wondered what this was they had him drink? He sighed in a wash of sedation. The hand of Nammais settled upon his arm. The cornbear was smiling to reassure him and that whiskered face had never seemed so like a bogfoke to Skag.

"You may sleep," whispered Nammais.

He led Skag to a small grassy hollow between the knees of the willow. Skag sank gratefully to the soft ground, cradling his head on his arms. The nunnehi brought him his cedar stave, placing it beside him.

"We will talk again when you are rested," whispered the founding-spirit.

Skag managed a nod, but all he wanted was to sleep. Sleep. No worrisome witch, just a gentle darkness to wash away the weariness.

***

The smell of grass was sweet and persuasive. The smell of the soil intruded rich and moist. Skag felt as if he were being pulled into the earth, becoming part of the soil.

He felt no fear, just a detached curiosity.

The darkness receded, giving way to an endless gray mist. Now Skag was startled and sat up. There was no grass beneath him. Had he dreamed all that? Or was *this* the dream?

He held tight to his cedar and stood. There was nothing in any direction except mist, and that had become so thick he could not see his own feet. Yet, it was not moist. It had no feel at all.

Before him the mist began to swirl. Skag stepped back a bit, bringing up the stave. Features began to form in the mist. Skag stared hard, not believing what he was seeing, Jeremiah Simms.

"I had not thought to see you again," said the wraith.

"I hadn't thought to see you either," replied the bogfoke.

Jeremiah Simms was smiling, and he tilted his head as if listening to something. A spectral eyebrow raised in reaction to some notion. "I understand you have accomplished much, my friend."

Skag shrugged. "Have I? I am lost in this place. Where or what is this?"

Jeremiah Simms spread his hands, "We are in the veil between the worlds. I have been sent, I think, to comfort you. I am the only thing familiar to you that can be in this place."

"I hope it is not an inconvenience," the bogfoke apologized. Jeremiah Simms laughed.

"It is not allowed that I should remember if it is or not. I suspect that I was willing to come," replied the wraith. He cocked his head again, with a look of concentration. "There is much that is portentous about what you have done, and might yet do. There is something for us to see."

Jeremiah Simms gestured theatrically with his arm, even giving a wink to Skag as he did so. The mist was swirled by his motion and dark forms began to emerge. They took shape like a slowly evolving dream. Skag felt his heart skip. The forms were those of the cemetery wall. He would have tried to flee, except for the words of the ghost-man, "Do not be disturbed, Skag. This is nothing more than an image. It is a tale woven in the mist. Look at the wall."

Indeed, the wall began to melt away. The tombstones faded into nothing. Trees and shrubs began to emerge. It was as though the years were rolling away. Skag saw movement from amongst the brush. A bogfoke moved there, carefully, as if to elude the eyes of some hidden watcher. It was a female. She was clad in a gown made from a material much like the clothing of the cornbears.

She was moving toward a wide path that swept through a bog and into the dense growth that would one day be the cemetery. Almost she was into that growth when another shadow separated itself from the dark beneath the trees, another bogfoke, with a cruel smile gleaming past whiskered lips. He held an iron bar in his hands. It was an irregular length of impure iron, as though some freak of nature had brought it into existence.

"Where do you go?" he asked in a language much like that of the cornbears. The darkness in the voice startled Skag.

"When was it decided that we should answer to you, Daugth?" asked the other. Her voice was gentle and smooth. It seemed almost to crack the darkness around Daugth.

Daugth held up the bar, smiling all the broader. "This has decided."

"That? That which you see as a weapon?" sighed the other. "That which is the contrivance of a dark spirit? That which is, in reality, the shackle that bind you to the dark?"

The argument was disrupted for a moment by the sound of movement along the cemetery path. Three more bogfoke came scurrying through the undergrowth. Two of them were males, the other a female. The female carried a young bogfoke in her arms. It was a mere bogling and lay helpless against her bosom. The bogling recognized the female bogfoke confronting Daugth and reached for her.

She who carried the bogling bore a worried frown. "Come away, Sloe, now is not the time."

Sloe of the golden voice turned away from Daugth, moving to take the bogling in her arms. She looked then to her friend and whispered, "It must be, Crabba. A great darkness has descended upon my brother. I will take my son and go from this place. All of you should leave. You should take back your true names and get from this place before the darkness descends upon you."

Sloe turned to face Daugth again. She was smiling gently, as though her eyes saw past the iron, the darkness and the hatred, as though she saw a young bogfoke playing in the forested aisles. "I must go, Daugth. They are waiting for me."

She moved to pass the iron bearer. Torment raged in his eyes. Then he screamed. All the other bogfoke shivered and cringed, except Sloe. She turned to face him again, even as the iron bar descended.

Skag closed his eyes against the sight. He felt the arm of Jeremiah Simms around his shoulder like a cool mist. The ghost-man whispered, "Only a few moments more, Skag. It is important that this be unveiled to you."

The bogfoke opened his eyes, staring at the form of Sloe lying upon the ground. Daugth stood over her holding the iron bar to strike again. His eyes were wide and filled with hatred that struggled with anguish. His gaze settled on the bogling still held in Sloe's arms. He moved toward it with the rod rising again.

"No," hissed Crabba, scurrying to pull the young one to her. "Look, Daugth. Look at what you have done."

Her words forced his eyes to the ground. They forced him to look upon the fallen Sloe. Tears filled his eyes, but the hatred blazed as if to engulf them. "Her head, so filled with dreams not meant for a bogfoke. So arrogant was she and so self-important, because of the sight given to her by the dreaming manitoh. But I am more powerful. The gift given to me has brought her dreams to nothing."

Daugth turned his head to glare at Crabba, "The bogling must die. It was fathered by the cruelest of lies. Never more shall we know the anguish of false hope. We shall be made great! And we shall take back what men-kind has taken from us."

"False hope," spat Crabba. "The dark chimera you would have us serve, *that* is falsity."

"We will *not* be the pawn of the nunnehi!" howled Daugth. "The bogling must die."

"Then you must kill me to do such a thing," Crabba rebuked him. The other two bogfoke moved hesitantly to support her. Daugth's eyes glittered with dark intent, but as he moved toward them their gazes went to the open path.

Daugth whirled, snarling like a beast. The form was tall and seemed impossibly thin. Its movement was so smooth it appeared to glide over the path before bending over the form of Sloe. The limp body was taken into slender arms and the green sea-foam eyes looked upon Daugth. "Give to me also the bogling."

"It is not yours, Mankatoh," spat Daugth as he backed away from the nunnehi.

"Whose is it? What life belongs to another, save to Getchemandou?" sighed Mankatoh. "He is the son of Sloe. He is my son."

"Perversion," growled Daugth. "Look at what you have become. Look at what you would have had Sloe become. I will keep the bogling. I will drive from it any vestige of what you are."

The eyes of the founding-spirit grew achingly sad. "You have let yourself become the tool of Amhomag. I cautioned you against the willow swamp, but your contempt for me led you into the lair of darkness. You have turned against your kith and kin. Now you are a creature of servitude, kneeling before Amhomag."

"Get from this place, spirit-thing," laughed Daugth. His smile was cruel and arrogant. "All you river-folk, are a diminishing people. The forest-folk might be deluded into following you, but never the bogfoke! What are you? Even your form is an illusion. Well I have raised a binding against you! You cannot come any further into this bog. You cannot best the warding of the lord of the willow swamp.

"We shall keep the bogling. We shall drive from it any hint of whatever might have come from you."

"Will you keep the dreams from it?" asked the nunnehi. The spirit-father looked past the iron-bearer, gazing deep into Crabba's eyes. "Remember. Bury deep in your heart the seed of hope so that no darkness may crush it. Many of your folk have come to live with the forest-folk. There will come a time for the rest of you."

Then the nunnehi turned with Sloe in its arms and moved like a dream into the night. Then the mist began to swirl before Skag's eyes. His vision was obscured for a moment while the images shifted and changed. Slowly he made out the walls of the cemetery again, but they were not complete and the tombstones fewer.

A dream of the city was unfolding. Daugth ran forward to pound at the gray wall, but the force of his hatred caused the iron bar to shatter. The pieces that flew beyond the wall touched the dream of the city and melted into nothingness. In his rage he hurled the piece remaining in his hand at the dream while shouting aloud virulent curses. Then Daugth screamed in impotent rage as the iron bar melted away.

From out of the night came the stooped form of a wiry built black man. He walked to the nearly completed arch. His eyes shone with distaste as they fixed on Daugth.

"You have buried yourself with darkness," he said to the bogfoke. "I know something of such things. I carry it with me, a sin that only a grim purgatory can cleanse from me."

"Get from here," hissed Daugth. "Who are you, worthless dog of the white men, to speak thus to me?"

"I too saw the dream of the city," replied Cornbread Jack. "I have seen. I have seen your sin. I will finish this wall and it will bind you within as surely as you sought to ward the nunnehi. You will not go again to your devil-spirit. This will be my purgatory. We shall never be released, you and I, until the city unbinds us."

"I spit on your city," snarled Daugth. "This is the place of the bogfoke! I rule here, and we shall never leave."

Then Mother Crabba came from among the tombstones. The years of tormented sorrow had ravaged her and her eyes held no spark of hope. Cornbread Jack looked at her and asked, "Do you know me?"

"Yes. You are a brave man, but in a moment of anger you took the life of another," she sighed. "The city and her terrifying master have set the terms of your atonement."

Cornbread Jack nodded. "So our fates are entwined. But the master of the city is terrifying only because our sins burn within us. Nurture as well you might what remains of the dream among your folk. Somewhere in your heart, remember, there lies freedom for us all."

The Mother closed her eyes and as she did so the images faded into nothing. Skag felt the wraith's arm release him. Jeremiah Simms squatted before the bogfoke so that their eyes were level, "Are you all right, Skag?"

"Yes," the cedar-bearer managed to reply. "But, it is as if many doors are opening in my mind. I haven't the brain to hold so many memories, all the lies and all the false tales."

The wraith stood again, looking down with sympathy upon the bogfoke. "The nunnehi, your father, will help you. I must go, but who can tell what whim or greater purpose shall bring me to you again? I wish you good fortune, Skag."

The image of Jeremiah Simms dissolved into the mist. The mist itself began to fade into black. Skag did not fight this darkness. He welcomed this restful oblivion, however brief it might be.

***

A patch of sunlight had moved across Skag's face, shining red on his eyelids. The scent of the grass and the soil came to him again as wakefulness crept up from the dark. Memories of the dream rushed to fill the void and he half expected to awaken and find himself in the forest barrow, or perhaps even the cemetery, or upon the witch's table. His dreams were becoming as jumbled as those of the city.

He saw a willow root and stretched as he turned onto his back and sat up. The founding-spirit was standing motionless nearby, gazing steadily at the bogfoke. Skag returned the gaze, scratching his stubbled cheek as he asked, "Are you the same nunnehi as the one in my dreams?"

The founding-spirit nodded.

"Then tell me, what happened to Sloe? Where did you take my birth-mother?"

The founding-spirit turned slowly, allowing Skag's gaze to follow his to the willow-nunnehi. The bogfoke got stiffly to his knees, leaning on the cedar stave as he considered the willow-spirit. "Can't she talk?"

"Certainly," laughed that which had been Sloe.

The voice was smooth, and as golden as morning sunlight. Skag recognized it immediately. The images from his dream became all the more vivid when she spoke.

"Why did you leave me?" he asked with simple curiosity rather than accusation.

"I had been struck upon the head," she reminded him with the goading thread of bogfoke humor woven into her words. "The Mankatoh could not challenge Daugth's warding at that time. I was grievously wounded, dying. He had to ease my transition into what I was to be. Later, we considered an attempt to cast down Daugth's warding. The dark spirit of the willow swamp had weakened by then, but the city dreamed of other considerations. We knew that it was not the will of Getchemandou that we should try."

The spirit-father nodded at her words and added, "The mothers and fathers of Gristel, Tegmina, Slignan, Robbis, Kribble, Weart and Welken all perished at the hands of Daugth. Their spirits were trapped in that place. But we knew the possibility of what you might become. In you there was something of the light alive beneath all the dark and despair, like a seed in the dark earth. You were born into the right moment and place.

"I was not yet as I am now when you were brought into the Song of Getchemandou. But soon my transition began, and in the manner and nature meant for our folk. I became what I am while you were still in your mother's womb, and some part of this new founding was upon you. You think me wise, perhaps, but even I cannot hold in my mind all the ways of Getchemandou."

"I did not bring any spirits from the cemetery," fretted Skag.

"No, but you released them when you felled Daugth and broke the bonds that Cornbread Jack had made. You freed the mason himself as well. Still, there is more to be done and you are the most likely instrument."

"I do not understand," muttered Skag, looking around the world of Ahkomaic. "I have asked to be nothing more than a bogfoke left in peace. You speak of me as some sort of hero. I know the realities of such things and I want no part of that."

Sloe-nunnehi smiled. "You are to be nothing more than a bogfoke. Yet, that means so much more than you ever realized. You shall be the focus of the dreams of your kind. You can be a dagger into the heart of Amhomag."

"A pawn," snorted Skag, shaking his head.

"Perhaps, but it might also be the only way the bogfoke can ever know peace. It has to be obvious to you now that the outside world is no longer a place for our kind. Would you risk your life for your folk?"

"I would lay down my life for the others," bristled Skag. "I owe them that, after having led them from the cemetery."

"That may be your fate."

Skag laughed. "So, I have no choice in the game?"

The founding-spirit chuckled lightly. "We all have the choice to join the game, as you would put it. You need not be a simple tool in the designs of others. You can choose to sing the Song of Getchemandou. You can choose to be part of, or apart from the singing, but to be not of the Song is to no longer truly exist.

"It is because you are a bogfoke that the task falls to you. Change is inevitable, Skag. You must surely see that, whether or not you choose to confront Amhomag."

Skag got to his feet. He looked long and hard at Sloe-nunnehi, and then at the founding-spirit before speaking, "I will not deceive you. I do not believe I am likely to succeed at what you propose for me. But, if it means that I might possibly save my kith and kin, then I am willing to perish in the trying."

The nunnehi nodded solemnly and motioned for the bogfoke to follow him. The founding-spirit led him through the grove. Skag turned to look again at the willow-nunnehi. Sloe was watching him and her golden eyes reflected the bittersweet joy of her heart.

"She who was Sloe is pleased with what you have become," said the nunnehi. "So am I. It is difficult to believe that we could have found so much courage within ourselves as you have discovered within your own heart. We watched the dreams of the city as she sought to assure us that you were worthy of this endeavor, but it seemed to us that you have been given so little to sustain you. Yet, from somewhere you found the courage."

"Courage? I've known only a single path away from despair and hopelessness," said Skag as he turned his gaze from the willow-spirit. "What choice was there but to stay or go? It was only fear of what *was* that drove me to the way of what might be."

Skag was silent a moment before turning his gaze from beneath his feet and toward the nunnehi. "If Ahkomaic is not the place for cornbears and bogfoke, why is Sloe here?"

"It is difficult to explain," the nunnehi sighed. "While her former existence had an untimely ending, it had been a natural progression. As a single entity, and long ago, she flowed seamlessly into the song of Ahkomaic. This land, Skag, it grows with us. In truth, we are closing upon another change, a move beyond even all Ahkomaic, whilst cornbears and bogfoke are just preparing to reach this level of existence, and not prepared for the next."

"Is there any end to changes?" asked Skag.

The nunnehi smiled. "Finality would be such a boring thing don't you think? That said, the finality is an eternity of one thing flowing into another. The finality is a paradox of distinctive sameness. It is difficult for us to grasp the great reality."

"Yes, so it seems to me," admitted Skag as they were nearing the ancient oak. The founding-spirit turned and put one hand on Skag's shoulder.

"You must go with Nammais. You must know the ways of the cornbears because your fates are entwined. What you are to become, they shall become. It will not take so long for you to understand them. They are much like your own folk."

"But my own folk have been left in great danger," protested Skag.

The nunnehi looked into the blue dome of the sky. "They have met well the challenge. It is not without cost, but they survive. The witch's own impetuous anger has caused the lord of the lake-wood to be freed from his binding. For a time his spirit will ward the darkness so that he may be atoned."

The bogfoke frowned. "Stump? What cost?"

The nunnehi looked back into Skag's eyes. "In time you will understand. You have the possibility to help make right many things, but none of us can make things perfect. That is a power and possibility beyond us and even beyond time itself. However, I urge you to always remember this. Amhomag has no power beyond its ability to subvert what is in us. It can manipulate the hearts and minds of human kind, as well as our own. That is not to be dismissed. The threat of this spirit is what it finds in the hearts of others. Mark you well that Daugth himself was once a bogfoke of great promise, but Amhomag found the dark seed that became the evil thing you bested beneath the monument of the gray cloaked warrior."

The nunnehi turned away toward the great oak. Nammais came to lead Skag away, but the spirit-father turned again to speak, "Now, go and learn."

The cornbear's eyes were filled with mist as he led Skag away. He gnawed at his bewhiskered lip in great concentration until Skag finally asked of him, "Are you ill?"

"No," replied Nammais, managing a smile. "It is only that we have waited for so long, and now, at last, we have a chance to be what always we should have been."

Skag sighed, "What if I fail?"

Nammais shrugged, "It will not be you alone, Skag Bogfoke. Even if we fail, at least we will have had a chance."

***

Skag stayed at the hut of the coquanon. It was larger than the other dwellings and was used by all the translators. The bogfoke soon realized that there was more to the coquanon than just their skill with many tongues. Like Mother Crabba they were masters of lore. They acted as arbitrators and healers. They sang. They sang songs that strove to mirror the song of Ahkomaic, which strove to mirror the Song of Getchemandou.

Nammais took Skag to the river with him to scrounge for clams, and also to show the bogfoke how to cast a net for fish. The bogfoke was intoxicated with the freedom of Ahkomaic, the freedom of open air and the freedom from fear.

"How big is this place?" he asked one day of Nammais, gesturing with his hand as though to encompass all Ahkomaic.

"Big," shrugged the coquanon. "Maybe as big as the world outside. Perhaps larger. There are seas and lakes and mountains. There are great arid lands and vast swamps."

"You know, Nammais, I wish I could just take off to explore," mused Skag. "No witch, no men."

"It is not without danger," cautioned Nammais. "As the spirit-father tells us, we are ignorant of this world and ignorance is danger."

Skag smiled. "That may be, but ignorance can be mastered. In the other world, perhaps the witch can be mastered, but I do not think we can ever hope to overcome the kith of Cornbread Jack."

"They are many," agreed Nammais. "They breed like rabbits. I wonder, when do you think they will begin to fall off the edge of the world?"

"A ghost-man once told me they were reaching for the stars," laughed Skag.

"Ah, then I suppose they will not be happy until they have filled all the worlds in the dreams of Getchemandou," said Nammais. "The spirit-father tells us that the other world belongs to the humankind. We should have been gone from it long before now, but the humans disrupted the song and the entire world was damaged. That is why we must free ourselves of Amhomag, free ourselves of the witch, and then we can join in the song and dream of our own world."

Skag did not reply. He looked around Ahkomaic. That would be a lot of dreaming, he reckoned. He chose not to think of all that stood between them and that dreaming.

***

On the third day, down by the river, Skag noticed an elderly cornbear sitting beneath a pine tree. It occurred to him that the old fellow had been there every day, hardly seeming to have moved. The hair on the ancient head was sparse and he had a long wispy beard.

Skag nudged Nammais and motioned toward the old one. "Who is that?"

Nammais looked up from the net he was inspecting. "We call him, *old one waiting by the water*. He has a real name, of course, but even the coquanon do not remember it. He has been sitting beneath that tree since before we entered this place. He never moves from it and hardly stirs at all. The last time he spoke, he said only that he was waiting. The spirit-father says that he was the first cornbear to ever enter Ahkomaic, and that he holds in him the first dreams, from the dawn of our kind and even from before the spoiling of the other world by the human kind.

"I asked the spirit-father why he has not become as the nunnehi. He said only that the old one is waiting."

"Waiting?"

"That is what the old one says. That is what the spirit-father says. So it is our guess that the old one is, in fact, waiting," shrugged Nammais. The cornbear began folding the net, frowning slightly. "We've torn this one on a root. I'll go fetch another."

"Take this," said Skag, handing the cornbear a basket of fish they'd caught. He then looked up into the hazy sky. "You had better hurry, it'll rain shortly."

"How do you know that?" asked Nammais as he took the basket and stared into the sky.

Skag shrugged. "Can you not feel it? The air moves differently. The birds begin to quiet. The trees seem to be expectant. I can smell it on the wind, can't you?"

Nammais shook his head. "No, I smell only fish. Sometimes I can read the signs of this world for changes in the weather, but never so early as this. Perhaps it is what the nunnehi spoke of to me, 'He shall know the ways of wood and world.'"

Skag chuckled. "I said only that it would rain. I could even be wrong."

Nammais laughed also, but he shrugged as he hefted the net onto his back and began walking for the village.

Skag waded out into the river, poking for clams with his cedar stave. He did well, filling half a basket. Shadows began moving across the land as dark clouds spilled up from the west. Skag smiled. Nammais would never make it back from the village without getting wet.

Then he frowned, realizing that *he* wouldn't make it back to the village without getting wet. A few big drops began splattering the ground. Skag looked around, finally deciding that the old one's tree offered the best shelter available.

He was barely beneath the spreading branches of the pine before the rain began in earnest. A sporadic pattern of drops made it through the canopy, but Skag pressed near the trunk and remained relatively dry. He was sitting to one side of the Old One and watched the rain sending circles spreading across the surface of the river. The circles struggled against one another, reminding him of the lives of men, or of bogfoke for that matter.

A strange feeling crept over the cedar-bearer. He turned and found the Old One staring at him. The bogfoke nodded. "Hello, I am Skag."

The Old One's head nodded slowly as he spoke in the tongue of Cornbread Jack, "They call me the old one waiting by the river. But my name is Askuwhetaeau."

"Well, that's a mouthful. What are you waiting for?"

"I am waiting for the final release. I am waiting for the next path I am to travel. I am waiting for the dreaming to begin. I am waiting for you."

"Me?"

"You are the one who will lead us from this place. You are the one who will begin the dreaming. Then shall I let go that which I have held, so that things may be as they should have been from the beginning."

Skag frowned. "Do not be sure. What if I fail?"

The Old One sighed. "You will not fail. I am weary of waiting. You must not fail. I have dreamed of your victory. I have sung of it. That will help make it so. Then we shall all join in the song and dreams of Getchemandou."

The bogfoke was about to reply, but the Old One turned back to stare at the river. Skag shook his head, also looking to the river. The circles continued to move across the water, some overwhelming others. Skag pursed his lips, thinking that he also was tired of the waiting.

***

Skag and Nammais meandered beneath the apple trees. They were half-heartedly searching the boughs for a few ripe fruit. Each carried a sack, but they had only a half dozen apples between them. It was still peculiar to Skag that tree should bear fruit in all seasons.

"I do not believe the founders have very original dreams," decided the bogfoke, a statement that nearly sent the cornbear into apoplexy. Skag chuckled and continued, "Why apples? Why peaches?"

"Because they love the dreams of Getchemandou," explained Nammais. "They are part of that dream, of the song, and so it stands to reason that their joining in the dreams should reflect that. However, there are places in Ahkomaic that are different from anything in the other world. I have seen them in glimpses, but the spirit-father tells us that those places are not for us, but that when we join the dreams and songs of Getchemandou to build our own world we will have places unlike anything of the other world, or this one."

"It is very confusing," Skag sighed.

"Yes, it is," admitted the cornbear.

The bogfoke's mind was not on apple picking. It had been months since he had entered Ahkomaic. The cornbears had proved to be much like the bogfoke. They sang more than the bogfoke ever had, and with a similar gift of mimicry they needed no musical instruments as some would sing while others created nearly instrumental sounds. But this similarity only reminded him of the danger looming over his own folk. He had been dreaming of them. In his dreams he saw one or more of them calling out to him. He sighed and, looking up into a tree, pointed with his stave.

"There is a ripe one up there," he told Nammais.

The cornbear squinted his eyes, peering hard into the green canopy. "Where? Way up there? How can you possibly see such a thing?"

Skag paused, letting his stave slowly drop. His brow drew into a frown. "I don't know. I didn't see it really.

Somehow I just knew. Would it startle you if I said it was almost as if it had sung to me? Well, yes, of course it would startle you."

Nammais smiled wide, taking Skag's sack. "Enough gathering for you, Skag Bogfoke. It is time for you to leave. This was the last of the signs for which the founding-spirit instructed me to wait."

The cornbear motioned back toward the hamlet. "First, the nunnehi said my folk must accept you. They have. The nunnehi told me that you must accept my folk. You have done so. The nunnehi told me that your sleep will become troubled by dreams. Lo, these past two weeks you call out as if to answer a summons. Lastly, the spirit-father said to me, 'He shall know the ways of wood and world.' So you tell me when it will rain. You speak with the Old One. Now you can sense the presence of a ripe apple!"

"You make it sound much more impressive than it is," protested Skag, but a notion came to him. "Why are your folk so intent on leaving this place?"

Nammais drew up straight, curling his lips and nodding at the sense in that question. He looked over this realm called Ahkomaic with his hands on his hips. "Why indeed? In truth, friend Skag, we do not want to leave. Yet, this is not the place for us, and we are taxing the strength of the founders. They must mold their dream around us and though there may be no malice in us, such a thing is a blemish on their creation. Well, they call Ahkomaic a sub-creation and consider calling it their creation to be near to blasphemy, but still it is plain that we must find a place of our own.

"Surely you have felt the strangeness of Ahkomaic? That feeling that you have stumbled into a place alien to you despite all its beauty? And, even then you and we have seen only that part of this place most fitted to us."

Skag considered this. "The Great Wood is a place removed from the homes of men, but it has been more difficult for us to hide there than it was at the cemetery. How can all the bogfoke and cornbears hope to hide there?"

Nammais gestured to encompass the world around them. "*This* is what is intended. Our time in the Great Wood will be short. We must dream a new realm, forever safe from the grasp of men. Should an army of men descend upon the Weeping Hill and reduce it to nothing with their tools and might, Ahkomaic would be untouched. What we must do is dream of a world born of Getchemandou's song, but removed from the world of men."

The bogfoke arched his eyebrows and scratched his whiskers uncertainly. "All this? That is some task. I can't even think of a way to rid us of the witch, not to mention Amhomag. I suspect they won't like us dreaming a new world in the middle of their domain."

"It does not belong to them," countered the cornbear. "It is of Getchemandou. The founder says we will find a way to overcome Yolande and the dark spirit. In any circumstance, it is now time for you to leave this place."

Skag crossed his arms, tapping his stave against his thigh as he looked at Nammais. "There is only one thing I ask. You must teach your folk the language of Cornbread Jack. They will learn quickly, I think. That is the nature of our folk. My own kith know something of your tongue, but none so well as I do -- perhaps I would have been a coquanon if I had been a cornbear. When the time comes for us to join together, we must be able to understand one another. Who can know the circumstances?"

"Knowledge of language has always been the trade of the coquanon, and our secret. Still, the moment is upon us," Nammais sighed. "It is our humble sacrifice to share that secret. We will just have to learn to fish better."

"Language is the gift of Getchemandou to men," decided Skag suddenly.

"That is so," nodded Nammais. "Our kith never spoke until first we heard the words of humans. It was to be the seed that sent us dreaming into a greater world, but the gift was marred."

"I can assure you that as difficult as it may be," said

Skag. "The language of Cornbread Jack is the most expansive and among the most beautiful of them all."

"Other than sounding like the hissing of snakes, I agree," replied Nammais.

Skag laughed. "The coquanon have barely scratched the surface to the great depths of many words. Indeed, if there is to be a dream time for us, we would do well to reflect on the meanings of words."

Nammais nodded, beginning to realize the enormity of what lay ahead. Then they turned back toward the cornbear village, slowly and pensively into the fate that awaited them.

TEN

AMHOMAG

The light was golden around Skag as he sat cross-legged beneath the veil of green-gold willow branches. Outside that veil sat nearly two dozen of the eldest cornbears in Ahkomaic. They had been singing quietly, nearly a whispered chant.

The bogfoke had let go into the song, allowing his intuition to absorb the power of it. The spirit-father and the willow-nunnehi had been singing as well, but now Sloe-nunnehi sang out of the song and began speaking to him, "The time has come for your naming. Always shall you be Skag, but also shall you be that which defines you in spirit. You shall be called *Narak*, the cedar. That was your first and truest name, before the great crime of Daugth. As Narak-Skag you shall go from this place."

Her long fingers touched his forehead with water from the pool. As she did so, she began to sing back into the greater song, even as the Mankatoh-nunnehi sang himself out of it and began speaking to Narak-Skag, "Now you understand the singing. You know how we join into the song of Getchemandou and begin our own singing. We can make only from what Getchemandou has formed. To try otherwise is to become that which Amhomag has become.

"When you begin the song, we will be near in a way you cannot understand, unseen we may be, but overlaying your sub-creation, as Getchemandou overlays this world of ours. We are nearing the day when we shall be wedded more completely with the Song of Getchemandou. So it will be with your world in another time. So it will be with every world created with the Song of Getchemandou."

Narak-Skag opened his eyes, understanding. "This dreaming, it is *thought,* and the singing is the doing. The singing is to the dreaming what speaking is to thought. It transfers the dreaming between us."

The nunnehi nodded. "So it has been since the beginning. The song is what binds us. In the end, we shall all be as one, and yet still as many. The understanding of that will elude us until it *is.*

"Now, rise, Narak-Skag and the coquanon will take you back to the *Singing* Hill, for it weeps no more. The song of the elders will go with you. It will be in your mind, and in your spirit."

Nammais came forward to embrace the bogfoke, whispering in his ear, "Now is the day that the glory begins."

Sloe-nunnehi sang herself from the flow of the song and spoke again, "We will be with you always, my son, in the song. Know also that time in this place is different, being closer to the timelessness of Getchemandou. So when you step into the Great Wood, there will not have been months that have passed, perhaps only days or weeks.

"We will be sending our song to strengthen you. In the end we shall, all created things, be with one another again."

Nammais took Narak-Skag by the arm and led him through the green-gold fronds, past the singing elders, and into the twilight world of Ahkomaic. Then they made their way through the song toward the hill that wept no more.

***

Skag felt himself pushing beyond the gate of Ahkomaic. The wards of Yolande and Amhomag set to keep anything from coming out of the Weeping Hill could not withstand the surge of the song that flowed from Ahkomaic. Suddenly the bindings failed and Skag stumbled into the Great Wood.

The tree trunks stood stark, quickly disappearing in the thick mist that filled the forest aisles. The bogfoke's whiskers bristled and the cold drove deep into his heart. Something was wrong here. From the wood around him he could sense it was early autumn, and midday. Why then so dim and cold?

He felt the unease of the forest around him. This part of the wood had gone dormant, as if withdrawing from the malignancy that haunted its aisles. Skag watched the mists swirling and congealing thicker around him. Already the form of the Weeping Hill was being obscured. The bogfoke used the stave to feel his way through the fog and struck out toward the west.

His progress was slow as he tried to keep a straight line. He realized the path had turned northward when he came upon the waters of the lake spreading before him. The sky was masked by a thin overcast, but the lake was free of the forest mist. The water was calm and gray, appearing nearly as dormant as the trees that marched to its edge.

The air was fresher, however, and the bogfoke felt less claustrophobic along the shoreline. He began to follow that line as a guide westward toward the barrow. The lay of the land forced him away from the water on occasion, and the mist would rush greedily over him like a gray shroud. Skag couldn't deny the cold fear, and he struggled back to the lake as quickly as possible.

He had stumbled along for perhaps two miles when a sharp sense of alarm cut through his thoughts. He realized that his fear had begun to cloud his mind. He pulled himself up and took a deep breath of air and exhaled it slowly. He concentrated on allowing the awareness of the song from Ahkomaic to flow again in his mind.

He reached with his thoughts toward whatever had alarmed him. Something was nearby, in the wood. He took a few cautious steps and felt the tension flowing from whatever was out there. It was stalking him. He could sense its confusion, and its frustration at the blinding mist.

With as much stealth as he could muster, Skag continued working his way along the shoreline. He tried to keep the vague tendrils of awareness upon whatever was following. Occasional bursts of insight came to him as he felt the pursuer's consternation. It was finding him a difficult prey.

There was something else, as well. There was a sense of suspicion. He was not what it had expected and there came a tingle of excitement as the search intensified. For all the uncertainty the pursuer felt, it was pulled along by a powerful compulsion and none of Skag's efforts at mimicry had any effect.

Skag pulled up ankle deep in the water, studying the skeletal forms of the trees. Something was familiar here. He thought perhaps he was nearing the wood around Remus Wolfe's dwelling. He nodded to himself. This part of the wood had indeed known the hands of men. It had to be part of the old homestead. Somewhere, in the wood behind his pursuer came steadily on.

That it might be Scarred-cheek haunted him. Yet, he knew the man would have had to of recovered much of his strength and wits for Skag to receive such an intense impression filtering into his head. He decided the best bet was to angle deeper into the wood and to seek help from the man-wolf. Skag smiled grimly because this would be tricky business to reach the old farm house without becoming lost in the mist.

He felt out with his senses once again for any sign of his pursuer. Whatever it was had wised up and was following the edge of the lake. It was either an adept tracker or just taking the easiest route. Skag turned from the water and headed toward the farmhouse.

The mist lightened as his progress lengthened. He was relieved on the one hand that the power of the mist seemed lessened, but alarmed that the gap between him and whatever was following had narrowed. He also sensed a heightened tension from the pursuer as he drew nearer the farmhouse.

The gap narrowed more. Skag was running between the trees, hoping that he was headed in the right direction. That which followed moved with easy speed, and faster than Scarred-Cheek could have run in his prime. It did the bogfoke no good to be evasive because the undergrowth was too sparse.

At last Skag saw the hunched, vine-tangled form of the farmhouse. He scrambled beneath the tumbled porch roof, but found his way blocked by a newly fallen timber. He backed against the rotting clapboards and peered across the mist-swirled homestead. The pursuer was near and Skag could sense burning anger from it.

He heard footsteps from his right, beyond the periphery of his vision. His grip tensed on the cedar stave. The footfalls sounded closer and then from the forest aisle to his left there came another sound. Skag's heart leapt in hope that it might be Remus Wolfe. His pursuer surged toward the new presence.

Skag caught a glimpse of booted feet and knew that now was his chance. He shoved the stave forward. He heard the sound of someone falling heavily to the ground. Then he darted from his shelter with stave raised high for a quick strike. Above the sound of the falling man, the bogfoke shouted, "Here, Remus! I've got him here! It's me, Skag! Help me--"

The words choked off and Skag shifted his swing so that the stave struck into the ground. Green eyes glared in bewilderment at the bogfoke. Then a slight smile touched the lips set amidst the narrow features.

"A case of mistaken identity, it would seem," chuckled Remus Wolfe as he shifted himself onto his elbows. "I've been chasing what I thought to surely be one of Yolande's creatures, and it turns out to be the long lost Skag!"

The bogfoke rolled his eyes and stepped back from the sprawled man-wolf. "And I have been fleeing what I thought must surely be one of the witch's underlings, but it turns out to be the very man I was seeking."

"What is going on here?" asked Skag as he gestured toward the misted wood.

"To begin with, you are supposed to be dead," replied Remus Wolfe as he climbed to his feet. "Where have you been? There is something very different about you. Your presence triggered the wolf senses, but somehow you didn't feel so much dangerous as simply alien."

"I'm sorry to disappoint concerning my proof of mortality," snorted Skag, but then his expression turned serious. "What has happened to me is a long story. Months long in my experience, though only weeks by yours, but what of my folk?"

Now it was Remus who became somber, "They are well enough, given all the circumstances. You would have been proud of them. However, I fear that Welken has been mortally wounded. Mother Crabba keeps him clinging to life against all the odds, but her skills cannot hold him much longer. He may already have passed from this life. I haven't seen them for two days."

"How did such a thing come about," asked Skag in a whisper.

"There was a confrontation with Father Daugth," the man-wolf sighed as he put his arm around Skag. "Come inside, it's drier and warmer. We have much to discuss it would seem."

The bogfoke followed him into the comfort of the kitchen. They seated themselves close to the cook stove after Remus had stoked the dying fire. The man-wolf looked around the room and Skag guessed they were sharing a reminiscence of their first meeting. Remus cast his gaze to the floorboards. "There is something else, a most curious thing. There was a confrontation between Yolande and Stump. The witch's men set ax to the troll."

Skag nodded. "I feared such would happen. He was a good friend, as good as ever I have known. Something of me has surely died with him."

Remus Wolfe looked up, brow furrowed. "He is not dead, not exactly. Yolande tried to stop the blow that felled him. Surely his flesh is dead, fallen like a tree before the barrow. But, that is when all *this* started. The woodland was thrown into a chaotic storm, a storm of leaf, limb, and a rippling earth that drove Yolande and her men into retreat."

Remus shook his head in wonder. "I believe the blow that felled him released his spirit from its binding. I do not think he is so powerful as he was before the binding, but he still influences the forest."

"What of all this mist?" asked Skag.

"The work of Yolande, I'd guess," replied Remus Wolfe. "I think she is trying to subdue or at least counter the release of the lord of the lake-wood. It ebbs and flows as if forming the indistinct line of a battle. The greater part of the lake-wood is free of it, but I fear for you if she has so much power. Even over the lake-wood the sky is obscured by the mist, for all that the aisles are clear of it."

"She has access to such power," the bogfoke sighed. "It is as grim a portent for her soul as it is for our safety."

Remus Wolfe leaned forward with characteristic intensity in his eyes. "How do you know this? Where have you been? We thought you taken by a dog."

"And so I was," replied Skag quietly. "I was taken by a dog named Ralph. I have been with a woman named Nannela Walker. I have been a captive of Yolande. I have been hiding in the Weeping Hill. Though, it weeps no more."

"You have done so little?" asked the incredulous Remus. "Has Nannela sided with Yolande? Did she turn you over to the witch?"

"You should know better," the bogfoke scolded. "She will never hate Yolande; for all that she hates what her grandchild has become. I fell into the witch's hands when I tried to return to the Great Wood."

"When your tracks ended at the field, I couldn't help but harbor some hope that you might have found refuge with Nannela Walker," explained Remus Wolfe. "But then, what

Daugth told of you to the other bogfoke seemed to end all hope."

Skag pursed his lips a moment before speaking, "Father Daugth was a liar. He became, in the end, nothing more than a lie himself."

"Did mother Walker speak to you of Yolande and me?"

Skag nodded. "She told me much. She is not without some bitterness, but wise enough to know that the judging of such things is not for her."

"Much of what passed is my fault, "Remus sighed. "I had a little shop where I mended nets and sold bits of tackle. It wasn't much but it was a living. I could have made more money by moving to a larger town, but I was tired of people and perhaps a little afraid of competition. It was hard on Yolande because most all the folk of the village were white and most all the folk of the village looked down their noses at her on account of her being of mixed race.

"A strange thing about my people, Skag. It was mostly the *good folk* that were the worst. The gamblers and drinkers didn't seem to mind so much the color of her skin.

"She complained one day about how little money we had. I think she thought money would fix everything. She intimated that I shouldn't be so lazy and such as that. So I snapped back as how I was the one actually earning a living.

"So she asked me for a corner of the shop to use, and she began to sell good luck tokens that she would craft. None of those so called good folk would buy 'em from her, but they'd buy 'em from the less good folk that would. That's how it all started, all the charms and hexes and curses. We don't, any of us, know what sting our words might inflict, or what wounds they might open."

Remus shook his head, dispelling the memories as he looked over to Skag. "How did you win free of Yolande?"

"Nannela Wolfe," sighed the bogfoke. The man-wolf's gaze was suddenly distant. "A courageous girl is your daughter. I had thought Jeremiah Simms the bravest soul

I had ever known until I met your Nan."

"It breaks my heart," said Remus in a fading whisper. "I lie awake at night and think of them, my children. It is like trying to sleep with a great weight pressing upon my chest and stealing my breath. Did you see Owen?"

"Oh, yes. He is learning well from his sister. They are safe, for a time, but I do fear for them when the blackness upon Yolande's soul is complete."

"Then I shall take them from her, or die in the trying," snarled Remus Wolfe. "Maybe Nannela Walker will care for them."

"If we cannot stop the darkness upon Yolande, then I doubt any place will be safe for your children."

"You know much of such things now," noted Remus Wolfe as the anger faded into resignation upon his face.

"I learned many things within the Weeping Hill," explained Skag. "Most importantly, I learned hope. I cannot speak of that now. I must go to the barrow."

"I'll go with you," said Remus Wolfe. "There was that noise we heard earlier."

"What do you suppose it was?" asked Skag as they were leaving the house.

Standing in the clearing outside the house, Remus Wolfe looked through the gloomy forest aisles. He shrugged at Skag's question. "Who can know? Perhaps an animal, though most of the large ones are only outside the ward now. It could also have been one of Yolande's spies, or very possibly, Jake Collanmore. He's been haunting the wood like a wandering ghost. The forest is crawling with such creatures, human and otherwise."

"The mist doesn't seem so thick here," observed Skag.

Remus had chosen a path and was leading the way toward the barrow. "It isn't so thick wherever the presence of that which was Stump asserts itself. The clear area forms a narrow crescent stretching from here to the northern shore."

"She is spreading the realm of Amhomag," muttered

Skag as he studied the mist. "This is a far more tangible power than I'd have thought possible of the dark one."

"I know that name," replied Remus Wolfe. He was frowning, trying to recollect the memory. "Yolande has used it before; when she was going on the way she sometimes did about old superstitions."

"It is more than superstition," asserted Skag "It is Amhomag that gives Yolande her power. It is Amhomag that she allows to twist her soul."

Remus Wolfe nodded but did not reply. The gloom of the forest reflected in his eyes. Both man and bogfoke held to themselves as they tramped westward toward the barrow.

***

As they crossed the spreading marshes Skag felt his skin crawling at the sight of what lay before them. The marsh reached beyond the hold of that which had been Stump and the mist rose like a gray wall stretching to a heavy overcast.

The fog curled tendrils through the aisles of the lake-wood but they would soon recoil or fade into nothing. Skag sensed the tension and the watchful anger of the forest. He knew some part of this to be illusion, but not such as ever he would have thought possible. The gloom of the descending evening replaced that of the mist as Skag and Remus sloshed past the clumps of marsh grass.

The cypress swamp rose ahead and a feeling of recognition washed over the bogfoke. There was something here that he knew. He smiled. Stump. Certainly the grim foreboding of the misted wood was vanquished by the staunch defiance emanating from the cypress wood.

They paused beside Stump's burrow. Skag smiled again, feeling that somehow the old troll had out smarted Yolande in the end. If Remus Wolfe wondered at the smile, he said nothing. The cedar-bearer turned away, anxious now for the last stretch to be covered.

A natural dark was filling the wood, but it was much warmer without the clinging mist. A few dark forms moved high above the lake-wood but none of the birds descended.

Skag felt sure they were Yolande's spies. The lake-wood was strangely quiet. He supposed that the spirit that was the lord of the lake-wood kept Yolande's creatures at bay, while others had probably fled the pending confrontation.

Something stirred in Skag's musings. Something was wedged in the feel of the lake-wood. Skag slowed, trying to concentrate but unable to define what he sensed. Remus Wolfe drew to a halt, with his green eyes glowing in the forest shadows. "What is it, Skag?"

The bogfoke shrugged. "I cannot be sure. There is something watching us."

He turned to his left even as a clump of wax myrtle was drawn apart. Slignan stepped from the shroud of leaves and his dark eyes glittered as they locked on Skag. The hatchet-bearer was wary and his blade was poised defensively.

"Can this be?"

Skag smiled and nodded. "Indeed it can be, ol' black-heart."

Slignan looked at Remus Wolfe who was also nodding. An unsure smile crept beneath the crooked nose. Then the hatchet-bearer reached out for a friend he had thought forever lost. The bogfoke embraced, with Slignan rocking Skag in his arms, and Skag muttering that he should be careful with the hatchet.

Skag managed to pull away. Slignan sheepishly hung the hatchet on his belt. It occurred to Skag that he couldn't remember ever having been moved to embrace another bogfoke. Stirred by this revelation he reached out and hugged the hatchet-bearer again for good measure.

They started laughing, while Remus Wolfe stood patiently with arms folded. Slignan looked as if he thought the cedar-bearer was an illusion that might fade suddenly from the world and his hand squeezed Skag's arm, testing the reality of what his eyes saw.

"Where have you been? Look at how you're dressed! We must get you to the others," declared Slignan. "I begin to think the world as full of wonder as it is of grim despair."

"Perhaps it is, indeed," laughed Remus Wolfe. "Certainly there was a time when I'd have never thought to be standing, with a curse upon me, whilst two bogfoke embraced one another and rambled on and on in their wordy way. Come! I'd reckon it is time we let the others in on this, or they're not likely to forgive us."

They covered the short distance quickly and the other bogfoke swarmed around Skag when he stepped into the clearing around the barrow. Grinning faces and back slapping blended into a flood of questions. But Skag noticed that Mother Crabba stood away from the others, looking at him from the doorway of the barrow. Her eyes were wide, seeing more than just the return of a lost bogfoke.

When the others noticed Skag gazing toward the barrow their exuberance faded. The cedar-bearer walked to the entry without taking his eyes from the Mother's face. The ancient bogfoke straightened her wig with nervous hands as he approached.

"I see it. I see it upon you. I see it in your eyes," she rasped as her own gaze sought out memories she had nearly buried forever. "The aura of the other-world is upon you, but you are bringing back the pain and the sorrow."

Skag took her fat hands in his and squeezed them as he whispered, "The hope, Mother Crabba, also the hope."

The Mother's eyes filled with tears and they flowed down her cheek, dampening the strands of her moss-wig. Skag looked past her into the barrow. "Welken?"

Mother Crabba turned. The glow of the fire within the barrow filled her misted eyes. "He is nearly gone. He did a brave thing. I wish you could have seen it Skag. I wish you could have seen the standing of Welken, but now he is lost to us."

Skag slid by her. The fire burned low and the light it cast was faint at the edges of the barrow, lost in the smoke clinging among the rafters. On a bed of moss and dried grasses lay Welken. The sight of him caused Skag to pause. The grinning and jovial Welken was now little more than a shriveled hide stretched thin over a skeletal frame. Weart sat hunched beside Welken. His presence provided a grim comparison to his womb brother's decline.

"Skag," whispered the grieving bogfoke. His expression looked as if he were talking to a wistful dream, "You have come back to us. Did you see Welken whilst you were gone? Will he be returning to us also?"

"Weart is half delirious," explained Crabba in a whisper. "He won't eat and has not slept since his brother's wounding."

Skag placed his cedar stave beside Welken and squatted so he could look into Weart's eyes. He put his hand on the other bogfoke's shoulders. "Welken is lost to us for a time. There is something I must do. He must be released, but I ask you to trust me, Weart. I cannot bring him to us, but in time perhaps I can lead us to *him*."

Weart's eyes began to clear and grew wide with wonder as he asked, "How is it that you speak to my heart, Skag? I trust you to do what you must."

Skag turned then toward Welken. He went to his knees, bending over the stricken form. He put his hand on the dying bogfoke's forehead. He began to quietly chant a song older than even the memory of the bogfoke as he closed his eyes, searching.

So distant, but he recognized the feel of the spirit immediately. A sad smile appeared on Skag's face. Welken was frightened, but he was not alone. The cedar-bearer spoke softly into the fallen bogfoke's ear, "I must leave you for a time, my friend, but you are not alone. The lord of the lake-wood is here. You can feel his presence, do not fear it. There are others too, sparkling and glowing like stars and you need not fear the darkness.

"This flesh can no longer serve you and binds you overlong to this world of misery. Let go now Welken, your standing has served your folk. Go to those who wait. You can move beyond the dark and part the veil. Let he who was Stump guide you."

Skag opened his eyes and slowly removed his hand from Welken's forehead. The wounded bogfoke's chest rose and then expelled as a sigh its last breath. Death long denied settled softly upon the battered flesh.

Skag took up his stave and helped Weart to stand, "Long will we sing of the Standing of Welken."

Mother Crabba stepped forward, enveloping Weart in her flabby arms. He buried his face into her shoulder, weeping. The cedar-bearer looked to the others as they crowded the doorway.

"Where did you bury Stump?

"Here," replied Gristel, motioning for him to follow.

She led him to a mound just outside the barrow. A thin covering of pine needles had already fallen upon the soil. Skag stood over the grave reflecting upon his lost friend.

"We had to bury him where he fell," explained Gristel. "His feet were rooted into the soil, and his flesh was like wood. We couldn't move him."

Skag nodded. "This will do fine. It is fitting that we should place that which was Welken beside him. They are together now."

"For a time, you have said," whispered Gristel

Skag looked at her with his eyes glittering. "I must rest for the night. On the morrow I shall confront the witch and the darkness that strengthens her."

"Rest then," said Robbis as he came up to them. "We will put Welken to his rest."

Skag shook his head. "It was I who released him from his flesh. I can help that flesh to its rest. We must do it soon, for that which was a bogfoke returns quickly and utterly to the earth. Then there are things I must explain to you. I will have time to rest later. The witch won't be leaving anytime soon."

They turned toward the barrow. Remus Wolfe stood nearby and called to Skag, "I shall come with you on the morrow. Ol' Stump, he sings to me in my dreams. He sings to me of atonement."

Skag looked for a moment at the man-wolf. Shadows that only the cedar-bearer could see swirled around the man, but from within him was the glowing aura of the other-world. Skag nodded to his friend, for he sensed that Remus was destined to stand beside him in whatever may come.

Remus Wolfe began raking away pine straw from the earth beside Stump's mound. All the bogfoke joined in the task. Skag began to sing of the standing of Welken and the release of the lord of the lake-wood. Soon all the other bogfoke were chanting the song with him as the voice of their folk was raised from their memory.

Around them, however, the forest was unnaturally quiet, waiting for a storm beyond the understanding of nature.

***

The wind had risen with the sun. Skag stood by the lake watching the wind rout the mist from the wood. Remus Wolfe was with him, watching it all with a grim expression.

"I'd reckon it won't be so easy as all that, Skag."

The bogfoke shook his head. "No, but it will be easier *because* of all that. The dreaming spirit of the city is assaulting Amhomag. It is singing the Great Song of Getchemandou and the dark spirit retreats."

Then Skag shrugged as he folded his arms before continuing, "But she cannot root him out from his dark wood. It is you and I, flesh and blood creatures of the Great Song, who must do that thing, or perish from this world in the trying.

"It is a good sign, however. The witch has shown the power to manipulate the weather, but something has weakened her."

"Stump has happened," guessed Remus Wolfe as he looked over the forest.

"Yes," nodded Skag. "The lord of the lake-wood has risen fierce against the great lie."

The mist clung in peculiar tendrils to those forest aisles most thickly choked by undergrowth, but the wind was like an insistent terrier rooting out rats from a tumble of stones. It was a chilling thing to watch, this unnatural hunt. Juniper and myrtle trembled seemingly of their own volition as they shook off the remnants of the fog.

"It is time we began," said Skag.

They walked back along the trail to the barrow. A second mound had been raised beside that of Stump. Wild flowers had been strewn upon the newly raised earth. Skag stood for a moment surveying the scene. He smiled softly. Usually the bogfoke didn't care much about flowers, but Welken had been different. Skag remembered that even in the cemetery Welken would sometimes sit and stare at the funeral wreaths. Welken and Weart had always shared an affinity for such things. They had coaxed the corn and potatoes from the forest soil.

The cedar-bearer turned toward his kith and kin as they sat clustered around the barrow entrance. Their faces were eager, sensing that at last their fate was to be decided one way or another.

"I will go now to seek the heart of Amhomag," explained Skag. "Robbis shall come with me, if he will. He is the tracker and his skills will help me greatly."

"He wills it," replied the tracker with a nod.

Slignan fidgeted. "Mightn't cold steel be of help?"

Skag gazed into those dark eyes. The blackness was gone from Slignan's soul. Now he was protective and determined. Skag smiled proudly before replying, "You are the hatchet-bearer. You are the warrior. Your cold steel is nothing to Amhomag, but it is much to the witch's men. You must stay with the others so that your steel is between them and the servants of Yolande."

Slignan's shoulders slumped a little, but he nodded. Skag shifted his gaze to the others. "When noon has come you must make for the Weeping Hill. Follow the lake's edge to the south and east. The Mother has the sight, when you are close she will find it. Should I not return, perhaps the nunnehi will shelter you in Ahkomaic. If we three are successful and the cornbears emerge from the hill you must lead them here. All of you must return here as quickly as possible."

"And then?" asked Gristel.

"Then? Then we shall *see*," promised Skag. He motioned for Robbis to come along. The two bogfoke fell into place behind Remus Wolfe as he led them down the forest trail.

They were moving past the cypress knees near Stump's burrow when Skag turned to Remus Wolfe. "We must get south of the lake, near the source of Taterbarge creek. It is there we will find the lair of Amhomag."

"The willow swamp," replied the man-wolf. "A dreary enough place for such evil, I would reckon."

"The nunnehi told me that it was in the most dismal portion of the Great Wood," explained Skag. "Amhomag will sense our intent and it will beckon Yolande. They will be formidable together, but they might also be the weakness of one another."

"I suspect they hate one another as much as they hate everything else," Remus sighed. "I've only ever skirted the willow swamp. I won't be much help to you when we enter."

Skag smiled and said, "That is why we have Robbis with us."

They trudged then across the great expanse of marsh in silence. The wall of mist had been torn ragged by the wind and sun. The forest around them was completely free of the mist, but still it managed to rise with some solidity beyond the lake-wood.

Remus Wolfe led the way. This was his realm and he was barely challenged herein by the witch herself. As he stared ahead along the forest path his gaze took in more than splashes of sunlight and gray trunks. The glow of memory filled his eyes as he sighed, "We are bringing this to a head, to an ending."

Skag nodded as they passed onward along the curve of the lake. "The ending of one thing might be the beginning of another."

The sun was over half way to the noon hour when they reached the homestead of Remus Wolfe. The man-wolf fetched apples, nuts and cool well water.

As they continued on, the sun was burning fiercely at the mist. They were not so far from the Weeping Hill now, and Skag could feel the song of Ahkomaic. The same call he was sure would reach Mother Crabba.

"We might as well cut to the south now," suggested Remus Wolfe with a tug of regret at leaving the fresh breeze from off the lake. "The willow swamp is within the ward so the going shouldn't be too bad. If we go any further along the lake shore we'll likely run into some of her men."

"It is important that I confront Amhomag before I deal with Yolande," replied Skag, though he spoke from intuition rather than any plan of his.

They took a southerly trail. The path began to descend and become soggy beneath their feet. By mid-afternoon they were in the midst of a pocosin swamp, slogging along beneath towering cypress trees draped in Spanish moss. The air had become dreadfully still.

"This is dismal enough for me," muttered Robbis as they made their way through ankle deep water that flooded the lower stretch of land.

"It doesn't smell that good, either," allowed Remus Wolfe. "But at least it might be so stagnant that even water mocs and gators won't want any part of it."

"You say the willow swamp is worse than this?" asked Skag as he looked down at the green scum floating on the water.

"I don't know how bad it gets in there," replied the man-wolf. "But the edges of it are bad enough. I'd say there's no more water, but the willows grow so close that it seems even more tight and airless."

The swamp suddenly began to give way to a rise in the land. Tall pines and oaks rose around them. There was very little undergrowth. Late afternoon light filtered through the leaves in patches that shone on the rusty colored leaf mold.

"This is the deer-wood," Remus Wolfe informed them. "It about the only place left within the ward with a sizable herd. It's the deer that keep down the undergrowth. Too many of them confined in here by ward and swamp, I reckon.

"This rise stretches in a crescent about eight miles or so. The water drains off this more abrupt edge to form the pocosin swamp we passed through, but the larger part of it drains along a more gradual slope into the willow swamp. The swamp drains into Taterbarge creek. So much as it drains at all."

"Eight miles?" mused Skag.

"That's the length of it," replied Remus. "It is only four, maybe five miles wide. We'll be cutting across the width to get to the swamp."

"Still, four or five miles," said Skag. His whiskered face showed his dismay. "This is taking us longer than I'd thought. I don't relish facing Amhomag at night. Though, I suppose it makes little difference in reality."

"Day is dark enough in the willow swamp," said the man-wolf. "Couldn't we wait until the morning?"

"Perhaps, but if Amhomag has already some sense of our approach I don't think waiting is wise," replied the cedar-bearer. "I wouldn't want Yolande and her men to fall upon us in the night while we rested."

"We can make torches," suggested Robbis. "Kribble and I have become very good at it."

Remus Wolfe chuckled. "If worse comes to worse, we can just burn down Amhomag's swamp."

"I would not make light of Amhomag," cautioned Skag as he surveyed the open forest they were passing through. "At least this last stretch should be fast and easy, as open as it is."

"We'll head off toward the southeast," suggested Remus. "If my memory serves, that's the narrowest part of this high land."

It took them less than three hours to reach the edge of the willow swamp. The sun had sunk beneath the western trees but they still had several hours of twilight before the dark of night would become absolute.

The willows were lean, scraggly things with branches entwined with one another like a net. The ground wasn't as waterlogged as the pocosin had been, but the web-like lacing of willow fronds brought premature gloom, and the twisting roots of the willows made footing uncertain.

Skag stood at the edge of this darkness while Remus Wolfe and Robbis fashioned torches. He could feel the malignancy of Amhomag in this place. The oppression was powerful and stirred claustrophobic emotions. The sins of Amhomag threatened to smother the bogfoke's hope and courage.

Then a slight breeze stirred, pushing into the dark willow wood. Even that bit of moving air reminded Skag that they were not alone in this endeavor. He felt a hand on his shoulder, causing him to start. It was Remus Wolfe, looking down on him with green eyes glittering. "Come, friend Skag. For good or ill, it is time we got on with the deed."

Each of them carried a torch but they lit only the one that Robbis carried. The tracker carefully began picking a passage through the gloom of the swamp. The place stretched before them like a skeletal cathedral and there was only the sound of their own movement. No wind stirred now, no birds sang before the coming of the night and no animals scurried in the shadows.

"This is difficult," muttered Robbis with his voice hushed into a whisper by the weight of the silence around them. Little in the way of undergrowth was evident but the willows crowded close upon one another and their tangled fronds draped toward the earth.

The feel of Amhomag was everywhere. It was choking in the still air and leering through the twisted limbs and gnarled roots. The earth stank of decay. The pools of water were black and devoid of life. Not even insects were to be found and the dark itself was laden with malice.

Skag felt as if he were drowning and staggered beneath the weight of the malevolent presence. He leaned heavily on the cedar stave, but reassured the anxious glances from his companions. The cedar-bearer withdrew from the touch of this place. He drew into himself trying to find the strength to keep one foot following the other.

"What would choose to live in such a place?" hissed Robbis in a whisper.

"That which has no choice," said Skag as quietly and composed as he could manage. "It has become so evil that it is becoming the not-being. Its substance comes from that which it is not. Beware."

"Oh, I am being ware," breathed Remus Wolfe. "I've nearly wet my pants with wareness."

The torch was an imperfect creation and the light spluttered and sparked. The shadows rose and fell in that inconsistent rhythm. The dark shapes loomed in a chaotic dance. Skag was so distracted by his own struggle to avoid the oppression of this place that he failed to notice its effect on his comrades.

Robbis was finding it difficult to concentrate and his gaze drifted to the shadows dancing at the edge of the torchlight. Remus Wolfe lifted wide eyes to the vaulted gray aisles surrounding them, but was unable to free himself of a gnawing dread. They felt as if they had stumbled into an endless hall of despair, or were caught in a dream that flowed in a current removed from that of world they knew.

Locked in the arms of this false dream they stumbled on. Robbis offered hardly a glance at the path beneath his feet. They were being guided instead by the reforming of the darkness around them. Remus Wolfe was sweating despite the cool of the evening now descended in full.

Something cautioned the man-wolf that all this was wrong, but buried deep within his mind the seed of caution was isolated. He continued on in his own personal mist as if the bogfoke existed not at all.

Skag was trying to remember the words of the nunnehi, but every reaching thought in his mind recoiled at the dark dread of this place. Then, suddenly, the cedar-bearer was jolted from his efforts when he walked blindly into the halted form of Remus Wolfe. Skag looked up, and then around. The man-wolf and Robbis both stood motionless. The tracker finally lifted an arm in a motion as if through liquid.

"A house," he whispered. Skag followed the pointing finger. It wasn't much of a house. Clapboard walls and a roof of rusted tin. It was in much better condition than the home of Remus Wolfe, though smaller by a good bit. It was also disjointed somehow, as if fabricated from sections of other dwellings. A glow of light shone past oil-cloth curtains from the lone window.

"Who would live in such a place?" asked Remus in an echo of the question Robbis had asked earlier, but his voice was filled more with marvel than with suspicion.

Amhomag, was the first thought in Skag's mind, but then he remembered that the dark one needed no shelter. Who, indeed? The willows had allowed room for the dwelling and gloom wrapped it like a cloak. Against this, the yellow glow from the window seemed comforting, and beckoning.

"Perhaps they will take us in," suggested Robbis in a whisper. "They might give us directions through this swamp, maybe even food."

"It might be warm inside and we could rest," offered Remus Wolfe despite the sweat beaded on his forehead. The man-wolf and the tracker both began walking toward the house.

"Who would live in such a place?" mused Skag in yet another echo of the tracker's question. He was trying to rouse suspicion within his own mind as much as in his friends. They paid him no heed and he felt himself pulled along by the gravity of their will. The torch flickered and died, bringing the dark close upon them so that only the square of greasy light from the window remained in their eyes.

Remus Wolfe was first to the door and he pushed it open as if expected. Robbis followed him over the threshold and Skag came stumbling behind. The interior was not as bright as the window had promised. The light came from a single lantern burning atop a table set to one side of the room. Something moved within the shadows on the opposite side.

Skag's eyes picked out the movement. For a moment he thought it a nunnehi, but it was far too corpulent. It seemed sexless, but with long hair appearing much like willow fronds and its bulk was firm as if carved from wood.

"Welcome," came the greeting from the shadowed lips. The voice was an elusive echo of whispers knit into one. "Rest yourselves and let go your struggles."

The voice seemed to change as it spoke, as if it were wrapping around their thoughts and seeking that which would touch each of them most. There was a hint of golden liquid in the voice, but the contrast to Sloe roused loathing rather than amity in the bogfoke's heart.

"Who are you?" he demanded of it as his companions moved toward the chairs set around the table.

Eyes glared in the dark for a moment beneath the thick fall of frond-hair. Then a smile. "Many names have I. Names of beauty, and alas, of fear. Call me Babiche, for I am the thong that binds."

Skag remembered the name as a cornbear word. It meant rope, especially when made of eel skin. They considered it strong and sometimes thought of it as symbolizing unbreakable bonds. The cedar-bearer turned back toward the door but found it shut behind him.

"Sit with your companions," suggested Babiche in a voice no longer golden.

Skag found himself walking to the table. Remus Wolfe and Robbis had seated themselves but stared into empty air as if in pursuit of distant thoughts. Skag wondered if the floor was crooked, because a bogfoke and a man shouldn't be sitting at the same level to the table.

He stared hard at his companions and realized they were not at the same height after all. Hadn't they been? This was disjointed, like the house itself. All was a pastiche of images that shifted and changed to whatever awakened in his mind.

A bird was perched in the shadows. At first Skag felt the familiar fear, but this was no crow. The body was too rounded and the postured slouching. Slowly it came to the bogfoke that this bird was a buzzard. It made him think of the cemetery and the despair he had once thought eternal pressed upon him again.

Skag frowned, thinking this had to be the work of that which he had sought, but the name for it could not be summoned. He saw Babiche set a pot upon the middle of the table. Thick fingers lifted the lid and steam wafted from within but rolled like mist rather than rising like smoke.

"Such a feast as this you'll never have had," Babiche chuckled as it backed away from the table. Suddenly the tangled head tilted and another smile crept across the featureless face. "A storm is rising, do you hear it?"

Skag listened but he heard only the steady breathing of his companions. Remus Wolfe suddenly shone consciousness in his eyes as he turned to Skag, "She is coming. She is the storm. Beloved Yolande who is still in my heart despite all that has passed."

"Are you one of her creatures?" Skag demanded of Babiche.

Irritation flashed across the bland face. Babiche glared with dark eyes for a moment, but then all was calm.

"Or, is she mine?" it asked in return with a voice of cold arrogance.

With the sting of that venom Skag was jolted back.

He closed his eyes. First he heard, indeed, a distant storm, but beyond it, through it, he heard *singing*. They were singing for him, and for his companions. They were reaching to him. Then he knew. He knew.

"I can name you!" cried the bogfoke, fastening his gaze upon that which called itself Babiche. "You are, *Amhomag*. You are without form and bind *nothing*."

Babiche began to grow larger. It grew until it dwarfed even the man-wolf. Staring down from shadowed heights it looked upon Skag. A snarl twisted into a smirk upon the thin lips, "Without form? Where are you now, cedar-bearer? Where are you now? In my house! What do you gaze upon? *Me!* Gaze upon my form, foolish creature. I am with form now, even more so than the accursed city with all her dreams!"

Skag startled even himself with a laugh before declaring, "This is nothing more than a sad imitation of the nunnehi."

His words did not diminish Babiche; instead, its form grew darker. A long arm swept out, gesturing to the darkened corners of the room. In each there sat perched one of the carrion birds and their forms began to alter.

"What is all this?" asked Robbis wearily, as if rising from deep slumber. Remus Wolfe came suddenly to his feet.

"Calmly," urged Skag, realizing that in whatever manner Babiche was manifesting its power it could no longer hold onto the man-wolf or the tracker.

The forms of the buzzards contorted and changed. Wings became arms and talons became feet. The eyes were naught save hollow sockets and the flesh was gray and rotting. The birds of carrion had become grim mockeries of the corpses of men.

Remus Wolfe was filled with terror and cringed as if to back away in all directions at once. The bogfoke were cautious but did not panic. They had lived with the dead of men most of their lives.

Skag slid to his feet and swung at the steaming pot

with his stave. The cedar sent the cast iron kettle crashing onto the bare floorboards. The steam swirled and rolled like a swarm of agitated bees.

"Enough! No more of these illusions," shouted the cedar-bearer. "I can *hear* them. They are coming. The Song of Getchemandou is upon their lips. Your storm cannot hold them back!"

Babiche shrieked in piercing anger. The four corpses trudged across the room. Remus Wolfe pulled his knife and was poised in wild-eyed defiance. Skag laughed.

"And yet you bring more of the same," he shouted as he leapt at the nearest form. Again the cedar darted out. This time there was no contact. There was only a squawk and the frantic flap of wings as the buzzard flew from out of the shadowed illusion.

The bird flew *through* the clapboard wall. Skag's eyebrows arched at the revelation. He strode into the closed door. A chill washed over him and he heard Babiche shriek again. Then there was only the hush of the willow swamp. Robbis and Remus Wolfe staggered as the sudden disappearance of the house disoriented them.

Skag chanced a cautious probe with his senses and he found that although the illusion had been dispersed, the feel of Amhomag still dominated this place. He turned to his friends and warned them, "We have survived but one test."

"You said they are coming," whispered Robbis. "Who is coming, if not Yolande?"

"She is coming, "Remus Wolfe sighed. "I thought I had dreamed it but she is coming."

"Not just Yolande," said Skag as he let his mind reach again through the biting cold malice. "We will not be alone."

"Then why are we here?" muttered Remus. "Why let us come into this place if they can do this deed themselves? These nunnehi, these spirits, why send us?"

Skag considered for a long moment before reaching out to clasp the man-wolf's hand. "*This*, I think, this touch.

The movement of matter sprung from the Song of Getchemandou. I do not know why it should be, but I can sense that it is."

"What was all that?" asked Robbis, gesturing to where the house had once been.

"Just illusion," replied Skag. "The dark spirit was trying to lure us in with images that might comfort us. That is my guess. It was the discordance between the images in a bogfoke's mind and that of a man that disjointed the illusion, and may well have saved us. It is a most fortunate thing that Remus chose to come with us.

"I think Yolande has taught it this trick of material illusion. I'm not sure that Amhomag was even aware that it *was* illusion. If we are fortunate, Babiche will be angry with Yolande. We can hope."

"Divide and conquer," Remus Wolfe grimly surmised. "But, enough of that, where are the torches? It's blasted dark, dank and dreary in this place."

Skag realized that the night had descended in full. Darkness was rarely complete to the eyes of a bogfoke, but even despite his curse, Remus was nearly blinded in this swamp. Robbis fetched the torches from where they'd been dropped. The man-wolf quickly had one alight.

The sputtering illumination drove back the dark, revealing the willows that reached over the small clearing in which they stood. Other than the open ground there was no hint of a house. Remus Wolfe speared the end of the torch into the moist earth.

"What a dismal, dismal place," grumbled the man-wolf as he strolled to the edge of the torchlight.

"It's not so bad as that last bit of swamp," offered Robbis, trying to find a grain of optimism.

"Except for Amhomag," said Skag quietly. The feel of the dark spirit was intensifying around them. The cedar-bearer was trying to not withdraw from the touch of it, but the essence hung like a foul odor. He called to Remus Wolfe and Robbis as they stood at the edge of the light exploring the clearing. "Do not wander. Babiche has been shaken, but it could materialize again and it would be angry. Mostly it works with illusion, but it can manipulate the material world, though the cost to it is great. We are of the material world, and somehow our presence can make a difference."

"Well, I wouldn't step out there into the dark with *your* feet," replied Remus Wolfe with a shudder.

"I think I hear something coming," interrupted Robbis, staring hard into the darkness. "I don't know, my mind is so confused."

"The presence of Amhomag does that," said Skag as he went to stand beside the tracker. "It's as if it warps reality around us."

Skag listened intently for some disruption in the silence of the swamp. There was a sound. With the senses that had awakened in him during his time in Ahkomaic, Skag reached out as much as he dared to probe the night around them. *Yolande.* He could sense the coming of the witch.

"We must put out the torch," said Skag. Remus Wolfe and Robbis looked at him as though he were mad. The cedar-bearer nodded to affirm his intention. "Yolande is coming."

"Surely she knows we are here," Robbis pointed out.

Remus Wolfe was quick to agree with the tracker. "She is not without senses beyond sight. And the dark one will have revealed us."

"I do not intend to avoid confrontation, or we would not be here," replied Skag. "Be ready to relight the torch at my signal. For now, we will wait at the far edge of the clearing."

"Well, if you prefer the dramatic," relented the man-wolf as he extinguished the torch. "Just make the signal something I can hear because I can't see a thing in this dark. Some help please, so I don't wander into the swamp."

"Careful now," exclaimed Remus Wolfe as Robbis

chuckled and took him by the hand to lead him to the edge of the clearing. "It occurs to me that you bogfoke have a peculiar sense of humor."

"But without malice," insisted Robbis, though his reply only brought a skeptical grunt from Remus Wolfe.

"Hush," whispered Skag.

Skag heard the distant noise drawing closer. Robbis nudged him with an elbow and gestured toward an equally distant point of light. In a few minutes they could see the form of Yolande. She had with her two of her men and their eyes showed great unease as they moved through the dank vault of willow branches.

Remus Wolfe stirred, but Skag's hand upon his arm settled him. The beam of light from the lantern was soon bouncing against the trees of the clearing. Yolande slowed her pace and approached the glade cautiously.

"Babiche? Babiche?" she called. Only the silence answered. She walked hesitantly into the clearing. "Babiche, where are you?"

Skag felt the spirit of Amhomag flowing and concentrating in the middle of the glade. The lantern's glow showed a dark mist roiling where once the house of Babiche had stood.

Yolande cocked her head to one side and spread her hands as if she did not understand. "If you have no form, then it is of your doing, Amhomag."

Her men started at hearing her answer an accusation they had never heard. The one called Silas limped forward a bit and started to speak but then thought better of it. The second man stood confused and tense beside him.

Skag smiled at the confusion. He knew that Yolande was conversing with Amhomag. She was trying to cajole it back into the chimera that called itself Babiche.

"Amhomag! You have let one of the small ones deceive you and take from you your form."

The mist congealed and darkened into a vaguely

human form. Yolande walked cautiously toward it. Her men did not. The witch was smiling and holding out her hands as though to a repentant child. "Come back, Babiche. I will restore your house."

The mist merged into something resembling Babiche. The sight of it was enough to send the witch's men back a few paces. A movement from Yolande's hand froze them where they were. The chimera's eyes were black and angry. The frond-like hair trembled as the shadowed form gestured around the clearing.

"House? You? Have you forgotten the source of your witchery?" accused a dark and brooding voice that came from all around them as much as from the hulking shadow. Yolande's own eyes glared and she stepped toward Babiche.

"I have forgotten *nothing*," she challenged. "What were you but a defeated, impotent, and brooding spirit when I came across you? Who provided you with sustenance so you could recover your strength? Who gave you form so that you could focus again in this world? And you let a cornbear trick you?"

Skag nudged Remus Wolfe and as the torch flickered to life the cedar-bearer stepped into the clearing.

"It is *bogfoke*," said Skag, shaking his head as if disappointed at Yolande's inability to hold this gem of knowledge. As soon as she saw the bogfoke the witch motioned. The man next to Silas stepped forward but halted at the sight of Remus Wolfe standing behind Skag.

"Man-wolf," smirked Yolande when she saw her husband. Remus Wolfe said nothing. Robbis was still crouched in the shadows cast by torch and lantern light. The vague form of Babiche stood brooding in the middle of the clearing.

"These are the ones who have robbed you," said Yolande, gesturing toward the bogfoke and his companions. The chimera turned toward them.

"Were we?" chuckled Skag. "How can we take what is only illusion? We can only expose an illusion, that

form, crafted by Yolande using your own power, what is it
but a binding? Not unlike the binding she lured the lord of
the lake-wood into taking upon himself. That form is limiting.
It diminishes your power more than it enhances it. Even as it
limited the troll, but now that he has been released the lord
of the lake-wood assails the very boundary of your power."

Skag shrugged then. "But if you desire it so, you had
best deal with us as the witch demands or she might punish
you."

A red light woke in the chimera's eyes. Yolande
gestured angrily. "Will you let this tool of the nunnehi deceive
you yet again?"

"Is Babiche as stupid as that?" asked Skag in mock
surprise. "Listen to her, Babiche. *She* has given you your form.
What are you without her?"

The chimera stamped the ground in rage. Its huge
fists shook in the air as it screamed in a tumult of voices, "I
am Amhomag! I am master!"

Babiche turned back to the witch. "You could not
have given this form but for the power I gave to you. What
were *you*? Save an herb gatherer and concubine to a net
weaver?"

"I have not to answer that!" exploded Yolande. "You,
the mighty Amhomag are letting this creature turn you
against me. You are behaving as if you were a child rather
than one of the great, proud spirits that dared to defy the
tyranny of the first spirit."

The form of Babiche wavered, losing its definition.
Skag stepped closer, chuckling and calling out, "Now you've
done it, Babiche. You've made her angry and she'll take away
your form. This is why she gave to you the shanty of a slave
rather than a great palace."

"Hold your form," hissed Yolande. "Ignore that
creature."

"Do as she says," warned Skag.

A roar shook the earth and set the willows to

trembling. Yolande's men fled into the forest screaming. The form of Babiche dissolved again into a dark roiling mist. The mist swirled toward the witch as she stood glaring at Skag. Like a shadowy shroud it swarmed around Yolande.

Skag began to softly chant the Song of Getchemandou. He knew that Amhomag was much more powerful and unpredictable in his truest form. The dark spirit was in a quandary because it was more focused and able to manipulate the material world in the form of Babiche, but was also diminished in that form and less able to extend its dark will.

"Listen to me, Amhomag," pleaded Yolande. "He has poisoned your thoughts. I know from where my power comes. You are the darkness and the darkness is fear. The fear is strength."

Another step was ventured by the cedar-bearer. He sought Yolande's gaze. The witch glared at him with hatred, but Skag softened his own expression and let go his mocking. He called out softly to her, "You have served Amhomag well, Yolande?"

"I have served *nothing*," spat the witch. Her form was obscured by the mist, but she seemed caught in a powerful wind that touched nowhere else in the glade.

"You have indeed served nothing," replied Skag after a moment of silence. "That is what Amhomag is becoming. Such evil is in the absence from the Song of Getchemandou. Getchemandou is being itself, to choose otherwise is to choose nothing. In the end Amhomag will be as nothing.

"That is your fate too, Yolande. Like Amhomag you cannot abide what you cannot completely possess. But those things that your folk call beauty and love, they cannot be completely possessed. They must be shared. They must be passed from one to another and to all, or they become no longer beauty or no longer love."

The dark coils of shadow flared then, but slipped a little away from off the witch. They moved limply along the earth as if feeling blindly for where the bogfoke stood.

Remus Wolfe and Robbis nervously drew nearer to Skag. The man-wolf looked with alarm at the groping tendrils of shadow. "Skag, we should move from here. How can we contest with that thing?"

The bogfoke looked in a sweeping arc around the clearing. His eyes grew wide as he replied to his companion, "We are not alone. *They* are here! Ah! Remus Wolfe, Robbis, I can see them now, the veil is so thin. They shine like the nunnehi! They are like a multitude of candle flames around us. Some I know. I see Jeremiah Simms among their number. Cornbread Jack! Some I think I know, Nathan Walker? Yes! He glows brighter at his name! I see Sloe of the golden voice, Mankatoh the spirit-father, and a host of other nunnehi. The world beyond is draped now upon this place and both our kindred have come to assail the dark. But I feel so inadequate in their great company. Every imperfection weighs upon me."

Then Skag staggered, driving his cedar stave into the soil to steady himself as he continued to gaze around the clearing. "Behind them, others! They shine like great stars; the lord of the lake-wood is among them, returned now to his proper place in the Great Song. The city of dreams I see! All of them are joined in the Song of Getchemandou."

Then the turning of Skag's head slowed and his eyes grew so wide his friends feared they would burst from his head. The very atmosphere around them seemed to pass in a wave over him. It appeared to Remus and Robbis that the world around them receded from the cedar-bearer so that they thought, for an instant, that he was actually floating mid-air in a fine silvery mist.

Then Skag shouted to them as if across a great distance, "Behind them. Behind them. Oh, such light and my heart aches. I cannot endure—"

Then the cedar-bearer lurched forward and went to his knees. He would have fallen flat upon his face except that he stayed himself with his grasp upon the stave. With his head bowed he spoke in a barely audible whisper, "Getchemandou. Such sweet dread is upon me. How can I endure such beauty? How can I behold such glory?"

His two companions moved to him, and Remus Wolfe squatted beside him to steady him with a hand upon either shoulder. Then it was that Skag looked slowly up to the man-wolf, and Remus nearly fell over backward when he looked into the bogfoke's eyes.

He saw it then, what the bogfoke had seen. It was but a lingering reflection, like a night sky upon a black pool of water. Remus Wolfe's heart and mind were wrenched in the sweetest anguish he could have imagined. He knew that this was only a fading image of what Skag had experienced, and the man-wolf was glad of it, because any more would have been the undoing of him.

The bogfoke used the stave to bring himself shakily to his feet. Then he surveyed the twisting form of Amhomag. It had grown more distinct, but had retreated from them and was coiled around Yolande.

"I am Narak-Skag," said the bogfoke. "Yolande, listen now to me. Around us is our salvation. You have only to reach for it. I cannot imagine what it will cost you to do so, but you must. Amhomag would drag you with it into the emptiness.

"Amhomag has seduced you into its service. All along you thought you were doing what is good. You thought you were helping others. You thought you were punishing a cruel world. Over time, in incremental steps, it lured you into being what you would never have wanted to be.

"That is what the dark one whispers to us. But what the dark one does is to isolate that which is good, to encapsulate what is good and beautiful so that it is no longer good or beautiful."

Narak-Skag stepped even closer. "It has to flow, Yolande, from one to another and to all. We are all flawed as Amhomag is flawed, but none of us are so utterly flawed as are the dark spirits. Because of their nature their choice is set beyond time itself. That is not true for us, we are creatures in time and can change course yet."

Yolande's breast rose and fell in deep breaths. The bogfoke could see the uncertainty in her eyes. He stepped to the very edge of the darkness. He turned around to gesture back to Remus Wolfe.

"What of your husband? You loved him. He loved you. You both still love one another because love can never be unmade. You can only seek to own it in a futile attempt to make it an eternal ornament. But love isn't a thing, is it? You know this Yolande. Love is a doing. It does. It never stops doing. It is an event that never stops unfolding.

"Your children, Yolande; so much you have done for your children. You have thought of them as you once were, powerless in a wicked and dangerous world. I ask you to think of them as you are *now*. Is that what you would have them be? Is this what you wanted to be when first you felt the thrill of the promise of power?

"Would you have your children do what you have done? No, you would not. You would not because you love them, and that love will not allow that you can delude yourself. You will admit the fallacy of what you have done. But do not despair, for your fate is not in your failings alone, but also in the very thing Amhomag used to seduce you, the compassion that he twisted."

Skag felt a presence beside him and looked up to see Remus Wolfe standing beside him. The man looked down at him and softly smiled as he spoke, "My friend, Narak-Skag. I know now why we are here. Why *I* am here."

He held his hand before him in the torch light and turned it so that they could both consider it. "This is why I am here. The other world is joined to us in what we are, *matter*. Now I will give. I will let flow from one to another what I too have shut behind the walls of my will."

With that Remus Wolfe stepped into the dark coils. As if he had passed into a great wind, a shadow seemed to fall from the man to be swept up into the winding coils of Amhomag. Narak-Skag knew then that the curse was ended upon his friend, man-wolf no more.

Remus grasped Yolande's hand in his own. Yolande jolted as if lightning had struck near her. She looked with marvel at the touch, and at the hand. Narak-Skag wondered how long it had been since last she had actually been touched by another person. Her head and her eyes lifted to gaze upon the face of Remus Wolfe.

For the barest moment her face darkened, but then a tear fell along her cheek. Remus brought his other hand up so that it could stroke the tear from her face. "Yolande, my love. Will you forgive me?"

The coils grew tense as Remus Wolfe *gave*. He gave what was both admission, pleading and acceptance. The man and the woman were battered by the spirit wind and leaned into one another for support. Even outside the shadow, the earth trembled. Narak-Skag began to softly chant the Song of Getchemandou as he steadied poor, confused Robbis who was standing to one side of him.

Then a sense of alarm burned through the cedar-bearer. He turned and caught sight of something moving like a flash across the clearing, Scarred-cheek. The bogfoke's heart sank as he felt a surge of dark gloating emanate from the writhing mist. In that moment Narak-Skag saw the emptiness of Amhomag in the crazed man's eyes, and at the same time he saw a knife in the deformed hand and tried to cry out a warning to Remus.

Scarred-cheek burst into the shadow-mist and the knife bit deeply into Remus Wolfe's lower back with an underhand blow. Viciously the clutching hand ripped the blade free and shifted so that it was poised for an overhand strike as he shrieked, "She is *mine*!"

"No!"

It was Yolande who had screamed and she moved swiftly between her husband and the descending blade. The force of the blow was so violent that the knife was buried to the hilt and drove her back against Remus. They both sank to the earth and as they did so the knife slid free.

Scarred-cheek stood stunned above them, looking at

the knife and his own hand, as if it belonged to someone else. Then he looked around in stricken panic and disbelief, "No! No! This is not what you promised! You have lied!"

A wretched sob trailed into a groan from the man's throat. He looked at Yolande as she lay prone against Remus Wolfe who was upon his knees rocking her in his arms. Scarred-cheek's head dropped forward as another groan surged from him, "No. No. No. Oh, Yolande, not this, never was it supposed to be this. Remus, what have I done?"

"What have I done?" repeated Scarred-cheek as he pulled himself straight and stared at the knife and the hand that held it. Almost he spoke, but instead the knife flashed as he drove it into his own chest.

Now it was Remus who groaned; a low, quiet thing of unbearable sadness. He managed to lift his head to look upon Scarred-cheek where he had fallen, "Oh, Jake. No. What fools have we all been, my friend. It should never have been like this. Forgive me my part in our falling."

Now Remus sank from his knees, pulling Yolande closer to him as he lay upon his side on the ground. Narak-Skag could see the blood spreading dark from the wound upon the man's back. Remus managed to lift his gaze to find the bogfoke.

"Where is the shadow, Skag?"

Narak-Skag dropped to his knees a softly said, "It has retreated. You have defeated it. It is slipping into that abyss from which it cannot return. It was such a simple thing to break it, really. Yet we make it cost us so."

"What a cost," sighed Remus, closing his eyes for a moment. Then he opened them, "My children..."

The bogfoke nodded. "I understand. I know what must be done, and I promise you that I shall do it."

"I will miss you," decided Remus. "But at least I die with Yolande in my arms. Both of us loved. I suppose that is as near complete an ending that a man such as I have been could have hoped for."

"It is not an ending of all things, my friend," replied Narak-Skag.

A puzzled expression passed over Remus Wolfe's face. "Are they still here, Skag? The others?"

Narak-Skag gazed around the clearing, and then he nodded slowly, "Yes. They are fading from my sight now. But still, I can barely stand the beauty of them. My time is not yet."

"My friend?" began Remus in a fading whisper as his strength failed.

"Yes," replied Narak-Skag. He knew what the dying man requested, and he leaned forward so that they could look into one another's eyes. Remus could not speak, but his eyes grew wide. Narak-Skag locked his gaze onto that of Remus Wolfe as life faded from the man. He knew what his friend saw, and that last, fading image of such heart wrenching majesty went with Remus Wolfe into the world beyond.

The cedar-bearer sensed Robbis standing next to him. The tracker seemed dazed, confused and even bemused. He looked at Yolande, Remus and Jake, then after a quick glance at Skag looked around the clearing as he asked, "That thing, that Babiche thing, whatever it was, is gone? Do I have to call you Narak-Skag now?"

"No, Skag is fine," smiled the cedar-bearer. "To you and all the other bogfoke I can always be Skag. And, yes, Babiche is gone."

"Forever?"

"I believe so," replied Skag. "But, there are other dark spirits at work in the world."

The tracker frowned as he considered the dead humans. "So that was all it took? To get Remus and the witch to hold hands? That seems stupid, too good to be true."

Skag sighed as he replied, "It *is* stupid that such a simple thing was so difficult to accomplish. In the end, it cost three lives."

"I just thought that Amhomag thing would be

tougher," said Robbis.

"How tough should it have been?" marveled Skag. "It took centuries to wear Amhomag down to where it needed Yolande. Centuries of bloodshed stretched across the land from the great mountains to the sea.

"What it cost Yolande and Remus even beyond their lives we cannot know. Even then it took an unseen host to drive Amhomag into the abyss. While we struggled here in this clearing, a much greater battle raged in the spirit world around us."

"Speaking of which," shuddered Robbis. "Please don't look into my eyes. I ain't ready for that just yet."

"No, neither was I," Skag sighed.

"Well we have won," decided Robbis as he put his hands upon his hips. Then his brows drew together as he continued, "But you are not finished, are you?"

Skag remembered his kith and he remembered the cornbears. He got to his feet and slipped an arm over Robbis's shoulder. "There is more to do. Return to the barrow. The others should be leaving the Weeping Hill now."

"What about you?"

"I have a promise to keep," Skag replied as he looked at the fallen Remus Wolfe.

"What of them?" asked Robbis looking at the dead.

Skag looked around the clearing. "The lord of the lake-wood will bury them. He will also turn this dreadful place into a beautiful glade. He will cleanse it, and their flesh will rest in beauty until their spirits are rejoined to it in a manner we bogfoke cannot understand."

"Just don't look into my eyes," protested Robbis again, waving his hand between them. "Not after looking around like that!"

"We should go now," chuckled Skag as the ground beneath them began to tremble.

"Ol' Stump has started work, eh?" replied the tracker.

Skag nodded. They left behind the willow swamp,

and arm in arm walked into the dreams of their folk.

ELEVEN

The Cedar And The Founding

Daylight was spreading beneath the forest canopy as Skag approached the edge of Stone's Creek. He moved cautiously from between the trees. He hadn't survived everything just to be done in now by a dog or some lingering servant of Yolande. The light was stronger as he stepped into the open. The village was quiet, with only the song of birds and the sigh of autumnal breezes.

The village was as still and as cool as a tomb. The last of the folk had fled, leaving the place to rot and fade back into the forest. Skag went from house to house searching for the children of Remus and Yolande Wolfe. Most of the dwellings had long been derelict but some showed signs of recent, hasty abandonment. The bogfoke sadly contemplated all those minions of the witch spreading like a puff of dandelion seed into the world outside the warding, each bearing some part of the evil that had fed Amhomag.

He found the witch's house and what must have been the children's bedrooms, but not the children themselves. He hastened to the church, thinking they may have sought refuge there. The building was boarded up so tightly that it defied even a bogfoke entry.

The cedar-bearer wondered if some of the Yolande's underlings might have taken the children as they fled. It seemed unlikely. Yolande had been surrounded by selfish and cowardly followers. He thought it doubtful any of them would have had the compassion or courage to think of the children.

Skag wondered if they could have struck out on their own. Certainly Nan seemed too smart for such a foolhardy venture. He could only stand and wonder, almost ready to give up the search and head for the barrow. Then he thought of something, and his bogfoke smile spread incredulously at his own slow-witted thinking.

He hastened back toward the witch's dwelling. The cluster of storage sheds stood at the edge of the picket fence. The bogfoke made for the one in which he had been held prisoner.

Skag dropped to the ground and squeezed beneath the jagged wall of the out building. The familiar scent of mildew and seed met him as he clambered to his feet. The place looked much as it had when he had been bound within. Rakes, hoes, and spades were stacked haphazardly in one corner, and the feed sacks were piled in the middle of the earthen floor. Nannela and Owen Wolfe were curled atop the sacks. Nan had draped a protective arm around her brother.

The sound of Skag's entrance had stirred her from an uneasy slumber. She shifted so that she leaned on one elbow as her eyes focused and her head cleared itself of cobwebs. Then she saw Skag and her eyes grew wide. "Somehow I knew it would be you. That's why I hid here when everyone started screaming that Mother was dead. They took off running, screaming that a monster was coming up from the willow swamp."

"There will be no monster coming up from the swamp," replied Skag quietly. Owen was awakened by their voices. He pulled himself into a sitting position, but shrank back defensively against his sister. Skag smiled, trying to reassure him, "Your mother and father won't be coming back. I promised your father that I would see that you were made safe. I never had a chance to tell you before, but your father was a good friend to me."

Owen had started crying. Nan wrapped her arms around him and rocked him gently back and forth, but tears fell along her cheeks as well. Skag did not know how to comfort them. He reached out to brush back the long strands of Nan's dark hair from her face as he spoke, "They went away together, Nan. Can you understand that? They were together and the darkness had no hold upon them."

Nan bit her lip and then nodded. "I am glad. Better that, than they should go on thinking they hated one another. They never did, you know. No matter what happened, Mother would never let anyone talk bad about our father around us."

"I think Owen is lucky to have a sister like you," said Skag. "Certainly my heart will rest easier knowing what a strong child you are, and what a fine woman you shall be. I told your father about you. He was real proud of both of you. I could see it shining in his eyes."

Skag took the girl by the hand and helped her to her feet. They each took one of the boy's hands. Then the bogfoke shoved open the door to the shed. "Come along. We've a good bit of a hike waiting for us."

The children gathered some of their belongings into burlap sacks. Skag led them northward away from Stone's creek. The ward of Yolande would not disappear overnight and the bogfoke was forced to lead the children between the marsh and the wood.

Nan was determined not to be a burden and helped urge her brother along. Owen managed to hold up well considering his age and the turmoil of the last few days. Skag was patient. His heart still ached over the pain these children had endured. Finally they were past the ward, a little scratched and weary but glad to be done with it.

They cut across an angle of marsh and entered the forest beyond Yolande's ward. The mid-morning sun had been hot on their backs and they welcomed the cool shade. Skag called for a rest and the children threw themselves onto the pine needles covering the ground.

Skag stood gazing into the forest. Patches of sunlight danced with shadow as the wind stirred the tree limbs. The bogfoke sensed something in the wood, something fresh. The

Great Wood was stirring now, free at last from the presence of Amhomag. It was like music to Skag's senses, sometimes joyous, sometimes reflective and sometimes possessed of a bittersweet poignancy.

There was a rustle of leaves and Skag's reflexes brought the cedar stave into a defensive position. Nan and Owen were quickly to their feet and they crowded close behind the bogfoke. A dark form separated from the shadows and strolled toward them in the sunlight. Skag laughed.

"Ralph, I'd almost think you've been waiting here all this time," the cedar-bearer chuckled as he scratched the top of the huge head.

"Isn't this Nanna's dog?" asked Nan as she vigorously rubbed Ralph's back until the dog shook from nose to tail. As her brother reached a tentative hand to rub the dog's muzzle, the girl became suddenly wide eyed and stared at the cedar-bearer. "Oh, Skag, I hadn't even thought of where you were taking us. All I could think of was an orphanage, and how much Mother hated them. You are taking us to Nanna! Thank you. Oh, thank you!"

"Nanna! Nanna!" shouted Owen, though Skag knew the boy had no real memories of the woman.

"I'm sorry," said the bogfoke. "I should've told you sooner. I wasn't thinking. I assumed too much. But now, let's get this done and get you safely to Nannela Walker."

They trooped through the forest with Ralph ranging ahead of them. The dog began to get excited as they drew near the farm and curled back toward them on occasion as if to hurry them along. The tangle of trees gave way to open sky and the dog's tail began whipping in fierce joy.

The fields stretched before them in long rows of browned, crumbled nubs of harvested crops. Skag saw Nannela Walker walking toward them along the work road. The children began a joyous dash in her direction. Skag could see her smile even from where he stood.

The children buried their faces in her dress as she

held them close. Old Ralph ran in circles around the trio with an unrestrained joy. Nanna was looking at the wood. Her gaze found Skag where he stood among the shadows. He could see the gratitude in her composure as she waved to him.

"A debt repaid, Nannela Walker," Skag sighed to himself as he raised his cedar in greeting. "Help them with the pain, good woman. May Getchemandou grant you the years that will heal them."

Skag turned back into the Great Wood. The old woman herded her great-grandchildren back to her house with old Ralph leading the way. Nanna ventured a gaze at where Skag had stood. She smiled sadly at the realization that she might be the last of her kind to ever look upon his kind until the end of time.

***

Skag made his way back to the barrow along much the same path as he had once fled from Jake Collanmore. His passage through the ward was not so difficult when free of urgency. The day was nearing mid-afternoon when he came to the paths near the barrow.

The sound of voices drifted to him. He recognized an occasional bogfoke amid the more guttural chatter of cornbears. Nammais and Gristel appeared through the forest aisles. They began waving at him, each with a wide smile.

"You've done it!" shouted Nammais. "We're free."

"*We* have done it," replied Skag. "All of us and a mighty host from the world beyond."

Nammais tilted his head as he considered Skag. "You have changed, Narak, grown."

"Robbis spoke of this," added Gristel, almost as much to herself as to Nammais or Skag.

"The tracker and I saw much," admitted Skag softly. "I saw things I cannot put into words. Still, we have much left to do."

The coquanon and Gristel escorted the cedar-bearer through the milling cornbears. The newcomers parted like a deferential sea before this procession. Many of them whispered, *Narak*, as he passed and it caused Skag a lingering embarrassment.

He saw his fellow bogfoke scattered throughout the throng. They all smiled and waved at him with a familiarity that soothed him. Slignan sat atop the barrow gazing over the congregation with a bemused expression.

"What are we going to do with this lot?" Slignan shouted down at him with a hearty laugh.

Skag smiled in reply as he glanced around. "We will take care of this shortly. Nammais, I need you and the Old One to come with me into the barrow. Gristel, where is Mother Crabba?"

"She is inside," replied Gristel.

"As is the Old One," added Nammais.

"Ah, good, Nammais, you come with me," said Skag before turning to Gristel. "Keep everyone else out of the barrow for a time, Gristel. Keep them from wandering off. Curiosity is a kindred trait."

Gristel nodded as Skag and Nammais disappeared into the cool dark of the barrow. The Mother and Askuwhetaeau sat facing one another in the middle of the barrow. They were conversing in a strange mixture of tongues, including some Skag did not recognize. Nammais stopped, with an amazed expression on his face.

"The Old One is talking," he observed.

"Well, he is of our kind," noted Skag. "We may never shut him up again."

The cedar-bearer went to sit at the side of the two elders and motioned for Nammais to sit across from him. He then drove his cedar stave into the earthen floor between them. He looked for a moment at the red veined wood, thinking of a frightened and frustrated bogfoke who had found courage within despair.

"What is to come must be part of each of our two folk," said Skag. The others understood but said nothing in reply. "It will not be a perfect place. The time for that has not come. Even Ahkomaic was not perfect, or why would a cornbear get rained upon whilst fetching a new net?"

Nammais smiled and Skag continued, "That will do nicely, friend Nammais. Let us craft a realm of contented smiles."

Skag reached so that each of them held the hand of another. The cedar-bearer looked then at the Mother and then Askuwhetaeau and said to them, "You are the eldest among us. In your memories is the Song of Getchemandou, from before the sundering of our folk. Find the song for us. Lead us in the weaving, the great making."

For a moment nothing was said. They sat in a quiet circle breathing easy and deep. Then Narak-Skag whispered, "Let the dream begin."

Darkness, but they weren't alone. Each could sense the other. Skag was the first to feel the presence of someone else. The others sensed it after a moment. Skag smiled in his heart. "It is good to be with you again, Welken."

"I have been waiting, Skag, but I do not know if I have waited a long or short time."

"Wait no longer," replied the cedar-bearer. "Join us in the Great Song. It is time now for the dream of what lies beyond for our folk."

Then, as one, Crabba and Askuwhetaeau began chanting the Song of Getchemandou. The singing pulled the song from out of Nammais, Narak-Skag and Welken. Then, in the darkness they shared they saw a sudden point of light. The song caused it to grow and their hopes gave it form within the song. The dream awakened and slowly spread until the dark was no more.

Skag could feel himself changing, growing with the dream. Now there came the song of calling. Outside the barrow the other cornbears and bogfoke heard and responded with their own voices. Then was the procession into the dream of a world that lay beyond.

***

The young bogfoke moved carefully through the forest. They were not physically in the world and no one could have seen them, but they were haunted by the tales told in their earliest years. They approached the mounded hill swathed in honeysuckle and juniper. As they drew up before it, the darkness between the brush formed into an arch. They turned to the mighty cypress that rose only a little way from the hill. The limbs stretched high above the forest which was its domain and each of the bogfoke respectfully bowed their heads to its presence. Then they slipped into the shadowed arch. When they had done so the arch disappeared and the forest was like any other.

***

The two bogfoke where suddenly within themselves again and burst laughing into the land the cornbears had named Rahnweygo, *the beautiful dreaming*. Running gleefully along the grassy hills they made toward a distant wood. They became more sedate as they slipped beneath the arching canopy of the great trees.

Their paths led them to a narrow stream winding between the trees. They could hear the water singing. A rather humble cedar rose on the grass covered bank, spreading its scattered boughs as if to test all airs at once. They sat beneath the tree, trying to be as patient as ever a bogfoke could be. Finally the shadows of the wood took form and a slender figure appeared. Its skin was coppery, like cedar wood, and its hair and beard were close cropped.

"What did you see?" it asked of them with a voice like sunshine filtering through the green canopy.

"We saw the city of men, Father Narak-Skag. We saw many strange dreams tumbling through the streets," replied one of the young bogfoke.

"Dreams of despair and hope. Dreams of fear and courage. Dreams of greed and charity," added the other.

Father Narak-Skag smiled gently. "Those are the dreams of the city. They are the images of the souls of men. They are also our legacy and the source of our own dreaming. Take these dreams into your hearts. Ponder on them. Sing of them so that all things might be healed."

They nodded solemnly. The Father smiled again and motioned toward the open land beyond the wood. "And now, get home to your kin and to your play."

Off they scampered, leaving irrepressible giggles in their wake. Father Narak-Skag knew they did not completely understand. They had much to learn, much growing to do before they would join the coquanon.

He smiled then, because he knew this was true even now of himself. But, for the time, it was best that they just be bogfoke and cornbears. There was no urgency in their growing, save only that it should flow into the Song of Getchemandou. They would take such memories with them as they were folded into that great dream.

-END-

Pronunciation Guide

Early readers of Bogfoke have consistently and persistently requested a pronunciation guide. I resisted this at first, for a variety of reasons beyond even being lazy. It is perfectly acceptable to pronounce anything you run across in Bogfoke in any manner with which you are comfortable. I ask only that you do not envision the Bogfoke with pointy ears. They have small, round ears.

As for the pronunciations, if we were to be able to eavesdrop on the bogfoke when they were in conversation, we would struggle to make much sense of what was being said. We would recognize many English words, but also words related to a variety of Native American languages, and even Paleo-Indian languages, but all with bogfoke or cornbear slants to their pronunciation. More than that, being exceptional mimics, the bogfoke would incorporate onomatopoeia and more overt sound effects into their conversation at a rate the human brain cannot easily follow.

Obviously I have rendered their conversations into a more banal fashion by way of the English language. This worked best for me, a speaker of banal fashioned English. Still, having been sufficiently pestered, I offer the following non-professional guide to pronunciations in Bogfoke.

Bogfoke

Crabba: Easy enough, it sounds like the crustacean with an "ah" at the end of it.

Daugth: Dawth will be close enough. The bogfoke would have included a slight, soft "k" sound where the g is, rather like Dawkth. But there is no need to go to so much trouble, I don't. Dawth is fine.

Gristel: Like gristle combined with crystal. Gris-tal, or

gris-tell.

Kribble: Krib-buhl, like quibble, if that helps any. He would, quibble that is.

Robbis: Robe-iss.

Skag: Easy one, slag with a k. His truest name, Narak, would be nair-akk.

Slignan: Slig-nahn.

Tegmina: Tegg-meen-ah.

Weart: Wurt, or weert. He wasn't fussy about the difference.

Welken: Well-Ken.

Cornbears

Nammais: Nah-mayess.

Suquahan: Soo-kwa-hahn

Askuwhetaeau: I have no idea. Okay, Ahss-koo-way-tow

Nunnehi

Nunnehi: Either noo-neh-hee, or nunn-neh-hee. I used both in my head. The Cherokee word was probably closer to noon-eh-high, but the bogfoke/cornbears word was not identical to the Cherokee word from which it was borrowed.

Mankatoh: mahn-kah-toh

Sloe: slow

Other beings

Amhomag: Amm-hoe-MAG

Getchemandou: getch-eh-mahn-dow, or getch-eh-mahn-doo, but let's be honest, the first one sounds better somehow when we consider that it is the name for the Great Spirit, God, Allah, or YWH. Getch-eh-mahn-doo sounds like a Cajun stew.

Machamanitoh: mah-kah-man-neh-toh, or mah-kah-man-neh-too

Stump: Seriously? Dump, trump, bump. Although it might be entertaining to imagine yourself as a snooty Monty Python character and pronounce it stoomp-ah.

Yolande: Like Yolanda, except with a "dey" ending instead of a "dah" ending. Yoh-lahn-dey.

Places

Ahkomaic: Ahh-koh-mayek

Chautauqua: Chaw-taw-gwa. This is a variation of a common Algonquin place name associated with water. It is often translated as meaning "place of enchanting water" "place of beautiful water" "place of shimmering water" and so forth. Personally, I'm convinced those are just romanticized translations of what was probably a more pragmatic "good fishing spot."

Rahnweygo: Rahn-way-go